PICKING UP THE PIECES

JO WORGAN

urbanepublications.com

First published in Great Britain in 2018
by Urbane Publications Ltd
Suite 3, Brown Europe House, 33/34 Gleaming Wood Drive,
Chatham, Kent ME5 8RZ

A CIP catalogue record for this book is available
from the British Library.

ISBN 978-1-911331-62-9
MOBI 978-1-911331-64-3

Design and Typeset by Michelle Morgan

Cover by Michelle Morgan

Printed and bound by 4edge Limited, UK

urbanepublications.com

PICKING UP THE PIECES

JO WORGAN

A STORY OF LOVE, HOPE,
AND NEW BEGINNINGS...

For Andrew

"A CHILD WITH AUTISM IS NOT IGNORING YOU, THEY ARE WAITING FOR YOU TO ENTER THEIR WORLD."

Unknown

PROLOGUE

JUNE 2007

The air feels different here, fresher somehow. I inhale deeply and allow the salty air to fill my lungs, to invigorate me. This must work, there is no turning back now. I walk along the promenade, placing my hands protectively around the small bump that is strapped to my chest.

I can feel the baby's rhymical breathing, his warm breath on my cheek. He is fast asleep, rocked by the melodic movement of walking. I double-check the straps once again, making sure that he is safe and secure. He will come to no harm here.

The smell of fish and chips fills the air, making my mouth water. When was the last time I ate chips from a tray on a bench? Years? It must be.

Memories swirl around inside my head. Snapshots taken from another place in time. My gran, sitting beside me, a printed headscarf tied tightly around her head, crimson lipstick and a mischievous smile, as she sat and licked the salt from her fingers. Her happiness reflected on my own face. We had sat on a bench, greedily devouring a bag of chips between us from the unfurled newspaper covered in grease. It wasn't quite the same, eating your chips from a plastic tray.

I glance into the steam-filled air of the chip shop; there is only one person stood there, chatting to the man behind the counter, awaiting her order. I walk in. A tray of chips and a takeout coffee will be lovely. I'll have time before he wakes up. He is such a good baby, no trouble at all, and I need to sit and rest for a little while. I shall watch the boats as they sail past.

I wonder where they are heading? Who will be waiting for them on the shore? Or are they returning to a cold and empty home?

I will absorb the serenity, the peace.

It will make me whole again.

I will be reborn.

Part One
Now

CHAPTER ONE

MONDAY, SEPTEMBER 9TH, 2013

The alarm had long been silenced. Kate Sullivan lay still and listened; she listened for the sound of soft footsteps that would softly pad across the laminate boards of the bedroom floor next to hers. She listened for the inevitable creak that would sound from the opening of the bedroom door. Poking his head around the doorframe would be the sleepy image of her beautiful six-year-old son, a tangled mess of sleep encrusted eyes and messy blonde curls, as he bounced onto her bed. As usual, he would snuggle up under the covers with his thin arms wrapped around her body. *Morning Sam,* she would say, her voice thick with sleep. But all was quiet now; he had not yet stirred. She had another fifteen minutes of peace and quiet. She closed her eyes and surrendered to the silence.

The slow creak of his bedroom door alerted her to his presence. A shaft of light appeared on the landing, seen through the slit of her bedroom door that was not quite closed. She never closed the bedroom door; she slept with one eye open, ever alert. The door wobbled slightly on its hinges as it was flung open. Sam jumped onto the bed and over Kate, burrowing himself under the embroidered flowery quilt, bought as a bargain charity shop find, and then pressed himself into the small of her back. He relaxed.

Kate inhaled his little boy smell; the shampoo from last night's shower clung to his skin. She ruffled his soft hair. His leg flung carelessly over hers. Her chest tightened, filled with the mixture of emotions that were love, fear, guilt and joy for this little boy. This little boy that was hers. She squeezed her eyes shut, savouring the precious moment, fearing it could be taken from her at any moment.

'Morning Sam,' she mumbled into the pillow.

Their day had just begun.

The stairs creaked one by one as they descended them, not quite warmed up by the morning sun that streaked through the crack in the hallway curtains. The carpet was blue, faded, marked with muddy patches and years of wear and tear, the edges frayed. Kate led Sam into the living room, and quickly found his iPad. He firmly plonked himself down onto the worn brown leather couch, right at the end, where he could squish himself into the armrest. An indent showed that this was his favourite seat. The screen flickered to life, fully charged. Kate sat down next to him and wondered what app he would open. The theme tune from his ABC app rang out loudly from the speaker, filling the room with life. Sam stared at the screen, the light illuminating his face, completely immersed.

'I'll go and get you your milk, Sam,' Kate softly told him. Without waiting for a response, she headed into the adjoining kitchen. *Coffee*, she needed coffee; she could not function without it. She ran the tap to fill the kettle and flicked the switch. Sleepily, she spooned coffee haphazardly into a chipped red mug, then opened the fridge to find milk and Sam's soya milk, which she poured into his cow cup. She set the timer for thirty seconds and watched as the cup slowly rotated, the microwave buzzing, the light filling the room. The kettle beeped noisily, steam escaping from the spout, while the

microwave pinged. Kate had the timing down to perfection. She took the cup out of the microwave, allowing it to cool while she poured the hot water over her instant coffee. Reaching up to the shelf above the toaster, she grabbed a straw, a blue one, always a blue one, and plonked it in Sam's cup. She carried both cups into the living room. She looked at Sam; he had not moved.

'Sit next to me,' Sam told her, patting the leather seat, his eyes not moving from the screen.

Kate smiled. 'Move over then, Sam.'

She squeezed in right next to him, replacing his position at the end of the couch and placed her mug onto the lowest wooden shelf at the side of the couch. She passed Sam his milk. There were piles of books on the makeshift bookcase, all crammed together, fighting for survival. Most were crime novels, waiting to be read. Kate made yet another mental note to start reading one tonight, that was if she could keep awake long enough.

Sam drained the milk and passed the empty cup back to Kate, placing both his legs over hers and resting his head on her shoulder. She gently ruffled his hair, once again inhaling the little boy smell that she knew would soon fade.

Sam loved close contact, to be squeezed, the greater the pressure the better. He liked to feel and touch things; he craved touch, he craved textures. He liked to sit incredibly close to Kate, to feel that human contact. But she did not complain; he wouldn't always be so little. Soon she would miss those tight cuddles.

Kate glanced up at the clock; it was not quite seven and his taxi was not due until eight. They had plenty of time. They would have a leisurely breakfast and then slowly get ready for school. All they needed to do was to shovel down their toast and cereal and get dressed. But of course, all in the same order; they always had to do things in the same order – it's just the way it was.

The house was so quiet; all Kate could hear were the birds chirping in the trees outside and of course the cartoons that were now playing on repeat on the iPad. Sam was watching the same clip over and over again, but strangely it didn't annoy her. As long as Sam was happy, she was happy. She was prepared to do anything for a quiet life. She grabbed her phone and opened up her emails to see if there were any from her editor, who had the habit of sending emails late at night with regards to the stories that Kate needed to cover the following day. Sadly, he hadn't sent any. She would pop into the newspaper office once Sam had left for school.

Kate sipped her coffee; it was still far too hot. She blew on it in the hope of cooling it down; it never worked. Stretching her legs out in front of her onto the blue and white patterned rug that had seen better days, she tried to empty her mind of all the crap that she needed to sort through today. The house needed cleaning, but she just didn't have the energy. The housework could wait another day, or two. She needed to go food shopping and she needed to write something, anything, so that she could pay the rent at the end of the month. She also needed to call the landlord about the boiler, as it was playing up again, only heating up the water when it decided to do so. Mr. Jenkins should have bought a new boiler years ago, but he was too tight-fisted. So, it would be repaired, yet again. Kate sighed.

The living room was small but cosy. It was sparsely furnished, but that was the way Kate liked it. It was a safe space for her and Sam. The room was crammed full of books, a battered two-seater sofa that was a hand-me-down from the previous tenant, a small recliner shoved into a corner that was barely used and a small table where Kate sat and did her work; this was also where her laptop was permanently plugged in. The walls had been painted a bland magnolia, but they gave a feeling of calm, of space. Bold

colours were too draining, too claustrophobic, and besides, they reminded Kate of *him*.

Kate and Sam usually ate in the kitchen; there was just enough room for a tiny wooden square table and four chairs, two of which were never used. The set had been a charity shop bargain that she had found one rainy Saturday when Sam was a toddler. It was pure luck that the heavens had opened, meaning that they had taken shelter from the unforgiving rain that had drenched them both. Mr. Jenkins had installed a rather nasty looking plastic table in the kitchen and she couldn't wait to get rid of it. It wobbled whenever she touched it. Kate did not own a television; she didn't see the point. She mainly read or streamed movies. It was either that or write. Kate stretched once more and yawned. Sam had been unsettled last night; he kept waking up and had crept into Kate's room at least three times. She very nearly gave up and let him sleep in her bed, but she found the strength to walk him back into his room each time he had stumbled in. Kate was pretty sure that his being unsettled was because the new school term had started. This always happened after the holidays. He became anxious and his sleeping pattern erratic. Kate had painstakingly made him a visual timetable, that she had stuck to the fridge with colourful alphabet magnets. It showed Sam pictures of his taxi and school, as well as the children in his class and his new teachers, all smiling into the camera. But Sam showed no interest in it whatsoever over the summer holidays. He just kept ripping the pictures off the fridge; the one that showed the school was scrunched up into a tight ball. So, in the end Kate had hidden the pictures. What was the point? There was no use in upsetting him. Visuals usually helped Sam, those small clues that told him what would be happening next, what would be happening in his life. But for some reason the visual prompts of school did not help him, they just created more

anxiety. This was the reason why Kate had not yet mentioned the word *school*. It would just upset him. What she wanted more than anything in the world was for him to be happy.

Sam attended a small autism-specific specialist school a few miles away from the sleepy village of Muddletown; he'd been there for over a year. He enjoyed it there; it was just that when there had been a long break away from school, it could take him a little bit more time to adjust back into his old routine, to become settled again. Kate knew that the morning would be a difficult one, for him, and for her. There was nothing that she could do about it.

Sam looked up at her with his big blue eyes. Kate knew what he was going to ask, even before the words had left his mouth.

'Cornflakes Mum.'

Kate ruffled his hair. 'Okay Sam, I'll get your cornflakes.'

Five minutes to eight. Kate stood in the living room, waiting for the taxi, trying desperately to swallow down her mounting nerves. Sam was finally dressed in his school uniform, plus dressing gown. She was not too sure where this need to wear his dressing gown had come from, but he refused to take it off. Getting him dressed was a struggle, but she resigned herself to the fact that it was not his fault. None of this was his fault. Kate was well aware that she should remove his *Bob the Builder* dressing gown that was two sizes too small. She could barely fasten it and the sleeves ended at his elbows, but it was only for one day; it really wouldn't matter. If it meant that she could lure him into the taxi, and that he was settled on his journey to school, then there was no harm done.

Once Sam was quietly playing with his cars, Kate quickly got dressed. Luckily, she was very low maintenance. She usually wore comfortable, practical clothes, so in other words, *boring*. This usually meant she ended up wearing jeans and a t-shirt, or a dress

and cardigan. Kate never wore heels. It was difficult to chase after a small boy who was sprinting down the road in killer heels. This was the reason why Kate stuck to either her tatty and much-loved Converse or lace up boots. Her long curly brown hair had been combed, and a lick of lipstick applied. She was now ready to face the world. Or rather, the taxi driver, Sam's taxi escort and her boss. Kate checked her watch; it had just gone eight. She looked out of the living room window and noticed a large removal van pulling into the driveway next door. The house had been empty for around three months and she wondered who her new neighbours would be. Would they be a young couple who hosted loud parties? Or would they be a nice quiet retired couple? Kate secretly hoped that they liked children. It would make a pleasant change from the previous owners. She stood back from the window, aware that if seen she would appear like a prying neighbour. She adjusted the net curtain and turned to Sam. He still looked like the condemned man as he sat on the floor, wheeling his red toy car backwards and forwards on his car mat. He had not spoken to Kate since the whole *getting dressed incident*. She had not been forgiven for making him go to school. She took another quick peek through the net curtains and saw the familiar blue taxi at the top of the street; the honking horn soon followed. Why did they do that? They knew it upset Sam. She turned towards Sam, his hands covering his ears. and took a deep breath. 'Sam, the taxi is here.'

He looked up at her, clutching the red shiny car. 'Oh, no Mum,' he muttered.

'I know Sam, but we need to get shoes on now,' Kate told him patiently, her heart hammering in her chest, praying silently for no meltdown.

She reached out her hand and he took it. Together they walked into the hallway, so that Kate could put his shoes on for him.

Having grabbed his bag, coat, lunchbox and car seat, that was now tucked under her arm, she unlocked and then opened the front door, before heading down the short path towards the awaiting taxi. Sam tightly gripped her hand. Kate looked over at him, seeing what expression he was wearing. But he gave nothing away. Kate was met with silence. She greeted the taxi driver, the same lady who picked him up every single day and asked how she was, while positioning the car seat for him. The words drifted over Kate's head in a melodic hum. She smiled at his passenger escort who greeted Sam with a beaming smile. 'Morning Sam.' But she too was met with silence. Kate handed over all his belongings, kissed him on the top of his head, and slowly closed the car door. She stood on the pavement as they drove away. A huge lump formed in her throat. She looked up at the sky and blinked several times to clear her vision. He'd gone, handed over to others to look after him, and she suddenly felt redundant. Kate was fiercely protective of her little boy, maybe too protective, but she couldn't help it. At times, he just seemed so vulnerable. She turned and walked back into the now still and quiet house.

The kitchen was an absolute mess; there was no way that the housework could wait until tomorrow, but it would have to wait until she got back from the office this afternoon. She fleetingly thought about getting a cleaner, but then laughed, as one, she should be able to clean her own home and two, she couldn't afford one. Kate attempted to lift a stubborn stack of papers from the kitchen table, now all covered in sticky jam, and shoved them into her oversized satchel that was covered in bright blue flowers. Grabbing her pencil case, she shoved that in too, and made sure that her phone was in its designated pocket. She knew though that by the time she arrived at work, it would be buried underneath all the toy cars, pens, bits of paper and other accumulated junk.

Draining the dregs from her now cold cup of coffee, she dropped the mug into the overflowing sink, slung her satchel across her shoulder and headed out the front door. She inhaled the fresh air; it was good to get out of the house. She just hoped that her editor had some stories for her to chase up. The *Muddletown Muse* was hardly a hub of activity, but she enjoyed writing stories about the local area. In truth, she enjoyed chatting to people, even if it was only the local mad cat lady.

As she pulled away from the house in her ancient Mini, she glanced in the rear-view mirror to check that nobody was following her. She did this automatically, subconsciously; it was now part of her morning ritual. The shadow was always there; it had never gone away. It was just a matter of time before it caught up with her.

CHAPTER TWO

'That's the last of the boxes, Matt.' Brian carefully placed the small cardboard box on top of two larger boxes, all of them labelled *books*, and wiped his dusty hands on his jeans.

'Thanks for helping,' Matt told his best friend. He quickly whipped out a fifty pound note from his back pocket, pressing it into Brian's hand before he could object. Matt knew that Brian was strapped for cash. 'It would have taken me the best part of two days to unload all of this stuff,' Matt added quickly, before Brian could open his mouth to object with a '*no, no, that's too much.*'

'Thanks.' Brian took a steadying breath, raking his hand through his short brown hair. Matt couldn't help noticing that he looked uncomfortable as he quickly shoved the note into his wallet, not quite meeting his eye. Matt wondered why his friend accepted the money so awkwardly. He didn't mean to make him feel that way. He just knew he was having a hard time, work wise, and that he had turned down overtime to help him out. Shit! It was the least he could do. He'd let Brian buy a round at the pub.

Matt watched as Brian looked around the room, unsure of what to say or do next. He decided to help him out. 'Let's go to the pub, I'll buy you a beer.'

Brian smiled. 'Great idea, I'm parched,' he lost the smile for a fraction of a second, 'but I'm buying.'

Then it was Matt's turn to smile. That's exactly what he knew he would say.

Matt sipped his pint; it was not yet lunchtime. He shouldn't drink any more as he was a complete lightweight when it came to alcohol. He'd already got that slightly buzzed feeling. But he was more relaxed now, so mission accomplished. He'd start on the unpacking later, just the essentials. The rest could wait.

'When do you start at the uni then?' Brian asked before taking another sip of his lager.

'Not until next week, well, lectures start next week, but I'll sort out my office tomorrow, or maybe later today.'

Brian nodded in acknowledgement while shoving ready salted peanuts into his mouth as if he was afraid that it was the very last bag on earth. Brian was Matt's best friend, but he understood nothing about his work at the university. Brian worked as a mechanic, always had, ever since leaving school at the age of sixteen when he started out as an apprentice at the local garage. He was the best mechanic Matt had ever met. He smiled; he was also sure that Brian thought he was some kind of mad scientist, conducting weird and wonderful experiments in his overly warm and dark, dingy lab. But nothing could be further from the truth. Matt was a research marine chemist, so much of his work involved staring at sets of data and spreadsheets, although he did occasionally get to go out and about taking samples from streams and rivers. He was going to be doing some innovative research at the local aquarium, as well as helping with the local schools' educational visits, which was part of the reason why he had moved up north to this sleepy village nestled alongside the Lancashire coast. That and his divorce.

Matt drained his beer and looked at Brian over the rim of his glass, noticing how tired he looked. Not tired from a bad night's sleep, but rather, a whole month's lack of sleep. He was working too hard, more so now that his wife had lost her part-time job at the bakery. His brown eyes appeared dull; they had bags underneath them. Matt was just thankful that he had not yet mentioned Lisa, and to be fair to him, he didn't think he would. He could barely think of her and what she had done to him, what she did to *them*. There was no *us* now. He was still hurt and humiliated, *yes*, humiliated was the truth; no man could ever get over the fact that his wife had left him for another man, a *younger* man at that. Matt was hardly past it at age forty. Christ, they'd been married for twenty years; Matt thought they had made it after that length of time. That they would be together forever. Grow old and have matching Zimmer frames. He thought he knew her, inside and out, but obviously, he had been wrong.

Matt had treated her well, looked after her, shit, he loved her; he still loved her. He still wore his wedding ring; that's how not over it he was, even though the divorce was finalised over six months ago. Matt still could not take it off, not yet. He often wondered why she had left him? Why she stopped loving him? He was well aware that he was not the world's most handsome man, but he looked after himself. He exercised and ate healthily; he had not let himself go as so many men his age had done. He was of average height, average build, with short blonde hair and piercing blue eyes. Lisa always told him that she loved his pale skin, strawberry blonde hair, and eyes, his eyes that reminded her of the Mediterranean Sea. *So deep Matt, your eyes are such a deep blue that I could swim in them forever.* Well, no more, not now that she had found Dave, fifteen years his junior and an accountant. Matt ran his hands through his hair. These types of thoughts needed to stop. He had

to stop thinking about her. He had a new beginning here. A new house, a new job, all new, all fresh; she had no part to play in this new life of his. He needed to stop thinking about her, but he just didn't know how.

Children – maybe that was why things never worked out between them. It was always the unspoken thought, the missing link. They had tried, unsuccessfully, for years, had two rounds of IVF. Then there was the miscarriage.

Matt had accepted that they were just not meant to have children, that nothing more could be done. At the time, he hadn't wanted to put Lisa through anymore agony. But he also knew that his pretty wife had never accepted this, not truly, even though she said she had. He knew that she had envisaged a little girl with the same blonde curls as hers, and a little boy with his blue eyes. If he was being truthful, he had too. It had changed her, this not being able to get pregnant, to procreate. *Isn't that what women are meant to do Matt, have children?* It changed them both, the way they were together. The way they spoke to each other. Every day he had never been able to say the words that he so desperately needed to set free. That was when everything had gone bad, when everything had fallen apart and no amount of glue could put them back together again.

So, that was that.

'Another pint Matt?' Brian asked.

Matt looked up from his pint, no use in denying that his mind had been elsewhere. Brian's brown eyes were now starting to look even more tired as he unsuccessfully stifled a yawn.

Matt smiled. 'No, I'm done. I need to get back and start on the unpacking anyway.'

Brian leaned back in his chair. 'Do you need a hand? I don't mind.'

'No, no, it's fine, honestly. You've got a long trek back. I appreciate you helping me, especially on your day off, but you've done enough.'

They sat in silence as Brian finished his drink.

'Well, if you're okay then,' Brian said, while picking at the corner of the beer mat where it had started to fray. 'I can pop down this weekend if you like?'

Matt knew that he was being kind and looking out for him; he'd always looked out for him, ever since they were kids, but he had a family now. He needed to be with his missus and the kids – he only ever got every other weekend off, and the last thing Matt wanted to do was cause trouble between the two of them. He'd never forgive himself if something happened to cause them to split up.

'No, I'll be fine Brian. I've got loads to do here; it'll take me weeks to sort the house out. But I don't mind, it's just me, I can take my time. I'll still be unpacking boxes in six months knowing me.' He laughed, which seemed to be the first time in months.

Matt was amused to see that Brian looked relieved that he had declined his invitation, although he tried in vain to hide it.

'Do you need a lift back to the house?' Brian asked as he stood up from the table, shoving his black beanie hat onto his head. He wore it all year, even in the blistering heat.

'No, I'll walk back; it'll give me chance to snoop on the neighbourhood. I don't really know this area. I need to do some investigating.'

It was true, Matt had been given very little time to find somewhere to live. He had given the house in London to Lisa; it was just easier that way. He had used his half to travel up north, creating as much distance as possible between them. There was no way that he could stay in their marital home, sleep in their marital bed, live with all its associated memories; no way on earth could

he have done that. He needed a new life, a new start, in a new part of the country. Somewhere he could be invisible. Somewhere he could blend in.

The two men made their way out of the pub and onto the narrow pavement outside. A slow rumble of traffic passed them by; a young boy zoomed past on his scooter. The air was still, warm for the time of year. Autumn had yet to make its appearance. They stood in awkward silence, neither of them knowing if they should hug or not. Matt pushed his awkwardness aside; Brian had seen him cry and everything, so he decided to make the first move and gave him a massive bear hug while patting him on his back several times. 'Thanks mate, thanks for everything.' Matt felt his voice beginning to break. He looked away.

Brian too avoided his gaze. Then with a final nod and a promise to phone him soon, he headed to the van. Matt turned in the opposite direction towards his new home.

Matt thought about how the streets were different here; they were lined with trees on either side, so much greenery everywhere, unlike where he lived in the city. Everything there was tinged with grey, almost as if the buildings and people had been stained from the traffic smoke and pollutants that engulfed them; it seemed so much cleaner by the shore. He needed to get out sailing. He hadn't done so in years; maybe in a few weeks' time he could hire a boat and just go away for the weekend, moor up somewhere, before the weather grew colder.

But for now, he had to get settled into his new home. It still sounded strange tripping off his tongue, *home*. Matt thought once again about where he used to live, his old life. But he also believed that he would grow to like it here. He just needed to throw himself into work; being busy cured everything. More importantly, it would take his mind off *her*. Busy, yes that's what he needed to be.

He bought a sandwich from the corner shop. Surprised by how friendly the old lady was behind the counter who reeked of lily-of-the-valley, he was reminded of his elderly aunt who died years ago. The old woman asked him if he was new to the area. He smiled politely and told her that that he was. *'Oh, you'll love it here, everyone is quite friendly dear.'* He smiled in acknowledgment, telling her that he was sure she was right.

He'd make a cup of tea; that'd help to sober him up a little. Once he had unpacked the kettle and found the teabags, cups and milk that was. Then he would make a start on unpacking.

Life here may not be so bad after all.

But deep down he knew that he was fooling nobody, not even himself.

CHAPTER THREE

The offices of the *Muddletown Muse* where located in what was best called the middle of town. Muddletown would perhaps be best described as a sleepy hamlet in those publications that aim to attract certain people of a certain class to an area. But in reality, Muddletown really was only a small town with a handful of shops, a primary school, library, a few cafés, and the local pub. Situated on the outskirts was also a large industrial estate that housed DIY shops and a large supermarket. What attracted so many visitors to the area was the picturesque harbour and long pier with its rustic fishing boats and rock pools that little ones could search in for hours, hoping to see the sights of a monster crab. Then there was the smell of fish and chips that filled the salty air. In the winter, the area was desolate, with only the locals shuffling along the streets, scarves wrapped protectively around their necks and hats pulled low down over their ears. But come summer, the place was heaving, and that was how Kate liked it. She could blend into the crowds, become invisible. Just another number.

The office walls of the *Muddletown Muse* were drab; they had always been drab and uninspiring. Off-white walls with peeling paint greeted Kate as she exited the stairwell, puffing and panting from having climbed up the sixty or so steps. There was a lift, but she didn't like lifts; they made her feel hemmed in, trapped like a caged animal, so she had to use the stairs. The only time she stepped into a lift was when she was with Sam. She really needed to add exercise to her never ending *to-do* list; that was probably more important than hiring a cleaner, considering how out of breath she was. And sleep, sleep would most definitely help her. Kate couldn't remember the last time she had had a good night's sleep, what with Sam waking up several times a night and her recurring nightmares.

Kate stifled a yawn as she eventually stepped into the open plan office, greeted by the smell of stale cigarette smoke; the smoking ban did not seem to apply here for some strange reason. There was also a distinct smell of cheese and onion crisps wafting in Kate's general direction. She dumped her bag onto her tiny desk that she barely used and headed over to the feature editor's desk, aware of the steely glare emanating from the editor-in-chief, who sat permanently in her glass box. She reminded Kate of a pet goldfish she once had, with her bulbous eyes and bored expression. Kate quickly looked away, knowing that she had only delayed the inevitable. She reached the safety of Bill's desk, but before she could even mutter a '*hello,*' he looked up from his computer screen, ripped the top sheet of paper from his notepad and handed her a cup of takeaway coffee, all within a few seconds. Bill, it had to be said, was solely responsible for Kate's coffee addiction. She never used to drink so much of the stuff until she started working at the *Muse* two years ago. He was also her only true friend.

Bill was handsome in that rugged kind of way, but he was far too old for Kate. Always smart, today he wore a tie that was covered in tiny green dinosaurs. Kate raised her eyebrows at him.

'We have a few jobs for you; it's a bit quiet now though to be honest,' Bill told Kate with a shrug of his shoulders. He couldn't

quite meet her eye. He was only too aware of how much she needed the money.

Kate sipped the coffee, grateful for the bitter hit of caffeine, although it was far too hot and scalded her tongue. She looked at the list of names Bill had handed to her.

There were two: a lollipop lady who was retiring at the end of the week after thirty years' service, and a local man who had rescued a cat from a tree. Kate sighed, wondering if her life could get any more exciting.

She managed to suppress a giggle when she saw that Bill wore the same bored expression as her own. He used to be a commissioning editor for a national newspaper. He was just as disillusioned as she was, but unlike her, he would be retiring soon. What happened to him was so very sad. He lost his prestigious and well-earned job due to his addiction to alcohol, and as a direct result, also lost his wife and children. Bill was a good man, decent, and more importantly, he was now sober. But he still had no contact with his children. Kate couldn't imagine how that must feel, to not be with your child. Her thoughts automatically drifted to Sam, wondering if he was having a good day. She hoped he was happy. There had been no phone call as yet and she had resisted the urge to phone the school; she had very nearly pressed the call button twice. But she also knew that if there was a problem, they would let her know.

Bill stared at Kate with a bemused expression on his face, waiting patiently for a response. His eyebrows arched ever so slightly, the laughter lines present around his piercing green eyes. Kate sighed again.

'I'll chase them up today,' she grinned. 'When do you need them?'

Billy scratched his chin. 'There's no rush with them.' He dragged his hand through his greying hair and shrugged. 'A few days is fine; we'll be sending a photographer too.'

He passed Kate another sheet of paper, ripped from a different notepad. 'Here are the addresses and contact numbers.'

Kate smiled and took the paper from him. The two addresses were close to where she lived; she could visit them both today.

'How's Sam doing?' Bill asked as Kate turned to head towards her desk. She stopped and smiled; he always asked after Sam, he never forgot about him. Kate believed that he had a soft spot for her son. Bill's brother's son was autistic. She vividly remembered the time when Sam had started to rifle through Bill's pockets, when they had first been introduced. He was searching for pennies, to add to his growing piggy bank empire. Luckily, Bill had seen the funny side; he was good with kids. Kate once again thought that it was such a shame about what had happened to him.

'He's okay, first day back at school today. You know how it is,' she paused, 'We had a good break together. It just feels a little strange to be without him, after being cooped up together for so long.'

Bill merely nodded, acknowledging this as fact. He knew not to say anything. 'I'd call in and see Veronica if I were you,' he said, looking pointedly at the glass box. 'Just to warn you though, she's in a right mood this morning.' He grinned at Kate and his green eyes twinkled. Kate couldn't help grinning back. *Great*, a pissed off Veronica first thing on a Monday morning – just what she needed.

Kate picked up her coffee and crossed the noisy room to the editor-in-chief's goldfish bowl. To say that Kate didn't like her would be a huge understatement. Kate loathed her, but she was her boss; she only had to tolerate her. The problem was that Veronica Braithwaite didn't understand Kate, or her life. She knew nothing about her past. No one was aware of what had happened to her, no one apart from Bill, and that was the way it had to be. Nobody could ever know.

Kate stood nervously outside the glass door, clutching her coffee as if her life depended on it, fully aware that Veronica could see her hovering there. But she waited a moment to collect her nerves before knocking and hearing the inevitable bellow of, '*Come in.*' Kate reluctantly opened the door. A quick hello, that was all that was needed here.

Kate plastered a false smile onto her face – it was so tight that her jaw began to ache – as she strode towards Veronica's desk, then she abruptly stopped, unsure of whether to sit down on the chair opposite the desk, or not, so she stood there, like a five-year-old in front of the headteacher.

Veronica looked good today; she always did, in her expensive clothes bought from boutiques, not from Asda like Kate's. She wore far too much make-up, her cheeks flushed with rouge and her eyes painted a bright blue. Kate thought she would look so much better with less.

'Please sit for a moment, Kate,' Veronica oozed with practised, polished annunciation. Her smile was equally as false as she gestured towards the seat with a perfectly manicured hand. Both women were aware of what was going on here. Kate sat down as she was told and waited. She looked down at her coffee, now rapidly cooling, noticing that her hand was trembling slightly.

'How are you Kate? How is Sam?' Veronica asked these questions with her eyes glued to the laptop screen. Kate suppressed the urge to roll her eyes. Why was she even asking? Veronica Braithwaite couldn't care less about her personal life, or her son.

'We are fine, thank you,' Kate told her in a clipped tone, not quite able to hide her indifference to this woman.

They sat in silence.

Kate had no inclination of making small talk with Veronica. She felt strangely claustrophobic even though she could clearly see

everyone busy working outside. Veronica briefly glanced towards the door while idly tapping away on her keyboard.

Kate planned her escape.

Veronica eventually looked up. 'So, I believe that you have a few stories to cover then? I won't keep you Kate.'

She carried on typing. *Tap, tap, tap,* her talons hitting the keys.

Kate leapt to her feet, scraping the chair legs backwards across the stone floor as she did so. It was not until she reached the safety of the glass door and had her hand on the handle, ready to turn it, that Veronica added, 'Make sure you do a good job.'

Kate swallowed her very unprofessional remark and stepped out of the glass box.

'Another cup of tea love?' Mrs. Jones asked Kate. She was already pouring tea into the dainty china tea cup. Kate thought that her bladder couldn't possibly take anymore tea, but she didn't have the heart to say no to the old lady. She was probably lonely. Kate knew that she might be her only visitor all day. She glanced at the large, round clock on the kitchen wall, 2:00 p.m. She couldn't stay much longer. The interview with Mr. Rogers, who had heroically rescued the cat, didn't take that long, brisk and to the point was Mr Rogers. But Mrs. Jones was from an entirely different generation, where politeness ruled, and you simply *had* to drink copious amounts of tea. Kate smiled, took another gulp of tea, put the cup back down onto the table and looked at her notepad.

'Is it okay if I record our conversation as well? My shorthand is rubbish,' Kate laughed. It really was. Kate was a writer, not a journalist; she was self-taught. It was one of the reasons that she managed to land a job at the *Muse.* She was paid far less than a journalist.

'Of course, love, now what do you need to know?'

Later, back at home, Kate stretched her legs out in front of her as she lay on the couch, reading her scant notes. She had hardly written a thing, but she had managed to record the entire conversation – which had lasted a total of one hour – on her phone. It had nearly drained the battery. Mrs. Jones most definitely had the gift of the gab. Kate reached for the packet of custard creams and crammed one greedily into her mouth. Not quite four o'clock, Sam would be home in about ten minutes. Her phone started to vibrate, and she glanced at the screen; Emily was calling. Kate sighed. She neither had the patience nor the time to chat to Emily right now. Kate met her a few years ago, when Sam had first started school. At the time, she had felt that she needed to make some new friends, to get out more, *socialise*. But how wrong could she be? At the time, she was looking to meet other parents who had autistic children; she felt that they would share a bond, a common understanding. But they were just like any other group on the planet that were thrown together. She had been unlucky enough to be saddled with the mother who was in complete denial and who would eventually 'cure' her son of his autism. Kate was now sick to death of her. Luckily, she could get out of meeting her, as she had the excuse of a day job, albeit a very flexible one. Emily had the impression that Kate worked full-time. Kate realised that she should feel guilty, at the way in which she had behaved towards this woman, her friend, but she couldn't help it. It was self-preservation. If she heard once more about a bleach cleansing agent or the need to only give pure organic foods in the hope that the *autism will just go away,* she would scream. She loved Sam. End of story. She reluctantly picked up the phone and sent a quick text, explaining that she was busy working, but that she may be free sometime, perhaps next week.

Swallowing down the last of the biscuit, Kate unfurled herself from the couch and placed her notebook next to the laptop. She

wandered over to the bay window and looked out. Sam must have had a settled day, as she had received no phone call. She hoped that he had. Kate had planned to write the articles up before he got home, but there was no chance of that now. She'd have to make a start on them tonight; otherwise she would have Veronica on her case. Even though Bill had told her there was no rush, Kate was aware that the vile woman was waiting for her to make a wrong move, so that she had an excuse to sack her. She was treading on very thin ice. So, the sooner they were done, the better. Hopefully Sam would sleep well tonight; he usually did after his first day back at school. Although he would probably wake earlier than usual in the morning.

Pyjamas! Kate needed to get his pyjamas ready. The first thing Sam asked for as he stepped through the door were his pyjamas. As far as Sam was concerned, once school was over, so was the need for him to wear his school uniform. Kate slowly climbed the stairs to Sam's bedroom and opened his bedroom door that was covered in his certificates and artwork from school. His pyjamas were laid out on top of his Teletubbies quilt. She must have put them there before leaving the house; she just couldn't remember doing so. She looked around his room, all his cushions and sensory toys shoved into the corner, overflowing from the blue plastic box. She needed to buy a larger one but in the same colour. Sam liked to come and play in his room, especially if he needed a bit of time out. It was his refuge. He would come and sit on his cushions, emptying out the contents of the plastic box onto the wooden floor. He would feel the fabrics, gaze at the different coloured materials, and then rub the fabric against his face, his arms, his legs. He would then lie on them. Some of the toys featured coloured lights, others felt squidgy and tactile. He loved them all.

Kate looked out of the bedroom window at the street below. Although she had Sam, she sometimes felt so alone. It was just the two of them, wrapped in their own little cocoon, their own little world. She sometimes wondered if this was healthy for him? Did he need someone else? Someone else to share his life with? She shook her head, *no*, that wasn't the answer. It could never happen anyway. They were doing all right; they had survived six years. She could do this; she was strong enough to do this. *He* nearly ground her down, but she refused to let him, didn't she? He could no longer hurt her, hurt them.

From the top of the street she observed Sam's taxi as it slowly crawled towards the house. She closed his bedroom door and ran downstairs. She shoved her feet into her Converse that she had left by the front door and opened the door just as the taxi came to a standstill. She saw his little face through the glare of the car window. She let out a deep breath that she hadn't realised she had been holding. He was happy, smiling at her. She opened the door and like a ninja he jumped out. Kate quickly told him to go into the house, which he did, while she asked his passenger escort if he had been okay.

'He's been fine love, quiet on the way home, but I think he's just tired,' she said, as she began to pass Kate his book bag and car seat.

'Yes, he had a restless night last night. Hopefully tonight will be better.' Kate forced a smile and picked up the car seat and waved, saying that she would see them in the morning. She briskly walked down the path and into the house. Sam's socks and shoes where in the middle of the hallway, abandoned where he had kicked them off. As Kate bent down to pick them up, telling herself that she really needed to remind Sam once more about putting his shoes neatly away, he called out, 'Mum, put my pyjamas on.'

Kate smiled. Every day was the same.

CHAPTER FOUR

Matt stood surrounded by boxes, most of them unopened, stacked against the living room wall. The room was filled to the brim with their dusty smell, the particles like shimmering confetti dancing across the room. He had unpacked the essentials, meaning that he now had somewhere to sit, somewhere to sleep, and he could make a brew. He had only been busy unpacking for a few hours, but he'd already lost the will to live. He had no idea how he had managed to accumulate so much junk during the past twenty years of his existence. He thought he'd left most of it behind with Lisa.

Most of the unopened boxes contained books, which he could never bring himself to give away. A mixture of much-loved text and reference books, but also well-thumbed novels, most of which were crime stories and science fiction favourites. Matt planned to convert one of the spare rooms into a study stroke library. He now had the space to do so. He had never lived in a house with its own library; the thought excited him. He could do whatever he wanted. The house was his and his alone. Lisa hadn't let him convert the spare room into one; it was left for the baby, that was never to be.

It could wait for now. Matt needed to plan the room properly, to start making the shelves. It would be a big job. He rubbed his eyes, suddenly tired; he needed a change of scenery, or he would fall asleep. Glancing at his phone, he couldn't quite believe that it was only 2:00 pm. He decided to go to the uni campus and sort his office out. It was only a twenty-minute drive away, one of the main reasons he had chosen the area. He hadn't wanted to rent a room on campus, although it would have been the cheaper option.

He began to search for the box named '*work stuff*', as it contained all his notes, research materials, books, pens and posters, and most important of all, wall planner. It took him a few minutes of searching to finally locate it. He looked inside to make sure that it was the right box, before picking it up and heading to the front door. Balancing the box on his hip, he managed to open the door and manoeuvre himself through it, box in hand. His gaze wandered towards next door; he had not seen the woman or her little boy to talk to as yet. He had seen her waving the little boy off in the taxi. He wondered if he should call around and say hello, or would that seem creepy? But on the other hand, he didn't want to seem standoffish. He'd just have to keep a look out and say hello when he next saw them. He had already bumped into the elderly couple on the other side while he was unpacking the van with Brian. But he couldn't for the life of him remember their names, *Jim and Sarah? John and Sally?* They had invited him around for a cup of tea, but he'd politely declined. He knew that they were just being polite, but they seemed nice enough. They probably thought he would be trouble, owning a bachelor pad and all. He smirked; nothing could be further from the truth.

Matt locked the front door and headed to his car. A battered Nissan Micra that had seen better days, but it got him to where he needed to be, and he loved his wreck of a car; they'd been through a lot together. He opened the boot and put the cardboard box inside. Slamming the boot, he sighed, and wondered how he would get on in his new job, knowing that only time would tell.

'Hi, you must be Dr Harper.' A huge burly man with arms the size of tree trunks and a face well-worn and cracked from living life in the great outdoors walked towards Matt.

'Yes, I am. Please call me Matt,' he smiled and shook the professor's hand, noting that the older man had a strong grip.

'Well, welcome. I'm Professor Baird, *Callum*,' he smiled, 'we chatted on the phone.'

The professor let go of his hand and patted him on the back. Matt couldn't help smiling; the soft Irish lilt was a complete juxtaposition to how this man looked. The professor had been unable to attend Matt's interview as he was out on a research trip in the middle of the North Sea.

'So, what do you think of your lab?' he asked Matt with a raised eyebrow. 'Do you need any further equipment?'

Matt scanned the lab once more from the comforts of the doorway. He had to admit that he was quietly impressed. There was a brand spanking new GC-MS, fluctometer and nutrient analysers and most of the other stuff looked like it was fairly new too. The lab was massive. He felt like a kid in a sweet shop. 'No, I think that I have everything I need. The lab is very well set up,' Matt grinned at him.

Professor Baird grinned back, content in knowing that Matt was impressed. 'I'll let you get on then. Do you need me to show you where your office is?'

'No, I can find my way, thank you.' Matt shook his head; he just wanted to be alone, to find his feet, get settled, but he didn't want to appear rude.

'Good, good.' The professor handed him a massive bunch of keys; they weighed heavy in Matt's hand. 'Come find me later, before you leave. We can have coffee.'

Matt nodded, knowing that he couldn't get out of it. Professor

Baird smiled once more, gave a small nod, and strode out of the room.

Matt slowly walked around the lab, mentally absorbing all the different types of equipment and the chemicals that were stacked in varying glass cupboards. He felt the adrenaline pumping through his veins. He was itching to get started.

The research involved collaboration with the local aquarium, studying the effects of dune stability and acidification along the Lancashire coastline. But Matt would also be very hands-on too, helping to set up displays, talking to the kids and getting them involved, getting them interested in sea life. That was what Matt really found exciting.

He continued his examination of the lab, inspecting the various machines, the top of the range fume cupboards, opening the immaculate white cupboards and drawers to see what lurked inside. He was quietly impressed; it really was well stocked. He'd have to quickly make himself known to the lab technicians, take them out for a drink. That was the secret to a well-run lab, a happy lab technician. He should know, he used to be one.

He pulled out a lab stool and perched on the end, gazing at his surroundings, knowing that there was nothing more he could do today in the lab. On the other hand, he did need to set up his office space. So, picking up his cardboard box, he headed out into the hallway.

The semester hadn't yet started; there was only one more week until the halls would be crammed full of undergraduates, so the hallways felt far too wide and airy. The office was not far from the lab, just a short walk, and after a few minutes winding his way through the long corridors, Matt eventually located the row of offices belonging to the *Science Department*. He stopped in front

of his door. A shiny new nameplate bearing the name *Dr Harper* had been added, telling him that the office was most definitely his. He placed the cardboard box on the floor, dug the large bunch of jailor keys out of his pocket and attempted to find the right one. Fiddling with the lock, he finally managed to open the door. As he stared into the room, he couldn't help the grin that slowly spread across his face.

The room was huge, in fact far too big for one member of staff. A sleek mahogany desk sat in front of a wide window that overlooked the courtyard. On top of the desk was a computer and keyboard, allowing Matt access to the university's intranet. One of the walls was lined with ceiling to floor bookshelves and the remaining wall had been left bare, apart from a huge notice board that had been placed upon it. It was perfect.

A blank canvas.

He put the box onto the table and sank down into the plush office chair. Knowing that time was of the essence, he stood up again and began to slowly empty the contents from the box. He had a strong feeling that he would feel very much at home in this office. He knew he'd feel more at ease at work than at home. That revealed an awful lot about the state of his life right now.

Matt immersed himself in his work, progressing methodically, putting posters on the walls and books on the shelves. He scribbled notes onto the dates of his wall planner and then pinned it to the notice board. He switched on the computer and accessed the staff intranet. After an hour and a half, he realised that he needed a cup of coffee and made a mental note to buy a small coffee maker to keep in the office. Then he remembered Professor Baird's offer of a cup of coffee, and so after locking the door behind him, he made his way down the corridor in search of the professor's office.

Matt stretched back on the sun lounger, his feet plunged into the still warm grass, the blades tickling his toes. He closed his eyes, enjoying the warmth of the setting sun on his cool skin. He contemplated his productive and interesting afternoon. He really did feel as if he had accomplished something and had somehow planted some roots. With mixed emotions, he realised that he hadn't thought about Lisa all day. He scratched his stubble and sighed once more; he needed a shave.

Matt would enjoy working with Callum, as he would pretty much leave him to his own devices, but he also knew that he would have to run ideas past him. At least he was an open book, a man with years of research experience. Matt could learn a lot from him. More importantly, he liked him.

He picked up his cold can of beer, the condensation making his fingers wet, and took a large swig, before placing it back down on the long grass. It was still warm for September.

He tilted his head up towards the sun. It was not such a bad life, lying in the garden with a beer, planning work. He started to run through what he needed to do, knowing that the first job on his list would be that of catching up with Dan at the aquarium; he'd do that first thing tomorrow, then he'd buy the coffee maker. He had a few ideas to run past him, especially about the marine displays for the children. He'd have to jot down a few notes.

He opened his eyes and absorbed his surroundings, the rustling of the trees, the sound of a lawn mower and a dog barking in the distance. He hadn't realised that the garden would be such a sun trap. It was a surprisingly large garden, with a raised decked area outside the conservatory's sliding doors and a long patch of grass that stretched to the very end of the garden, forming a V-shape. He was no gardener, but he knew that he would have to do a bit of mowing, weeding and planting.

Lisa was the gardener.

He paused mid-thought, squeezing his eyes shut once more. He mustn't think about her, he did not want to ruin a perfectly enjoyable evening.

Blinking, he opened his eyes and looked around him, thinking that he needed to buy a few planters to arrange around the decking area, just to brighten it up a bit.

While he was thinking these thoughts, enjoying the stillness of the moment, he heard a twig snap, or what sounded like a twig snapping. He sat up and scanned the garden, but there was nothing out of the ordinary to be seen. It must have been a bird. He laid back down, slowly closing his eyes, but then opened them once more when he heard another noise, as if wood were being split in two. He shot up and looked around the garden but once again couldn't see anything unusual. He shoved his feet into the flimsy plastic flip flops that he always wore outside. He swore that he heard something. Standing still, he listened once more, rooted to the spot. He didn't dare breathe.

No, nothing.

He slowly let out a breath, but then he heard it again, the same sound, coming from the far side of the garden, where the mum and little boy lived. He walked over slowly to where he heard the sound, then all of a sudden, so sudden in fact that he jumped back, a head popped through the gap. Two huge blue eyes stared at him, surrounded by a mop of blonde curls. Then ever so slowly, the rest of the small body emerged, squeezing through the tiny gap.

Matt watched spellbound as the little boy stood and looked around the garden. He noticed that he avoided his gaze. It was almost as if Matt wasn't there. Matt had no idea what to say to this small imposter, but before he could think of the right words, the blonde-haired boy strolled over to the now empty sun lounger and

flopped down onto it. Stretching out his thin body, he allowed his arms to drop to the side and then closed his eyes.

All Matt could do was stand and stare at the little boy from next door, the one who went to school in the taxi. He hadn't seen any other children in the house. He had no idea what to do; he wasn't used to dealing with young children, never mind one who was completely ignoring him. He approached the little boy ever so slowly and crouched down in front of him. The last thing he wanted was to frighten him. 'Hello,' Matt ventured.

No response.

Matt cleared his throat, tried again. 'Hi, I'm Matt. What's your name?'

No response.

Boy and man sat there in silence for several moments. Matt began to think that the little boy would not respond. But then he slowly opened his eyes, blinked at the brightness of the sun, and without looking at Matt responded with one word. 'Sam.'

Matt sat and thought of his next response, his next move, not entirely sure of how he was going to get this little boy out of his garden. It was while he was pondering his many options, that he then quickly rejected, that he heard a woman's voice shouting, trembling in fact, with what sounded like uncontrollable fear.

'Sam ... Sam ... where are you?'

Matt jumped to his feet, shouting in the direction of her voice, through the battered fence. 'Hello ... erm ... he's right here, in my garden.'

He looked towards the little boy, who was still stretched out like a cat on his sun lounger, his eyes closed to the glare of the sun, and he couldn't help but laugh.

At least he'd get to meet his new neighbours.

CHAPTER FIVE

EARLIER THE SAME DAY …

Kate sat down next to Sam and kissed the top of his head, his curls tickling her nose. She wanted to hug him so tightly but knew that now was not the right time. After his shower, once he was dressed, that's when he liked to be hugged, when he was wrapped up in his soft fluffy towel, his thin pale arms wrapped around her neck. She would hold him so tightly, so tightly that she sometimes felt that her heart would break in two. Instead, she forced herself up from the couch and went into the kitchen to sort out the leftovers from his lunchbox. Usually just his plastic drink bottle and a banana peel would be lurking inside, but she liked to check that he had eaten his lunch.

It was always empty.

Sam ate the same packed lunch every single day. Two slices of dry bread – Kate could not put anything on them as they would be too *sticky,* too *yacky* – a banana, a packet of ready salted crisps (always the same brand), two rice cakes and some breadsticks. All gluten free. All crunchy, dry, and brown in colour.

Kate turned to look at Sam; he was sat waiting patiently for his cornflakes, leafing through his train book, that apparently was his *best book ever.* She had to leave it in the same position on the couch; if it went missing then all hell would break loose. She checked every night before she went to bed.

'Did you have a good day at school Sam?' Kate shouted through to the living room, as she grabbed the cornflakes box from the cupboard.

'No Mum, *stop*,' came Sam's sharp reply, without him lifting his eyes from a picture of a steam train.

Kate sighed. She had to keep trying to engage with him, to get him to tell her about his day. It was just that he didn't want to talk about school. She knew in his mind that school was over, *finished*, so why did he need to talk about it? She just silently craved to be part of it. Instead, she poured a handful of cornflakes into his blue plastic bowl and placed it onto the kitchen table in the usual place. 'Come and get your cornflakes Sam,' she shouted.

'No, here!' he shouted back.

'No Sam,' Kate tried to keep the frustration out of her voice, 'cornflakes at the table.'

'Noooo,' Sam yelled, 'here, here, here.'

Kate quickly counted to ten before walking into the living room. 'Sam,' she said, kneeling in front of him with the picture cards of *cornflakes* and *kitchen*. 'Cornflakes in kitchen after school.'

Sam inched forwards towards her, closely studying the cards. Quick as a flash, he snatched them and then promptly threw them on the floor. Making a mad dash into the kitchen, he grabbed his bowl of cornflakes, then walked carefully back into the living room, before landing back on the couch with a thump. 'Cornflakes on couch,' he said stoically.

Kate stifled a laugh, looked away. Sometimes you just had to pick your battles. 'Sam what do you say?'

'Thank you,' he replied with a mouthful of dry cornflakes.

Not for the first time, Kate wondered how he could eat dry cornflakes by the bucket load; he ate them like crisps.

She left him happily munching and wandered into the hallway

to grab his school bag, so that she could read his chat book. At least this would give her some information about his day.

'Sam has had a settled day. He practised typing his name and address on the computer and enjoyed the interactive room ...'

Kate carried on reading, immersed in the words, soaking them up, trying to understand Sam's day. It looked like he had had fun and had been fairly settled. She swallowed down the tears that were threatening to spill over her cheek. She just wished that sometimes he would tell her about his day, what he had played with, *who* he had played with, *just like a normal ...* But she stopped herself. That wasn't fair to Sam and it didn't help her either. He'd had a good day and that was all that mattered.

Kate switched on the kettle. She'd have a cup of coffee with Sam before making a start on tea. Sauntering back into the living room, she placed her cup on the small table, then picked up her notebook. She began to read her notes. Sam sat quietly, engrossed with his trains that were displayed in full glossy technicolour in his treasured book. The only sound to be heard was of him crunching his cornflakes, *crunch ... crunch ... crunch.*

It was only when he had finished eating that the silence was broken. 'Drink Mum.'

Kate turned to look at her son. 'Yes, Sam, you can have a drink. I'll get you some apple juice,' she smiled at him. 'How do we ask?'

He looked at her with his huge blue eyes and smiled. 'Please,' he said, while doing the sign for please, touching his hand to his chin and then opening his hand out flat, palm upwards, like they must do at school. Kate thought not for the first time that she must learn Makaton.

'Good boy Sam, I'll get your drink.'

Kate picked up her coffee and took it with her into the kitchen. She quickly found his favourite blue cup from the cupboard and

after retrieving the apple juice from the fridge, headed back to the living room, placing her coffee cup once again onto the small table in the corner of the room.

'Here you go Sam,' she said as she gave him his cup.

'Thank you,' came his reply, his eyes still glued to the trains.

Kate's heart lurched; it was the little things, like when he said thank you without being prompted that meant so much to her. 'Good boy Sam,' she told him quietly, the words sticking in her throat.

They continued to sip their drinks, immersed in the silence.

Kate had finished drinking her coffee when Sam suddenly stood up and started flapping his hands up and down, as if he was trying to take flight. 'Go in garden Mum, go in garden.' He ran towards the fridge, picked up the picture of *garden* that was attached to his visual timetable, and gave it to Kate.

'Yes Sam, you can go in the garden, let's find your shoes,' Kate told him gently. She found that it was a good way for him to burn off steam and calm down before sitting at the kitchen table. Whenever the weather was warm, he was always to be found in the garden.

Kate took his hand and led him towards the back door that opened straight out onto their secure back garden. The garden was safe, as much as it was enclosed on all sides by a sturdy wooden fence. He just liked to run about in huge circles and bounce on the trampoline, located at the far end in the shade. She didn't know how she would cope without it. Before she bought it, Sam had already broken two of the wooden slats on his bed by bouncing on it repeatedly; she couldn't stop him.

Kate found Sam's sandals, which were buried under a pile of wellies and outdoor toys – she had no idea how they had got to the

bottom of the pile – and told him to sit down, so that she could put them on for him. He sat swinging his legs, perched on the wooden kitchen chair while Kate fastened the Velcro straps.

'Sam, you can have ten minutes,' Kate told him, as she set the egg timer. 'Then I will start to make tea,' she paused to check that he was listening to her. 'Is that okay Sam?'

He looked at her as she opened the back door and then shrieking with laughter, ran out into the open space and quickly unzipped the mesh netting that encircled the trampoline. Kate watched from the back door, as he scrambled in and zipped the cover up, just as he had been instructed to do. She stood and observed him as he bounced up and down, up and down, his blonde curls flying upwards, an expression of pure joy etched upon his face. He looked so happy, he was happy. He loved to be outdoors.

As she stood and watched through the open door, her phone started to blurt out Journey's *Don't Stop Believin'*. She hesitated for a second; she had left her phone in the living room. She looked towards Sam as he bounced up and down. He would be fine while she took the call; she would only be a minute. Decision made, she ran into the living room and rooted in her bag, before remembering that she had put it on the table. She quickly swiped the screen to answer the call before it rang off. She didn't notice that the caller number was withheld. That would occur to her much later.

'Hello,' Kate answered breathlessly.

Silence.

'Hello?'

Again, silence.

Kate stood and listened to the sound of static that echoed down the line, wondering who was calling her. 'Hello?' she asked again.

No sound.

Fear suddenly gripped her. She started to shake. Now she could

hear faint breathing through the line but nobody spoke. For some reason, she knew that it was a man.

'*Jake*?' The word came out as a hoarse whisper, forced. She hadn't said that name aloud in a long time.

Again, there was silence.

The caller hung up.

Kate's arm dropped limply to the side of her body, the phone falling to the floor. Her heart was beating ten to the dozen, thoughts frazzled. Could it have been him? *No,* it couldn't have; there was no way that he could have got hold of her number. She shook her head, cursing herself for being so silly. Just a wrong number, that was all it was, it happened all the time. Her breathing started to slow, and her vision cleared. It was only as she bent down that she remembered she had left Sam unattended, and she could no longer hear his squeals of delight.

Panic seized her once again as she ran to the back door. She looked towards the trampoline, but he was not there. Was he playing a game? Hiding in the overgrown bushes behind the trampoline? He had done that many times as he liked to go there to say hello to the bees. He called it the *Bee House*. She continued down to the bottom of the garden, pushing through the bushes, but there was no sign of him. Did he go back indoors? Kate told herself to stay calm. He couldn't have gone far; the front door was locked. She headed back into the house and started calling for him, as she ran frantically from room to room. Kate felt the hysteria bubbling up inside her as her skin turned to ice. *Where was he?*

He must be in the garden. Was he playing hide and seek? But he had never played those types of games with her before.

She stumbled along the narrow path that led down the centre of the garden, exploring carefully the edges by the fence, behind

the trampoline once more. She shouted his name, but there was no sign of him. Where was he?

Kate stood in the middle of the garden and shouted his name as loud as she could, unable to stem the rising panic.

Then to her relief she heard a man's voice coming from the garden next door.

'Hello ... erm... he's here in my garden.'

'I think that's your mum calling you Sam,' Matt said gently.

Sam did not move, did not even acknowledge that Matt had spoken to him. Matt's brow creased as he studied this peculiar little boy while wondering what was wrong with him. Something wasn't quite right.

'Yes, my mum,' Sam eventually replied, breaking the silence. He still lay on the sun lounger with his eyes closed.

'I'll come and open the front door for you,' Matt yelled towards the gap in the fence. 'He's safe ... he's erm ... lying on my sun lounger.'

'*Thank you so much,*' drifted the sound of the woman's relieved voice towards Matt. He noticed that the voice sounded strained and relieved all at the same time.

Matt looked at the little boy once more and realised that he was happy. He just wished that he wasn't in his garden. 'I'm going to get your mum now. You just stay there,' Matt mumbled, not knowing if Sam had heard or even understood him. He made his way into the house and took one final look behind him, before racing to the front door.

Matt took a steadying breath. He didn't know this woman, or her son, who was now sat in his garden, which made the whole situation way beyond awkward. What a way to meet the new neighbours. He just hoped to God that she didn't think he had lured her son into the house.

He opened the door and the woman stumbled into the hallway, catching him off guard. He quickly held out his arms to catch her, a reflex action, but she shrugged him off while attempting to squeeze past him down the narrow hallway that was a mirror image of her own. Matt let go of her arm as soon as he saw the openly hostile look on her face.

'Where is he?' she demanded.

Matt stood speechless for a moment before responding. He thought she was about to cry. 'He's still in the garden, I'll erm, show you.' He looked away from her, clenching his jaw. Why was she being so rude? He strode quickly towards the back door. Stepping into the garden, he could feel the warmth of her body behind him.

She pushed past him.

He watched as she stumbled over the grass in her haste to be with her son.

She crouched down and placed her hand on Sam's. Matt watched as she picked up her keyring and showed Sam something, an image, but he was not sure what it was; he couldn't see clearly from where he was stood. But he was hypnotized by their exchange.

It was somehow raw, something that he had never experienced before.

Sam slowly sat up while she continued to gently speak to him. Then he swung his legs over the side of the chair. Holding onto his mother's hand, they both walked over to where Matt was still rooted to the ground. What he had just witnessed was something quite special. He had no words. It was the invisible bond between them that was so raw. He ran his hand through his hair, feeling uncomfortable, feeling as if he were an intruder in his own home.

'Hi, I'm so sorry about all of this, –' the woman began as she approached Matt, but he shook his head.

'It's fine, not a problem.' Now that she wasn't scowling he realised

that she was quite pretty, in a bossy kind of way. Her features had softened, she looked relaxed. Matt then knew that she had just been worried about her son, of course she had, she must have been out of her mind. How old was he? Five, six? He also noticed a slight accent, one that he could not quite place; she wasn't from around here.

The woman continued to stand and stare at him, the little boy tugging at her to leave.

'No harm done,' added Matt in an attempt to lighten the mood. He couldn't help staring back at her. He noticed her pale blue eyes for the first time, so like the little boy's, fringed with long delicate eyelashes, and the way that she was biting her lip did something in the pit of his stomach.

'No, I was incredibly rude, I'm so sorry. I just panicked,' she paused, her cheeks reddening slightly. 'I didn't know where he had gone. I didn't know that he could get through the fence.' Her eyes wandered over to the broken fence slat and then to Sam's face. Matt saw that she tightened her grip on the little boy's hand.

'It's okay, I understand,' Matt said as he tore his eyes from where she held Sam's hand. 'No harm done.'

'Well,' she hesitated, looking at Sam, 'we'll be going now, so sorry to disturb you. Sam, say goodbye to the nice man.'

Sam looked at the floor; he would not meet Matt's eye, but he obediently mumbled, 'Bye.'

They all stood in silence for a few more seconds, until Matt realised that he was blocking the entrance to the back door. He turned and retraced his steps through the kitchen and the living room, then down the hallway. He opened the front door. It was only as they stood on the doorstep that he realised his blunder. He hadn't told her his name, and for some reason he wanted her to know.

'I'm Matt,' he shouted, a little too loudly.

She turned and smiled. 'Where are my manners today? So sorry, I'm Kate. Nice to meet you.'

But before Matt could utter a response, they were gone.

He let out a long-held breath while gazing at the space where they had stood. He could still smell her perfume. Slowly he closed the door.

CHAPTER
SIX

The book on Kate's lap remained unread, a Nordic noir thriller that no longer held her interest. She was restless. Shadows flickered on the walls from the glare cast by the small round lamp that was nestled among the yellowing paperbacks on the bookshelf. She should really be writing up her articles, but she couldn't concentrate. All she could think about was the phone call, and if she was being truly honest, those piercing blue eyes belonging to the new next-door neighbour.

The phone call had unnerved her, shaken her. It had taken her back to all those years ago, when she had been a different person, a completely different person to the woman she was now. She did not want to be that woman again. She had checked her phone, once Sam was safely tucked up in bed, to see if there was a number logged, but it had been blocked. That's what really bothered her. The fact that whoever it was didn't want her to know their identity. It had to be Jake; she couldn't think of anyone else who it could be. But how did he get hold of her number?

Kate pulled the crocheted blanket, a mess of woollen blues, yellows and reds, that scratched her skin, further around her shoulders. She was far too tired to think straight but although exhausted, she knew that sleep would not come.

Jake, her ex-partner, the man who had made her life a living hell. It could very well be him. She thought that she had got away with it. How stupid was she? Nothing was ever that simple. After six years, she had grown complacent. She was less careful; she should never have let her guard down. Paranoia was beginning to set in. Kate had made sure that all of the windows were locked when she came home with Sam; she had checked twice. Now, she could feel the fear overcoming her once more, and she could not let it, not again. He would never again have that power over her.

No, it wasn't Jake. It wasn't him. Kate kept repeating this mantra to herself, in the hope that she would believe it.

It was nearly 11:00 p.m., but Kate decided to make herself a cup of tea to take up to bed with her. Tea always had the power to soothe. She was not sure why that was so. Perhaps it was the ritual of making it? Or the fact that she could drink it from a sturdy brown mug, with two teaspoons of sugar. She switched the kettle on and hunted out the teapot. Staring out of the kitchen window, she saw the trampoline bathed in shadow; it looked so forlorn in the darkness. She shook her head; she would need to fix the fence tomorrow, meaning that she would have to go to the large industrial park at the edge of town and pick up some large wood screws, or whatever they were called. It was her responsibility, the fence; it was on her side of the garden. Perhaps she could ask Matt to help? But no, Kate thought, that wouldn't be fair. If she asked him then he would probably feel obliged to do the work, so no, she would fix it herself.

Kate heard Sam shuffling about above her in his room – he'd not yet settled. She had left him to settle himself. She would check on him in a little bit. Sometimes she found him asleep in his sensory den, lying on all the soft cushions, toys draped over his sleeping

body. It was always a military operation trying to gently lift him back into bed without waking him.

The kettle beeped. Kate picked it up and poured the boiling water into her bright yellow teapot. It was one of the very first items that she had bought when she moved into the house all those years ago. She loved the colour – it was bright, cheerful, carefree. It was how she wanted to be, how she wanted to feel.

She waited for the tea to steep, the water slowly turning brown.

She thought of Matt. His eyes, his eyes were so blue. She had never seen eyes quite so blue before and they stirred something deep within her, within her soul, something that had long been buried. It would, however, take her a long time to trust another man, and anyway, she had Sam. He was her priority. He was her life now.

She picked up the teapot and sloshed the brewing tea about a bit before pouring the scalding liquid into her favourite brown tea cup. She spooned in two heaped teaspoons of sugar and then taking the cup, went up the creaky stairs to the safety and warmth of her bed. She believed that there was something quite magical about lying in a warm bed, nestled under the covers. Nobody could get you there; the outside world was miles away. Maybe these thoughts stemmed from childhood? Hiding under the bedcovers so that the bogey man couldn't get you. Many emotions, thoughts and feelings came from those hidden recesses in the mind, locked away from childhood days gone by. Kate knew that they made us who we are.

Her thoughts then drifted to her gran, and of how she would tell Kate bedtime stories about the times when she was a little girl, growing up in the war. Kate smiled at the memory. She missed her gran.

Kate switched on the bedside light and picked up her tea. Everything was now quiet from Sam's room. She sipped her tea,

enjoying the sweet bitter taste. She briefly closed her eyes and an image of Matt appeared. She hated to admit it, but there was an instant invisible attraction between them. But she had been so flustered, so preoccupied with finding Sam and making sure that he was safe that she knew that she had come across as rude and almost aloof. What must he have thought of her? Did he see a worried mother, or a woman who appeared cold and uncaring? Kate had no idea, she just hoped that he didn't think that she didn't trust him. Could he have thought that? Kate held her head in her hands, suddenly weary with it all. She felt awful now; she didn't even thank him properly. She was just so frazzled, with the phone call and then not seeing Sam. If she hadn't received that phone call, then things would have played out very differently. He may even have liked her.

Matt was a good-looking man, in that honest, boy-next-door kind of way. So unlike Jake. The Jake she had known was dark and brooding, that nauseatingly classically handsome shallow type, who know exactly how good-looking they are. It was one of the things that had attracted her to him, his sheer belief in himself. She was younger then; looks meant everything, they no longer did.

Matt was tall, almost lanky, and the way he walked, the way in which he held himself was somewhat awkward. His vulnerability shone through – maybe that was why Kate felt attracted to him. He seemed safe. But she knew that she had made a terrible first impression on him. She had met him for all of five minutes and he had probably decided that she was unhinged. One of those mothers. But he never passed comment about Sam. No snide remark, hurtful words. That said an awful lot about him. Kate had been the target of many hurtful words, '*What's wrong with him?*', '*You are too soft with him*,' or '*He'll grow out of it*.' But Matt never said anything about Sam, about the fact that he had invaded his

privacy, his space, and why wasn't Kate watching him? None of this was said. Although of course, he may have thought it.

Kate got the impression that Matt was single; she saw no photographs of him with another woman, and the place was in utter chaos. But then perhaps she was being unkind. He had only just moved in; of course, the house would be upside down. And anyway, there may very well be a girlfriend; he might have just moved in before her, to unpack. But Kate didn't think so. She thought that he was all alone in the world and was once again ashamed of how rude she had been towards him.

She sipped her tea, now cooled, the liquid warming her bones, although the temperature inside the house was still warm. She smiled, wondering what secrets he had, if he had any skeletons lurking in his closet? Probably not. He didn't seem the type, but then again, neither did she. He would never find out her secrets. Nobody could know her past. It was probably best to keep her distance, the way she did with everyone. Life was much easier that way.

She contemplated turning the lamp off, just as Sam's bedroom door opened, and in he stumbled, rubbing his eyes, trying to climb over her into bed.

'No Sam,' Kate told him gently. 'Back to bed love.' Slipping out of the covers, the cool air hitting her legs, she took his hand and walked him back to bed, covering him with the duvet, tucking it around his small body. He seemed so much smaller when lying in bed. She bent down and kissed him gently on the top of his head.

'Night, night Sam,' she whispered, then slowly retreated from the room, to snuggle once more under her own duvet. But he would be back in. It was going to be one of those nights.

Matt couldn't stop thinking about them, well more precisely, *her.* He had tried unpacking more boxes, to keep his mind busy, but

they had slowly crept back in. It was getting so late now; his arms and legs ached and he was desperate to get to bed, but he knew that he couldn't switch off. He had such a busy day tomorrow. Instead of treading up the stairs to get some rest, he found himself sat in the lone armchair, in the dark. Thinking about her, and the little boy.

There was something not quite right about the little boy, he just couldn't put his finger on it. There must be for him to go to school by taxi, and then there was the fact that he turned up in the garden wearing his pyjamas. Matt had only registered that fact once they had left.

He thought about how the little boy did not look at him, not even once. It was almost as if he wasn't there. He thought that this behaviour wasn't normal, but then quickly swallowed down that thought; it wasn't the done thing, to think like that. What the hell was normal anyway? He had no idea anymore. It was just that the boy had no sense of personal space, of boundaries. He had broken the fence and shown no obvious signs of guilt. He didn't care. And then Kate didn't say anything to him; she didn't tell him off. Matt just thought that it was all a bit strange.

She had seemed so tired, black circles evident under her eyes, but they couldn't hide how pretty they were. She had incredibly pretty eyes, even when she was scowling at him. But she had been afraid, perhaps afraid that something had happened to her son? Matt got the impression that she didn't trust anyone, she was so nervous. She could barely keep still, and she couldn't get away from him fast enough. He thought at the time that he had done something wrong, but he now knew that was not true. It was because she was embarrassed, the fact that her little boy had just walked unannounced into a complete stranger's garden.

Matt laughed, it *was* funny. *He* was funny, the little boy, Sam. Perhaps he should send around a card, to tell her that what

happened wasn't a problem. Perhaps that would help? But then it may well be best to leave things as they were. She was only his neighbour after all.

He was being ridiculous, sitting in the dark. He used to sit in the dark years ago when married to Lisa. She'd often ask him why, and he wouldn't really have an answer. He'd mumble and look away from her. It just gave him time to think, he supposed. But then he had far too much time alone nowadays – too much thinking was bad for you.

He lay his head back against the coldness of the leather and closed his eyes.

All he could see were tired and lonely, pretty, blue eyes.

Chapter Seven

Tuesday, September 10th, 2013

Kate gently massaged her throbbing temple, trying to ease the stabbing pain that was gradually growing in intensity. It had started just above her left eye as a gentle ache. She knew it would eventually fade; her headaches always did. A common occurrence due to a lack of sleep and too much caffeine.

Sam had crept into her bedroom a total of five times. The first four times she had wearily put him back into his own bed, exhaustion washing over her, but on his fifth attempt, at two in the morning, she had given up and allowed him to stay. Getting some sleep was more important than trying to get him to settle in his own bed; there was just no point.

Kate sat at the kitchen table, head bent, slumped over a cup of coffee. She stifled a yawn. It was only 5:30 a.m. Sam was in the living room, playing on his iPad, making things on his Minecraft app, spawning Endermen, sheep and zombie villagers. Kate had no idea what it was all about. She really needed to research it. She knew it was something to do with blocks and building things, creating online virtual worlds. She would Google it later. It was Emily who had told her about the phenomenon that was Minecraft, and that Sam really must play it. Kate wasn't so sure, but she had downloaded the app for him and it certainly entertained him. He liked living in his alternative, imaginary world. Perhaps it was because he could control it?

He'd already had his milk, that he demanded once he had plonked himself down on the couch, at just gone five that morning.

Kate just needed five minutes of alone time, and then her day could begin, fuelled by coffee. Always by coffee. She cradled the mug, her hands welcoming the buzz spreading through her synapses. She listened once more to the sounds echoing from the living room. A cow mooing and Sam laughing. She ran her fingers along the surface of the kitchen table, that was covered in crumbs and tomato sauce from last night's tea. Should she ring a cleaning firm today? She kept putting it off because of the cost, and to be honest she was filled with guilt at the thought of having a cleaner. The truth was that she should be more organised, to make the time to clean her own house. But between work and looking after Sam, she just didn't seem to find the time, or the energy.

A weary sigh escaped her lips. She needed to clean the table before doing anything else. The cupboard under the sink contained all the cleaning materials. She quickly unlocked it using the key that she kept hidden in the plant pot on the windowsill and found the disinfectant spray. After rinsing out the dishcloth, she generously sprayed the table with the disinfectant and methodically wiped away the sticky mess. A comforting saying popped into her head, *a tidy home is a tidy mind*. She sat down, the cloth still in her hand. Her gran had always been right. She always knew exactly what to say. She needed to get her act together, to be more organised, to clean her house. No more excuses. She'd have a quick clean before leaving for work.

'Mum, I want cornflakes,' Sam hollered over the blare of the iPad.

'All right Sam,' Kate shouted as she washed her hands in the sink. She fetched his blue bowl from the cupboard, sprinkling the cornflakes into it. Picking up her now cooled coffee, she went back into the living room.

'Here you go Sam.' She gave him the cornflakes and sat herself down next to him. 'What do you say?' she gently coaxed.

'Thank you,' he mumbled while crunching.

Their day had begun once more.

Kate sipped her coffee and thought about how she had lain awake for most of the night, Sam stirring at her side, thinking about *him*, her past. She hadn't done that in a long time. She couldn't allow herself to think about him. Not anymore.

She sat and closely studied her little boy, drinking in his features. Thankfully, she saw nothing of Jake in him. People told her that they could see *her* in him, although the same people had never met Jake – they did not know about his existence – but she couldn't see him in her son. She was just grateful that he looked nothing like his father, although a part of her knew that his genes were an integral part of who he was, and that did worry her. She told herself that she was being silly, she had a beautiful six-year-old little boy. An innocent, with a golden halo of blonde curls and blue eyes. To her shame, he had been mistaken for a little girl on a few occasions because of his hair, but he wouldn't let her cut it; he wouldn't allow her to take him to the barbers. Kate had tried, but he had become so upset, so anxious, he had screamed and hit out. Kate flinched at the memory. It had been upsetting for everyone. The last time she attempted to take him, which was well over a year ago, even the hairdresser ended up in floods of tears, as Sam had screamed that she was hurting him and that he needed an ambulance. So in the end, Kate had just let his hair grow. You pick your battles and getting his hair cut was not one of them.

'Mum, more cornflakes!' Sam asked, pulling at Kate's sleeve.

She took Sam's bowl and headed back into the kitchen, in search of the cornflakes.

'Sam, just let me put this sock on, *please!*' Kate demanded, while trying to grab hold of a wriggling Sam's foot. She was quickly losing her patience; she could feel the frustration bubbling up inside her, about to burst at any moment. It had taken her half an hour to get him dressed so far, as he had flatly refused to put on every single item of clothing, of which she had finally wrestled onto his moving body.

She had tried to coax him into getting himself dressed, with the use of visual symbols, pointing to the pictures of *underpants* and *polo shirt*, but he had thrown the pictures onto the floor. The sweat was now pooling at her waist, her armpits damp. She'd need to take a shower once he had gone to school. Why must the mornings be such a battle? Kate knew it wasn't his fault; he just didn't want to go to school. He'd already done one day, and he now knew what was in store for him. His not wanting to get dressed was his way of telling Kate just that, his way of exerting power. But it was fruitless – he still needed to go.

Sam was now stretched out on his sensory rug, burrowing his head, arms and chest into the soft and fluffy cushions, with just his pale, thin legs sticking out. He had managed to wrestle the one sock off his foot, which he now flung at her.

Kate told herself to keep calm.

She got up from his bed and trudged downstairs to sit in the silence of the living room. He was safe, he just needed time to calm down. She was making matters worse by being with him. She glanced at the clock, 07:45. Fifteen minutes and they'd be here, that is if they weren't late, but if he was not ready, then she would

just have to explain why. They would have to wait. She sat and looked out of the window; it was drizzling, you could barely see it, but the pavement glistened like scattered glitter. She steadied her breathing, calming herself.

'Mum, Mum!!!' Sam roared from upstairs. 'Put socks on!'

Despite herself, Kate laughed. She headed back up the stairs and into his room. He was sat on the bed, clutching both grey socks. His tear-soaked face made her heart clench. She bent down in front of him and took the socks, then without a word carefully put them on his feet.

'Okay Sam, now let's brush teeth.'

Much to her amazement, he offered no protest but followed her meekly into the bathroom.

The taxi was late.

Sam was on the floor, rhythmically pushing his toy car forwards and backwards. They had chatted about Matt, well Kate had done the talking, telling him that he should not go into Matt's garden. Sam listened but did not say anything. She didn't think he understood, but at least when she had fixed the fence he wouldn't be able to get in again. Maybe she should do him a social story? Kate made a mental note to search for images later, and she'd make him one. That was, once she'd cleaned and written those articles.

What was far more worrying, even more worrying than vandalism and trespassing, was Sam's total lack of awareness when it came to personal space. He had no concept that it was wrong of him to go next door, into a stranger's garden, and to sit on his sun lounger. Although it was funny now, at the age of six, it wouldn't be so funny when he was sixteen. Kate thought once more about how vulnerable he was; he could get into so much trouble. That's what scared her. Luckily, Matt had seen the funny side, well, at least she

thought he had, but not everyone was like that. Not everyone was kind. Kate shuddered, and looked towards her innocent six-year-old, wishing in her heart that he would never have to grow up.

She shook those thoughts from her head, glancing at the clock again, 08:27. She heard the roar of an engine and when she stretched to look out of the window, she saw the taxi stop in front of the house.

'Come on Sam, let's get your shoes on.'

Thankfully, he did just that.

Once she had quickly vacuumed and mopped the floors, Kate had jumped into the shower, ready to start the day afresh. She needed to go out; she couldn't stay in the house all day, she'd go stir crazy. She didn't really want to go to the office, not until she had written up the articles, so she planned to sit in the library until they were finished, and then email them over. She would also make a start on researching Sam's social story. That'd keep her busy, keep Veronica happy, plus she'd be using the library's free Wi-Fi. She told herself to remember to buy those wood nails. She really couldn't have a repeat performance of yesterday. That would be too embarrassing. She'd fix the fence once she got back from town.

Kate double-checked that she had all her papers, pens, notebook and laptop charger, and was just about to open the front door when her phone started to ring. She was tempted to ignore it, but thinking that it could be Sam's school, as they sometimes rang first thing, she began to root inside her bag, her phone inevitably at the very bottom, wedged between tissues and matchbox cars.

It was not school but an unknown number. It was the same person, it had to be. Kate's finger hovered over the screen, unsure of whether to answer the call or not. But it was always best to know, wasn't it?

She swiped the screen.

'Hello,' Kate's voice wavered. She hated herself for it, for her weakness.

Nobody spoke.

'Hello, who is this?'

Again, she was met with silence. All that could be heard was the breathing of the unknown caller. Her body and mind were seized once more by panic, her heart racing, forcing her to take deep breaths *in and out*, to calm herself. Whoever this was, they were playing mind games, and she was not going to be part of it.

She was about to end the call, her finger hovering over the red *end call* icon, when she heard him, *his voice*. The room began to sway. Lurching to one side, her vision slowly began to fade. She dropped the phone, his words echoing in her ear like the buzzing of flies.

'It's me ...'

CHAPTER EIGHT

The ray swam past Matt as he loomed over the large and open pool. He loved the sheer stillness of the place. It was still early, the aquarium empty, devoid of squabbling children who were eager to dip their hands into the water and to run under the huge glass-walled tunnel where the sand tiger sharks and black tips swam high above them. Matt was hugely impressed with what they had managed to achieve with the place. It had only opened a year ago, and although a lot more work needed to be done, it was easily making a profit, especially with the school tours that had been recently organised. It was also enticing in both the locals and visitors from across the north west.

He was now a part of that planning process. Collating all the data that the schools would need for the kids, producing work sheets, photographs, and then giving the guided tours. He enjoyed working with the children. They were always so inquisitive, so full of life. He loved that they were like huge sponges just wanting to soak up information. Then, of course, he had his own research.

'Shall I show you where the office is Matt?' Dan asked. He was a tall imposing man with vibrant red hair that hung in waves around his face, a face that was full of freckles, and a cheeky charm that disguised his many years. Matt had at first took him to be in his late twenties, when in fact he was nearing his own age.

'I better had, thanks.' Matt had been so preoccupied when he had first come to see the aquarium, taken in by its well-stocked resources and how energetic Dan had been, that he had neglected to ask about where he would be able to plan his work. He had just assumed that it would all be done back in his office at the uni.

The two men strolled through the empty corridors that were filled with various tanks displaying fish of all colours, shapes and sizes. At the rear of the building they came to a large wooden door emblazoned with the words 'STAFF ONLY', and after fumbling with a mammoth set of keys, Dan opened the door into a large and open-plan office space.

'It's not much I'm afraid, but you have a desk, somewhere to plug your laptop into and of course a fax machine, photocopier and printer. You should have everything you need.'

'It's perfect Dan. It'll save me having to go back to the uni to print stuff out. I can do it all from here.' He hadn't thought much about the logistics of all the prep work but having a desk space here made so much sense.

'We have a party of children booked in for this Friday, and then after that you'll find a schedule that I have just emailed over to you in a Word doc. That should have all of the information that you need. If not though, just ask. There aren't that many booked in yet, but it'll pick up during December. That's when they all do their Christmas trips.' Dan grimaced.

Matt knew that this would mean a busy schedule for him, and probably a noisy one too. He placed his bag onto the table. 'I'd better get to work then,' he grinned, unzipping his bag and squeezing the laptop out, then dropping the bag onto the floor.

'I'll leave you to it. If you need me I'll just be at the freshwater tanks, I need to talk through the feeding regime *again* with Ken.' He shook his head, all humour gone from his features. 'He keeps over feeding them, the last thing we need is a tank full of dead fish.'

Matt remembered meeting Ken on his last visit. He had recently retired and was looking for something to fill his days. Sadly, he didn't have a clue about fish. He had been recruited to clean and keep a general eye on things, but he did like to help with the feeding schedule, much to Dan's annoyance. Dan should never had hired him, but that was his call, not Matt's. He would bet money that Dan felt sorry for him, he was a soft touch was Dan. He could still hear him laughing as he closed the door.

There was so much to do here, Matt just knew that he would enjoy the work. Although completely different to his usual research, he needed that human contact, otherwise he would become too engrossed in what he was doing, shutting out the rest of the world. That had happened before; for three whole months he had hardly acknowledged Lisa, so immersed with his own research findings. But they had worked through it, well, he thought that they had. Perhaps it wasn't the baby thing after all? Perhaps she thought his work was more important than her? He hoped that wasn't the case. She had to know how much she meant to him.

Shaking his head, he booted up his laptop and started to think about what information he would need for the kids. Thoughts of Lisa were temporarily put on hold.

All he wanted was a simple coffee maker. *Was that too much to ask for?* Matt looked at the various coffee makers, all shiny and bright on the rows of shelves before him. All singing and all dancing. Whatever happened to just pushing a button, he wondered? He just wanted a coffee maker that he could plug in and brew his

coffee. Something simple. All the coffee machines that stood before him looked far too complicated. He was about to give up, thinking that he would just buy a kettle, and use instant, when he saw her. At first, he thought that it was a woman that looked like her, as why would she be here? Miles away from home? He stood and watched her out of the corner of his eye, his back pressed against the shelving unit. She hadn't noticed him. She turned her head slightly, in his direction, and his breath caught in his throat. It was Lisa. *What was she doing here?* Her slim fingers reached out to pick up a shiny red kettle. They had had a similar one at home, well, what *was* their home. Metallic, highly impractical, Matt had thought at the time, but she had insisted on buying it. He noticed the diamond, glinting on her ring finger above the gold band, and although it came as no surprise, he felt a sudden ache in his gut. She looked the same, but not quite so polished if that were at all possible. Her cream dress was her usual style, but it hung from her now too thin frame. She wore matching shoes with a slight heel. Her hair was tied up into a top knot, loose, blonde tendrils escaping, framing her face. It took all of Matt's power not to reach out and touch her, to put the strands of hair back behind her ear. He swallowed; he needed to turn away, she could not see him. But it was too late. Their eyes met, just as he was about to look away.

'Matt,' she breathed, so quietly, that Matt saw, rather than heard his name.

He looked down at the floor. What should he say? He had no idea. *How is your wanker new husband?* That probably wouldn't go down too well. But he was an adult, and they had both moved on; he needed to be civil with her.

'Hi Lisa, how are you?' His tone was flat; he was just going through the motions. How had things become so sour?

'Fine Matt, just fine,' she replied, in an equally measured and flat tone.

But Matt noticed that she wouldn't meet his eye, the slight twitch that alerted him to the fact that she wasn't telling the truth. He knew her too well.

Why are you here?

'Buying another red kettle then?' Matt laughed, instantly regretting his words as he saw the look of hurt on her face.

'The other one blew this morning, I need a kettle Matt,' she answered tartly. Her words clipped.

He shoved his hands into his pockets. 'Can we start again?'

This time Lisa smiled. 'Yes of course,' she sighed. This time she met his eye. 'How are you?'

'Good, I'm good,' Matt wondered when he had become such a good liar, he had never felt more wretched in his life. 'Just looking for a coffee maker,' he told her while gesturing wildly with his arms at the array of contraptions that were on display.

'Well there are lots to choose from,' Lisa laughed, her eyes scanning the shelves. She lost the smile. 'You need some help?'

Matt slowly shook his head. Lisa would be perfect in choosing one for him, but he didn't want her help, not now, not ever. 'No, I'm fine thanks. It's just for the office.'

'Oh.'

The comment was left hanging in the air. Matt had no idea what to say and it became very clear to him that Lisa had no intention of asking where his office was or what his new job entailed. Did she even care? He wondered once again why she was here in this part of the country. He had moved away so that he wouldn't have to see her.

'You on holiday then?' he asked. He knew that he shouldn't care, and that Lisa had probably been waiting for him to ask this question the moment their eyes had met, but he couldn't help it. It was just too bizarre, too much of a coincidence.

'Something like that,' she replied far too quickly.

Matt wondered where Dave was? In the car park? Surely, she wasn't alone?

'Well then, I'll leave you to it.' Lisa took a step backwards and paused. 'It was nice seeing you Matt.'

Matt tried to swallow, his throat still dry, a huge lump forming in his throat. 'Yeah, you too,' he managed to get out.

She wrapped her arms tightly around the large box with the kettle inside and slowly turned away from him towards the tills, but not before he caught a glimpse of what he thought to be sorrow flash in those beautiful blue eyes of hers. But then, he thought, he had probably just imagined it.

Kate's hands were trembling as she tried to type, her words on the screen incoherent. She couldn't concentrate, but she had to. She had a deadline, she had to write these articles. Why had he phoned her? To torment her? To tell her that he had found her, and could see her whenever he wanted? He had no idea where she lived, she was sure of that, but he could find out. She wished that she could phone her gran, ask her what to do. She would know; she had always known the right answer to every single question Kate had asked. But that wasn't an option now. She could only rely on herself. She had fleetingly thought about phoning Bill, but he would only worry, and she wasn't sure of what exactly had happened anyway. It had only been a phone call. That was why she had decided not to phone the police, as what could they do? Nothing, nothing at all. She didn't want to have to go through *everything* again. She had tucked the past neatly away into a box and had tightly sealed it. The troubling thing was that he had said hardly anything, other

than, '*it's me*.' Why taunt her like that? She was even doubting that it was him. She had no proof, none whatsoever. It just sounded like him, and she knew that she could never forget his voice, even after six years. And that's what he wanted, the control, for others not to believe her. Yet again, he had won.

She was frightened. Not for herself, but for Sam. He would want to see him, but she would never let that happen, not over her dead body.

The library was noisy today. It was usually a quiet haven where she could sit and think, write, but for some reason the room was full of children singing and babbling away. This usually wouldn't bother her, but her nerves were a jumbled mess. With a heavy sigh, she closed the lid of her laptop. She needed a quick break. There was a coffee vending machine somewhere. She remembered that they dished out luscious hot chocolate. She needed to taste the sweetness of the drink. She needed the sugar rush. Shoving her belongings back into her bag, she went in search of the machine and to then browse the shelves for a while. Maybe there was a thriller that she could immerse herself in? Just for a little while.

Her phone rang while she was standing at the machine, ready to insert her fifty pence. Should she answer it? It could be Jake. It could be school. She pulled the phone from her bag; the lock screen displayed *Emily*. Her pulse rate slowed. She'd have to answer it, she had fobbed her off far too many times. She swiped the screen and braced herself for the adrenaline rush that was her friend.

'Hi Kate, I thought you were ignoring me.' Emily's slightly high-pitched voice carried down the line.

I was, Kate thought. 'No, no, just busy as per usual. How are you?' Kate hardly recognized the sound of her own voice.

'Oh, you know, not good to be honest.' Emily paused a moment. 'You know what it's like.'

Kate had no idea what it was like to be a neurotic mother who only focused on the disasters and how you could cure your child, but she kept quiet. 'Oh yes, I know, how is Isaac?'

She had asked the question before fully realising that she shouldn't have asked it. She'd never get off the phone now.

'Oh, you know, Isaac wasn't too happy about going back to school. Absolute nightmare. Full meltdown before getting in the taxi this morning, and then he kicked off at school and smashed a window. I nearly died when his teacher called. What could I say? *Sorry* doesn't cover it, does it? Luckily I don't have to pay for any damages.'

'No, well that's … good,' Kate suggested. What else could she say?

'Are you free for that coffee tomorrow?' Emily continued, 'it's just that I read this fantastic article about cutting out all food colourings from the diet and then giving them an enema once a week to cleanse the colonic system. I could show you the clipping from the newspaper?'

'Erm … I'm at work tomorrow,' Kate lied. Well, she would have to work but not all day, and she could make time for coffee with a friend if she wanted to. 'Sorry, perhaps next week?'

'Oh, Kate, you work too hard; you need to rest you know.'

Kate could easily detect when someone was being insincere. False sympathy oozed down the line.

'Well, if I don't work then the bills don't get paid, so you know, needs must.' Kate recognised the tightness of her words, but she couldn't help it. Emily always managed to wind her up the wrong way.

There was a pause, and Kate knew she had won this one. Always play the single and poor parent, although she hated doing so.

'Yes, it must be so *very* difficult for you. I forget how lucky I am sometimes to have Gerald.'

Kate suppressed a laugh. No matter how bad her life got, she would always be thankful that she didn't have a Gerald. The man was a controlling and manipulative bastard, and Kate should know. Absolutely useless. Emily would be so much better off by herself. She knew for a fact that he blamed Emily for Isaac's autism. He was a vile man full of self-importance who was ashamed that he had an autistic son. Hence the need for a cure. Kate had told Emily once that she needed to leave him, a conversation that hadn't gone down too well as she refused to talk to her for over a month. So she no longer mentioned him, but she quietly mourned for her friend. Annoying as she was, she deserved better.

'Look, I can make this Friday, how does that sound?' Kate said the words quickly before she changed her mind. Swallowed them down.

'That sounds fantastic.' Emily sounded cheerful, eager.

Kate bit back a feeling of guilt. 'I'll see you then. Bye for now.' Kate ended the call and inserted the coin into the vending machine. She stood and waited for her hot chocolate to be dispensed, thinking that meeting Emily was bound to be a disaster. It always ended in a heated argument. She picked up the cup, the thin plastic bending in her grasp, the heat seeping through. Jake couldn't get to her, she was safe. No need to panic, no need to panic at all.

Matt stood back and surveyed the fence. Perfect. It hadn't taken him too long to fix the loose slat. He'd bought a few nails on his way home. He knew Kate would have felt obliged to do it, but well, he didn't mind. At least his garden should now be Sam-proof, he chuckled. The evening was once again warm for September. He took pleasure in sitting out with a cold can of lager and a book. He could hear Sam playing next door, his shrieks of laughter as he

bounced on the trampoline, catching the sight of his blond curls as he rose above the fence. He picked up his can, drained the dregs and decided that he should have one more. It had been a long day and, he had fixed the fence.

It was only when he went back into the garden and looked towards his sun lounger that he noticed he wasn't alone.

He blinked.

Lying there, eyes closed to the low sun in the sky, was Sam. He looked very much the same as he did yesterday. Only today, he was wearing Batman pyjamas. Why did she let him play out in his sleepwear? He stood looking at the little boy, unsure of what to say or do. The film *Groundhog Day* sprang to mind. He cleared his throat. 'Hi Sam,' he said in a gentle tone, aiming to sound calm and friendly. He didn't want to frighten him.

'Hi,' came the mumbled response.

Matt walked towards him, crouched by the side of the lounger. 'You okay Sam?'

'Yes.'

'Why are you in my garden?' Matt asked, but he secretly thought *how did you get in*?

Sam opened his eyes and looked upwards. 'Like your chair.' And a huge grin stretched across his face.

Matt stifled a laugh – he too liked his chair when he could sit in it. 'Mmm, yes well, it is a comfy chair, but we really need to get you back home, your mum will be worried.'

'Okay,' Sam replied, swinging his legs around the chair and jumping up. To Matt's surprise he grabbed his hand, making him feel like a giant, and pulled him towards the open kitchen door.

'Oh okay, yes well, yes, I'll take you home then.' They stood for a moment while Matt stretched his head to look at the newly fixed fence slat. It was still in place, so how had he got into the garden?

No other panels seemed to be missing. This child really was a mystery. Maybe he had bounced over?

Feeling awkward, Matt led Sam through the house. He wasn't so sure how Kate would react to him once again *letting* Sam into his garden. Although he had obviously invited himself. Would she even believe him when he told her that he had fixed the fence?

CHAPTER NINE

Kate could not believe that once again Sam had managed to get into the next-door neighbour's garden. This had never happened with the previous neighbours, an elderly couple to whom she hardly ever spoke. Just as well really, she couldn't begin to imagine what their reaction would have been, probably not a happy one. The worst of it was that she hadn't even realised he had left the garden until he had turned up on the doorstep. He must have escaped when she nipped up to the loo. What must he think? *Incompetent*? She *was*, allowing her six-year-old autistic son to wander wherever he liked. Feeling flustered, she ushered Sam into the house and mumbled an apology to Matt, who she noted looked equally embarrassed. He couldn't meet her eye.

'Look, do you want to come in and have a cup of tea? I feel terrible for him disturbing you again. It's the least I can do,' Kate asked.

Before Matt could offer a reply, she stood aside to let him past her and shut the door, remembering to slide the bolt across. 'I really meant to fix the fence but just haven't got around to it yet,' Kate told him as they entered the living room, inwardly cringing at the mess they walked into. She hadn't bothered tidying up when

Sam got back from school and there were clothes, books and papers everywhere.

She noticed that he suppressed a smile. 'Err actually, I did fix it, but he still managed to get through,' Matt told her as he stood in the middle of the room, hands shoved inside his pockets. 'I think he may have bounced across … from the trampoline?'

'Oh god, I am so sorry.' Kate felt mortified. 'How much do I owe you? The fence is my responsibility, I'll pay for the nails and any bits of wood you used.' She ushered Matt onto the end seat by the bookcase, towering with books.

'No, it's fine, honestly. I had all the bits and pieces anyway,' Matt told her, as he slowly sank down into the chair. 'It was no bother, really, at least I must have fixed it properly as he found another way in.' Matt glanced towards Sam, engrossed in his iPad at the other end of the couch. He suppressed a smile. *How did he get into the garden*?

Kate stood hovering, unsure of what to say or do. She noticed that Matt placed his large hands onto his lap and it was then that she noticed his wedding ring. So, he was married. 'I'll go and make the tea. Are you okay with Sam for a minute?' Kate looked towards Sam, his eyes still locked onto his Minecraft world; he wouldn't be any bother.

'I'm fine,' Matt said as he looked towards Sam once more.

Kate made a quick retreat into the kitchen and busied herself making the tea. She wondered if the day could get any worse?

Matt eased himself back into the comfy couch, listening to the sounds of Kate clattering about the kitchen, him at one end, Sam at the other. The room was a mirror image of his own. But this house was homelier and just full of stuff. He had never seen so many books before in one room. From a quick glance her book

collection looked rather impressive, and by the looks of things not just chick lit. He spied some Nordic noir novels and grizzly crime thrillers nestled among the popular romances of the day. He hadn't taken her for the crime reading type of woman. Looks could be deceiving. He had noticed her slim fitting jeans, the way in which they hugged her hips. His eyes also took in how her t-shirt skimmed her body in all the right places. She was a good-looking woman. He had also noticed that she wasn't wearing a wedding ring, but again, that didn't mean she wasn't in a relationship. Looking about the room, he couldn't see any photographs of her with a man, just pictures of Sam. Perhaps she was single? What he did notice were funny little symbols dotted around the room, and pictures of everyday objects. The door to the kitchen had a weekly planner attached to it with various symbols, and he wondered how they helped this little boy. Was he autistic? He had heard of autism but knew very little about it. Sam didn't make much eye contact though and his speech wasn't like that of a boy around his age. So perhaps he was?

'Do you take sugar?' Kate bellowed from the kitchen.

'No thanks, just milk,' Matt replied, his voice suddenly sounding far too loud in the small room.

Sam looked up from the screen. 'I like milk in my blue cup.'

Matt nodded, not sure of how to respond to this serious little boy's statement, but he was saved by Kate who wandered over to the couch with two cups of steaming tea.

'Here you go,' she said as she handed him the cup.

'Thanks.' Matt took the cup and balanced it on his knee. There was no coffee table to put it on. It was only as he took the cup that he wondered where Kate would sit, but his question was answered when she walked over to the small table in the corner of the room and pulled the chair out.

'So, how are you settling in?' Kate asked.

This was the one question that Matt hated to answer; he knew that people could see right through the lie. 'Oh, you know, it takes time,' he said as he moved the scalding cup to his other knee, but I'm slowly unpacking those boxes.' He tried to offer a small laugh, but it sounded more like a wheeze.

Kate laughed and he noticed the way in which it changed her entire face. It lit up, making her look years younger. 'I know that feeling, I still have boxes upstairs to unpack.'

'Really?' Matt was surprised. He thought that they had lived here for years.

Kate just stared at him with a fixed expression painted on her face, as if what she said had not meant to be said out loud.

Matt sipped his tea.

'So, what do you do then?' Kate asked.

Matt liked this type of question, non-personal. 'I'm a marine chemist. I'm doing some new research at the uni. Then in my spare time I help at the aquarium, mainly taking the kids on tours, that sort of stuff.' His voice trailed away. His answer seemed rehearsed, non-personal, even to his own ears.

'Wow. You mustn't get much time to yourself then. What does your wife think about all this?'

Matt could tell from the expression on her face that she instantly regretted her choice of words. She must have seen his puzzled look. Her face flushed bright pink. Her eyes darted from his face to his wedding ring, then back to his eyes, before lowering to her cup of tea that she was holding far too tightly.

'There is no wife, just an *ex-wife*.' Matt tried to keep his voice light, as if the words came easily to him. He knew he wasn't fooling anyone.

'Oh, erm … I am sorry,' Kate said quickly.

'I'm not, please don't apologise. We've been divorced six months.' Matt was wondering why he was telling her all of this. She wouldn't want to know about him and Lisa. He felt more foolish than ever, for stubbornly wearing his wedding ring. This could have all been avoided if he had taken it off.

They sat in silence, both sipping their tea; the only sound was that of Minecraft villagers in the background, emitting their zombified cries.

'It must be difficult for you though.' Kate gestured towards the ring. 'How long were you married?'

'Too long,' came Matt's curt reply, 'no, I didn't mean that. A long time, and we were happy. I suppose we just drifted apart.'

'Yes, that sometimes happens.' Kate looked towards Sam.

Matt was unable to read her expression clearly. What had happened to her, he wondered? 'So, how long have you lived here then? Not that long if you still have unpacked boxes.' He asked the question casually, trying to change the subject, so her expression puzzled him.

'No, we've lived here for just over six years now. Just been too busy to properly unpack.'

She attempted a small laugh and a slight shrug of the shoulders before directing her gaze once more to her cup of tea.

Matt thought this was a little strange, though he decided to probe no further. It was none of his business.

'Listen, I'll be popping Sam to bed in a little bit and I've made some chicken curry,' she paused, 'you're welcome to stay and have some if you want, you mustn't have had much chance to sort the kitchen out yet.'

Matt thought about his empty house next door, with no food in the fridge. 'Thanks, I'd love that,' he grinned.

Kate grinned back at him then sipped her tea.

Whatever had prompted her to ask him to stay for dinner? Kate had absolutely no idea. She just knew that she was fed up of eating alone every night and she wanted to say thank you to him for being so understanding about Sam. Anyone else would have probably kicked up a big fuss about it.

Sam was safely tucked up in bed but for how long, who knew? Kate warmed up the curry and heated the naan bread in the oven. Sometimes she was truly surprised by her culinary skills. Her gran had taught her well. She missed her so much. A dull ache in her chest. It was always there. Gran would have been such a help to her with the whole Jake situation. She would have known what to do. But as ever, Kate was alone; she would deal with it.

'Do you want any help?'

She turned to see Matt standing in the doorway; her heart leapt at the sight of him. He truly was a good-looking man. Her eyes locked onto his and for a moment she was lost for words, as if hypnotized. She blinked and turned away. She stirred the curry.

'I'm fine Matt. Won't be much longer.'

'Do you always cook this well?' Matt asked with a smile.

Kate turned to look at him more closely as she took the pan off the stove.

He was smirking at her, his eyebrow raised.

'Yes, I do. I like to cook,' she said, hands on hips with a glint in her eye, 'I find that it helps me to unwind. It also makes a change from eating chicken nuggets.' Why had she said that thought out loud?

'Nothing wrong with chicken nuggets,' Matt laughed. 'Well, it smells wonderful. Let me take that from you, shall I pop it next door?'

Kate thought of the tiny table next door with the single chair. 'We'll eat in here I think, more room. Just pop it on the table for me.'

Kate busied herself preparing the salad and then retrieved the naans from the oven before they burned. After placing everything on the table she opened the fridge to retrieve the bottle of white wine she had bought the previous weekend and had not yet got around to drinking. 'Let's have some wine to celebrate us as new neighbours.'

'Sounds like a plan,' Matt said, 'here's to new neighbours.'

He raised an imaginary glass.

The evening was going well; Matt was great company, he was so easy to talk to. It felt as if Kate had known him for years, which was stupid. She knew absolutely nothing about him, but she trusted him. Her gut told her that he was safe, and her gut was very rarely wrong.

It was while Kate was having these thoughts that the phone rang. She knew it was *him* before she even looked at the screen. The wine stuck in her throat, suddenly sour.

'You not going to answer that then?' Matt enquired, looking at the vibrating phone on the table between them.

'No, whoever it is will leave a message if it's important.'

The phone stopped ringing; Kate breathed a sigh of relief. She had no intention of speaking to him.

She picked up her wine glass and had a sip, her hands shaking slightly, when the phone rang again. The glass nearly slipped from her fingers. Her throat tightened; she heard the glass clatter onto the table as she tried to place it down too quickly. She willed the phone to stop ringing. She couldn't deal with this right now. Not with Matt staring at her.

'You okay, Kate?' Matt reached across the table and placed his hand onto hers. She jumped, not realising he had spoken. The touch alien to her.

The phone continued to buzz on the table like an insistent fly.

‘Excuse me,’ she told him, ignoring his concerned stare, her voice barely a whisper. With trembling hands, she took the phone into the living room, and stood in front of the bay window. Glancing at the screen she noticed that the number was blocked. It was him. She closed her eyes and swiped the screen.

‘About time.’

His voice was oily, charming. She hated it. She hated him. ‘What do you want Jake?’

‘That’s a fine way to talk to the father of your child.’

His words were clipped; she could hear the annoyance in his voice.

‘I don’t want to talk to you, I have nothing to say.’

‘Oh, I think that you do. It’s been six fucking years. We need to talk about Sam.’

Kate gripped the phone tighter, trying to control her breathing. This couldn’t be happening to her. She wanted no contact with this man. ‘Just leave me alone Jake.’ She couldn’t keep the tremble out of her voice. What was she going to do?

‘Seriously? What the fuck are you on? I have a right to see my son.’

‘I can’t deal with this right now Jake.’ She needed to collect her thoughts, to regain control. ‘Can I phone you tomorrow? Now’s not a good time.’

‘Not a good time? Seriously? For fucks sake … I’ll phone *you* tomorrow.’

He hung up.

Kate just stood there, the phone in her hand.

‘Kate, is everything all right?’

Kate had completely forgotten that Matt was in the other room. He was leaning against the doorframe, arms folded, his face creased with worry.

'I'm fine, it was just a friend.' Where had that lie come from? Why didn't she tell him the truth? That it was her crazy ex-partner who liked to stalk and control women. *What the hell was she going to do*?

He took a step closer, lowering his head to meet her eye. 'You don't look okay.'

Without her realising, Matt took her hand and led her over to the couch. 'I'll get you a drink of water.'

She sat motionless, watching as he went into the kitchen. She heard the cupboards opening and shutting as he searched for a glass, the tap switching on, water running. All noise blurred into one. *What was she going to do*?

Matt placed the cool glass into her hands.

'Thanks.' Kate managed to mumble. She was about to lose it all. Her life was back on track; her and Sam were happy, they were safe. But now he had found them and that changed everything.

Matt sat down slowly next to her. 'Look, you don't have to tell me, but whoever that was, well, I take it the news wasn't good?'

His blue eyes seemed genuinely concerned for her and Kate very nearly spilled the entire story. It would be so cathartic to tell someone, to get it all out into the open. But she couldn't. Not yet.

'It was just a bit of bad news, that's all.' She offered a wobbly smile. She desperately wanted to be alone. She needed to think, and she couldn't do that with Matt sitting so close to her. Maybe if she had known him for longer then she would have confided in him, but she couldn't tell him. It would destroy everything she had built up.

She looked down at the glass in her hand, relieved that she had stopped shaking. 'I think we'd better call it a night, I've a busy day ahead.' She pushed herself up from the couch, legs as heavy as lead, relieved when Matt followed suit. She saw the worry in his

eyes and hated herself for it. But this was her mess and hers alone. She didn't want him getting involved.

'Are you sure that you're okay?'

'Yes, yes, just tired. Nothing an early night won't fix.' Kate forced a smile. *Please leave.*

She headed for the door, forcing herself to slow her steps. She didn't want to appear rude, but she needed him to go.

'Well, erm … thanks for dinner.' He raised his hand, then dropped it to his side, offered a smile. 'It was lovely.' As he stepped through the door, he turned to face her once more. 'I'm here if you need me … for anything.'

She watched helplessly as he walked away. Perhaps she should have told him the truth after all.

CHAPTER TEN

FRIDAY, SEPTEMBER 13TH, 2013

The children shouted questions in quick fire succession. All wide-eyed and with earnest expressions. Matt loved their enthusiasm, but as they were all talking at the same time, he couldn't hear them over the humming of the tanks. What made matters even worse was that their voices echoed around the room. He reminded himself never again to drink on a week night. It was Brian's fault, turning up unexpectedly with a crate of beers. He had wanted to check on his best mate and well, a few beers had turned into most of the crate disappearing. Matt knew that Brian would be in for an ear bashing when he got home, whereas he had only himself to berate, and quite frankly he was suffering enough for both of them.

Brian had helped to take his mind off Lisa, and if the truth be told, Kate. She was frightened, of what, or who, he did not know, but it had something to do with that unexpected phone call. No matter what she had told him, she *was* frightened.

He held his hand up.

'Okay, one at a time please.' He pointed to a little girl standing directly in front of him with shoulder length blonde curls and before he could even ask her name, she launched into her question.

He answered quickly, looking about him, desperate for the teacher, wondering where the hell she had got to. There was no way that he could control a group of overexcited ten-year-olds. This was not part of the job description.

Thankfully, as he finished talking, the teacher came back into sight and edged herself to the front of the crowd, smoothing her hair as she did so.

Matt released a long-held breath.

'Sorry, Dr Harper, didn't mean to be gone for so long.' The teacher smiled sheepishly at him.

Matt grimaced, wondering what on earth she was referring to, but let it go.

'Right children, who wants to see the rays?' Matt was met with squeals of approval as the children all ran towards the low-level tanks.

Why had Kate decided to meet Emily on Friday the thirteenth of all days? True, she had not realised it would be that date when she had reluctantly agreed to meet her friend, but it didn't bode well. The day had got off to a bad start as she had to wrestle Sam into the taxi.

She had then quickly gathered all her work stuff so that she could go straight to the office after meeting Emily at the café. Hopefully, she wouldn't stay too long. She could only usually stomach about an hour before she had to tell a white lie, such as having to dash off to an important interview. Kate had not heard from Jake. He had not called the following day after his surprise phone call, and although she had brought up his number on her phone, she had not been able to go through with it. Once the adrenaline rush had evaporated, so too had her bravado and strength. She willed him to go quietly away. Perhaps he would?

There really was nothing she could do. He was out there, and he had found her.

She pushed open the café door; inside it was heaving. The noise and steam hit her full on, making her want to turn back, to go straight to work. But it was too late, as she had been spotted. Sat in the far corner facing the doorway was Emily. As ever she looked immaculate. Her pale pink blouse fitted her snuggly and her hair had been coiffed to perfection. Kate noticed that she was one of those women who always wore make-up but managed to look like they wore none. Kate took a deep breath and ignored the fact that she was someone who wore supermarket and budget clothes, and who just about managed to get to the hairdressers once a year. Those aspects of her life, funnily enough, no longer seemed important. She had showered, washed her hair and was wearing clean and ironed clothes. A simple black t-shirt had been teamed with fitted jeans. She was also wearing her beloved Converse. She'd get another month out of them at least.

Kate sauntered over to where Emily was frantically waving and was greeted with two air kisses.

'Darling, it is *sooo* good to see you. How are you?'

Kate suppressed her initial answer of, '*I feel like crap, Jake has found us and has been phoning me. I am scared shitless actually.*' Instead she told her friend what she wanted to hear. 'Fine, just fine.'

'And how is Sam? Settling back into school?' Emily cocked her head to one side in that annoying way that people do when they wish to show false concern. Kate once again bit the urge to say something sarcastic. 'He's fine Emily. I'm just glad that it's Friday.' At least that part was true. She would spend the weekend having fun with Sam. Saturday was always spent wandering around the city centre and in the museum.

'Oh, me too, me too,' Emily said with forced cheerfulness.

Kate could detect the lie. She wondered if Gerald was home this weekend. She quickly shrugged off her coat, desperate for a large coffee. 'How is Isaac coping with being back at school?'

'Oh, you know,' Emily hesitated, swallowing before carrying on, 'he's struggling to be perfectly honest, but we'll get there.'

Kate felt a sudden surge of remorse. Why did she always think the worst of this woman? All she wanted was a friend and Kate knew that she was a crappy one. 'I'll go grab a coffee. You want another?' Kate asked gently.

'Oh, darling, that would be lovely.'

Matt leaned back in his comfy office chair, savouring the silence. Absolute bliss. That had been one busy hour, but he'd made it through in one piece. As they had progressed with their tour, he had begun to enjoy himself and the kids weren't as bad as he had first thought. Just excited, and that was a good thing. That was half the battle. Getting them interested in marine life.

'I think that went well,' Dan said while busily stuffing papers into his bag.

'Yes, I think it went well. They enjoyed filling out the questionnaire. The teacher said she was going to do a worksheet based on the answers for the class.'

'Did she get the info pack and image file?' Dan asked, hovering in the doorway.

Matt nodded, 'Yup, all sorted.'

'Fantastic,' he grinned. 'You here for the rest of the day?'

Matt shook his head. 'No sadly not, I need to get back to uni and finish off a few bits and pieces.'

'Sounds good. Well, I'm off to grab an early lunch, you want anything?'

'No, I'm good. I'll get something on my way to campus.'

'I'll see you on Monday then, have a great weekend.'

Matt smiled and held up his cup. 'You too, don't do anything I wouldn't.'

Dan raised an eyebrow. 'Ah, now what would be the fun in that?'

Matt slowly shook his head but couldn't help his slow smile. He liked Dan; he had got to know him over the course of the week. He was a passionate marine biologist who made everyone around him take interest in what he had to say. It would also appear that his charm crossed through into his personal life, as he had more than one girlfriend on the go. Matt wondered if they knew about each other? Possibly not. Or maybe they did? Matt had always been a one-woman kind of a guy and would always be so. He believed in marriage and monogamy. Perhaps he was old-fashioned, but that was the way he was.

He opened the file for the trip that was planned on Monday and started to work.

'I honestly don't know what to do Kate. Should I phone the school again?'

Kate nodded sympathetically. 'To be honest, yes I would. If you're worried, then talk to them. I just know that they have been fantastic with me.'

'I feel like I'm a nuisance when I phone them up,' Emily replied while slowly stirring her coffee, her face downcast. Kate fought the urge to reach out and touch her hand. She felt sorry for Emily, she really did, even though it didn't excuse her annoying ways. She really did want the best for Isaac, and he really was struggling at school. This was through no fault of the school's; it was just one of those things. Over time it would right itself as he settled back into school life. She had told Emily not to worry, that he would soon

settle, but her advice had been quickly shrugged off, dismissed. Maybe she would listen to the staff at school?

Emily sighed, rubbed her eyes, and stood up. 'I need another coffee. You want one?' she gestured towards Kate's now empty coffee cup.

Kate smiled; she did need to get to the office, but she had at least another half hour before she needed to leave. 'Yes please.' She watched Emily as she made her way over to the counter.

Kate looked out of the steamed-up window. Her eyes gazed upon the people walking outside. A tall, dark figure caught her attention. Something about how the person moved, the way they held themselves, their gait. Her brain was too slow to process what she was seeing. Staring back at her, through the misted-up window, were a pair of dark brown eyes. She watched in complete horror as the man drew the shape of a heart on the glass, with a gloved finger. Kate began to shake; she couldn't help it. She was trapped. What was she going to do when he came in to talk to her? She fumbled in her bag for her phone, her fingers too clumsy, too slow, the phone always buried at the bottom of her bag. It was only once the phone was firmly in her grasp that she looked up and saw that he had gone.

'Are you okay?' Emily stood in front of Kate with two cups of coffee. All Kate could do was slowly shake her head, her throat dry. She felt sick.

'Whatever is the matter? You're white as a sheet!' Emily said as she lunged forward to steady Kate, fearful that she was about to faint.

Kate swallowed down the bile that was threatening to escape; she could not cry now. She just needed to escape, to claw at the fresh air.

'I don't feel too well, I need to go,' Kate mumbled as she began to pull on her coat, fumbling in her rush to fasten the buttons.

Emily stood silently watching her, lost for words, waiting for Kate to elaborate on what was wrong. But Kate had no words to offer.

All Emily could do was stare after her friend, as she stumbled out of the café.

It was only when Kate reached the door that she allowed her tears to silently fall.

CHAPTER ELEVEN

SATURDAY, SEPTEMBER 14TH, 2013

Matt leaned back and observed the bright new paint that was now splashed across the front door of his new home. Not bad, he thought. He was no painter, but he had to get rid of the dirty brown colour that the previous occupants had chosen. Every time he returned home the colour had just depressed him. It felt like he was walking into someone else's home. Now the front door was a dark blue, which was more suited to his mood and general feelings about life.

The lure of the weekend stretched out before him, but he had no idea of what to do. He had ruled out going into work, as he wanted to stop that habit dead in its tracks. Once he started going into work of a Saturday or Sunday, then it would become a regular occurrence and he couldn't let that happen. It was a slippery slope to isolation and depression. He should know.

Matt had politely declined Dan's kind offer of hitting the town. He was aware that Dan felt obliged to ask him. Maybe next week? There was so much to do in the house. He would now have the time to sort things out, like making a start on the library, and painting the kitchen. He was determined to have a library. It was the evenings that he dreaded most. A takeaway pizza and a can of lager were all that he was looking forward to. As he dipped the brush into the tin to apply another coat of paint, his thoughts drifted to Kate. He still hadn't seen her since that awkward evening, and the strange phone call. Perhaps she was avoiding him? He hoped she wasn't. He still needed to find out what had frightened her so much but felt that he couldn't ask her.

As he began to paint, the paint glistening in the weak sunlight, Kate's front door was flung open and a whirlwind of blonde curls rushed through the gap.

'Matt, Matt … I help,' Sam screeched in Matt's direction.

Matt had just enough time to snatch the can of paint away from the very eager and excited Sam. He wasn't quite quick enough though to stop him from snatching the paintbrush and he watched, stunned, as Sam began to paint his front door.

'Sam, what on earth are you doing?' Kate yelled as she reached over and snatched the brush out of Sam's tight grip.

'No, no, I paint,' he yelled back at her, while attempting once more to wrestle the brush out of her hand.

'Matt, I am so sorry,' Kate said as she handed the paintbrush back to Matt. 'He has a thing about painting,' Kate muttered, her face turning red.

Matt couldn't help but laugh. 'It's okay, he's done a good job,' he gestured to the newly applied streak of paint. He turned back towards Kate, studying her more closely; he couldn't help but notice the way in which her hair was curled today, forming loose tendrils around her face. It was usually tied up in a ponytail. She looked tired though and distracted.

'You off out?' Matt asked, as he placed the paintbrush onto the open paint tin. She held his gaze for a fraction of a second, opening her mouth to say something, but then closed it again, before looking away. Matt swore that he saw an unspoken message in her

eyes. It was almost as if she was asking him something without words, but before he could ask, the moment had faded. Gone.

'Yes, we are,' she looked towards Sam. 'Tell Matt where we are going.'

Sam stood looking at his feet, arms crossed, clearly put out that his painting days were over. 'No, we go now Mum,' he shouted as he started to drag Kate towards the car.

'We're just off into town to do a bit of shopping and have a drink at the Book Café. It is Sam's favourite place to go.' She hesitated and shouted towards Matt from the car, 'You're welcome to come with us if you like?' Her hand hovered over the door handle.

Matt smiled. 'Sounds good, I would do but I'm covered in paint and you're clearly in a rush,' he shrugged, 'have a good time.'

'Thanks,' Kate paused, 'perhaps you'd like to go with us next weekend? We usually go every Saturday.'

Matt looked from Kate to Sam, unsure of what he should say. He'd love to go with them, but he wasn't too sure of how Sam would react. 'Would that be all right Sam?'

But Sam wasn't listening. He was now pulling on the car door shouting, 'Let me in.'

'I am sure Sam would love your company,' Kate shouted over the noise.

Matt nodded, unsure if what she said was true. 'Okay, I'd love to, thanks. Have a good time.'

Kate opened the car door. 'We will, as long as coffee and cake are involved, I'll be fine.'

Matt registered the words, but he noticed that something was off. The smile didn't quite reach her eyes; the words seemed forced, almost practised. Did she want him to go with them? He had just assumed that she was being polite?

Matt watched as she bent to buckle Sam in and then as she

slowly lowered herself into the car. He was still sat staring into space long after the car had gone.

'Sam, do you like Matt?' Kate glanced at him in the rear-view mirror, wondering what he thought about the handsome next-door neighbour. She had a feeling that Sam liked him. She cursed at her rudeness for not having spoken to him since the other night. She just couldn't bring herself to look at him. She could tell by looking at his face that he knew something was wrong; she just didn't want to lie to him. Anyway, would he want to know the truth? Probably not.

'I like him,' Sam piped up, making Kate jump. She had forgotten she had asked him a question.

'I like him too,' she grinned. While she realised that what she said was true, she liked him a lot more than she should. As she moved into the lane that would take them away from Muddletown and into the city centre, she glanced once more at Sam in the rear-view mirror. 'So, where are we going first then Sam?'

She asked the question, although she knew exactly where they would go and in what order. It was the same every Saturday. She made a mental note to tell Matt this, that he would have to stick to their routine. She hoped he wouldn't mind. But she had a feeling that he would just go along with it. He was that kind of man.

'The toy shop, then next museum, then next Bookshop Café, and then car shop,' he recited, clutching his key ring which showed all his favourite places that he liked to visit. This was a visual reminder of where he needed to be and what would be happening. Kate was completely lost without that keyring, and his ear defenders. She never went anywhere without them.

'Yes, we'll go to the toy shop first Sam. But remember the rule, no toys today. Okay?'

She observed his expression in the mirror.

'I know,' he said quietly, his voice resigned to the fact that he would be going home with none of his beloved toy cars.

Sometimes Kate felt like the worst mum in the world, but if Sam had his way he would buy a toy car every single weekend, and she simply couldn't afford it. Plus, she didn't want to spoil him.

The rest of the journey was spent in relaxed silence. Sam thinking about all the lovely toys he would see and his much-anticipated piece of chocolate cake, while all Kate could see were a pair of haunted brown eyes staring at her through a misted window, dripping with condensation.

When she fled the warmth of the café, she had gone looking for him, against her better judgment. She knew it was a stupid thing to do, but she swore it was him. But even as she had walked up and down the high street, she knew there would be no sign of him. Had she imagined him? Had her mind been playing tricks on her because of the phone call? No, he was real, she wouldn't let herself be fooled into thinking that he was simply a figment of her imagination. She had seen him, and he was in Muddletown. She had to be vigilant, always. She had thought about contacting the police, but again, what would she tell them? *I think that I saw my ex-partner looking at me through a fogged-up window in a café.* Hardly hard evidence, was it? And then she would have to tell of what happened in the past. Who would believe her? In the end, she had taken herself back to the office and had finished her articles, in readiness for enjoying the weekend with Sam. As she had typed away on the laptop she had felt Bill's eyes on her back, sensing that he knew something was wrong. She should have confided in him, but what could she tell him? She didn't want to worry him. If Jake contacted her again, or heaven forbid that she saw him in town, then she would tell Bill and she would contact the police.

She just hoped that Jake had no way of finding out her address. It was unlisted, but then he had managed to get her mobile number and he had found out that she was living here in Muddletown. The area wasn't that big. Knowing Jake, he would find out and what then? Kate gripped the steering wheel tighter, her knuckles turning white, trying to control her breathing. She had to keep it together for Sam's sake. He was all she cared about. She now wished that she had waited for Matt to come along with them. She'd feel safer with him in the car and when wandering along the city streets. Why hadn't she told him? He would understand. She indicated left as she turned the car into the one-way system, joining the heavy queue of traffic. She cursed both her stupidity and stubbornness. As soon as they got home, she would tell him about Jake. Feeing like a load had been lifted off her shoulders, she grinned at Sam in the mirror. 'Righto Sam, let's have some fun!'

Wandering around the museum, Kate tightly clasped Sam's hand as they followed the same route around the building. Always the same route, she would know her way around the museum with her eyes closed, but it didn't bother her. Routine was safe, calming, and if that was what Sam needed, then so be it. The curator gave Sam a friendly wave as they passed by. Kate smiled at her, such a friendly old lady. They had been coming here for several years and had always made the time to say hello and smile at each other; she was fantastic with Sam, giving him the space that he so desperately needed, but Kate was ashamed to admit that she didn't know the lady's name. Perhaps on their next visit she would pluck up the courage to ask her? It was while she was having these thoughts that her phone began to buzz. Making sure to keep an eye on Sam, she fished it out of the bottom of her bag. She let out a sigh of relief – it was Emily with a short text. *How are you? Up for another coffee*

next week? Kate quickly typed a reply, keeping an eye on Sam who was now busy looking at an ancient map of the local area. *Yes, coffee would be good. I am fine, feeling much better. I'll text you on Monday with a day*. She had felt so guilty about running off from Emily. She hadn't even bothered texting her that night, to tell her that she was feeling better, even when Emily had left several fraught voicemail messages. Kate had just needed a bit of space to think and breathe. She could not tell Emily the truth, so that was that. She dropped the phone back into her bag and walked over to Sam, gently taking his hand.

'Ready to go little man?'

Sam nodded as they passed the mannequin of the man in the stocks whom Sam had affectionately named the *Naughty Man* on their very first visit. Kate smiled at the memory. They walked past the Roman artefacts and archaeological finds from the local area, then rounded the corner to approach the stairs that led back down to the ground floor.

A tall man with dark hair wearing all black approached them. He made his way up the staircase, head down, eyes on the steps. Kate could not make out his features, could not see his face, but he reminded her of Jake. The way he had followed her around the shops when trying on clothes for a girlfriend's party. How he had sat outside the changing room, disapproving of every single item that she had tried on. He too had worn a black leather jacket, the sleeves rolled up. She could still smell the leather, feel the coolness on her skin. She blinked, taking in her surroundings once more. The man looked so like Jake that she was momentarily frozen, unable to move. Sam tugged urgently at her arm, trying to force her down the stairs.

'Mum, Mum, we go now,' he began to screech, alerting the attention of everyone in the building. Kate swallowed down her

fear and gripping Sam's hand, they started to slowly approach the man. It was only when the stranger raised his head and she saw his kind blue eyes, that she realised her mistake.

It was not him.

He was not here, they were safe.

For the entire time that they had wandered around the city, she had thought that she could see him. Hiding in alleyways, creeping up behind her. Her imagination was running wild, making her jumpy, skittish, and she could not afford to act in this way. It wasn't fair on Sam, He would eventually pick up on the fact that his mother was a jumbled mess of nerves, and it would frighten him.

The man passed her by, and she watched as a little girl slowly followed him, transfixed by all the large paintings that dominated the walls of the staircase. He was just a father out on a Saturday morning with his little girl. Once again, she told herself that she was safe. They approached the large oak door that opened onto the stone steps in front of the museum. She blinked several times at the bright light.

'Where to next Sam?' she asked, as she placed his blue ear defenders back on and then handed him his keyring.

He stood and thumbed through the pages, finally finding the one that she knew he would choose. 'Bookshop Café,' he grinned. Kate couldn't help grinning back and gave him a thumbs-up. Bookshop Café it was then, and a large latte was needed. She clutched his tiny hand in hers and off they set towards the café, all thoughts of Jake slowly fading away.

Matt listened to the beginning of the midday news on Radio Four, then leaned over to switch it off. He had heard the news headlines every hour since seven that morning; he needed a break. As well as painting the front door, he had begun to give the front garden a bit of

a tidy up, pulling out a few stray weeds and mowing the small patch of lawn. He was going to spend the rest of the day food shopping and then relaxing in front of the television, or maybe with a good book; he hadn't quite decided yet. It was only as he reached down to pick up his bag of gardening tools that he sensed someone standing behind him. He slowly turned, his gaze falling upon a tall man, aged around the late forties with dark stubble and equally dark eyes. The man smiled at him, but the smile, such as it was, did not quite reach his eyes. Matt instantly felt on his guard. *Something wasn't right*. He did not like this man who had invaded his personal space.

'Hi, can I help you?' Matt asked, his tone flat, to the point. He stood with one hand on his hip, the other still holding his bag of tools. He deliberately blocked the door to the house.

'Hi mate, sorry to bother you. It's just that I was told that Holly lives next door to you.' He made a sweeping gesture with his arm towards Kate's house and then shrugged. 'I've knocked but no one's in.'

For some reason the man-made Matt feel uncomfortable. Maybe it was the cocky nature in which he stood on his path, or the fact that he appeared to be smirking at him. He also hated the use of the word, '*mate*'; this man was no mate of his. But it was his eyes. There was something about his eyes that unsettled him.

'No one called Holly lives there. Sorry, I can't help you.' Matt turned to leave. Discussion over. He had no plans to tell this man anything. He felt sorry for Holly, whoever she was.

'So, who does live there then?' The stranger shouted, making Matt turn back round to face him. 'Listen, I haven't seen her for years – she has a little boy, blonde hair, he's beautiful. We lost touch and I just wanted to give her an early birthday present. Listen … erm … she may go by a different name now.' He shrugged, giving an apologetic smile.

Matt looked at the man's empty hands. There was no present, and why would he ask for a woman called Holly and then say that she may have a different name? Something didn't add up. 'I couldn't possibly say.'

'Well, either she does, or she doesn't. It's a simple question,' the man hissed. 'Do you know when they'll be back?'

Matt bristled. 'No, I have no idea when they'll be back. If you were such a close friend you would obviously know that nobody called Holly lives next door, so as you don't, well –' Matt left the statement hanging in the air. He wanted this man to go away. He regretted speaking to him. Had he said too much?

It was as Matt stepped into the house that he felt a strong grip on his shoulder, forcing him to spin around, a pair of dark brown eyes inches from his own.

'Does she live here with a little boy?' he snarled.

Matt's jaw clenched. His instincts had been right. Without another word, he stepped back into the safety of the house, shutting the door in the man's face.

Matt wondered what mess Kate had got herself into? More importantly, why had she changed her name?

CHAPTER TWELVE

Matt stared at the pages of the book with unseeing eyes, words unread. He closed the book, sat back and shut his eyes. What was he going to do? He would have to tell Kate. Was he the same man who had phoned Kate the other night? Something told him that it was the same man.

Matt hoped that Kate would be back soon. He had to tell her. There was something about that guy that made his skin crawl. The way in which he had grabbed him, trying to get him to tell the truth. Yes, he was trouble, and somehow, he was linked to Kate. That was not good, not good at all.

Matt wandered into the kitchen. He needed something to do, to take his mind off what had just happened. He'd make a snack. He needed to keep busy until she was home. He just hoped that she would take him seriously.

Matt pulled a loaf of bread out of the bread bin and cut two thick slices. He rummaged through the contents of the fridge, found the block of cheese that had been sat there since he moved in, sniffed it, and cut that into slices. He quickly made his sandwich and then grabbing the tub of Pringles, made his way back into the living room.

So much for his quiet Saturday at home. He should have gone with Kate even though he was splattered in paint. But then again, that guy, would he have tried to break in? Knowing that Matt was sat next door must surely have been a deterrent. He'd ask Kate if she had a burglar alarm and if the doors were secure. Come to think of it, he knew that she had locks installed, as he had seen them. They were there to keep Sam safe, but now they would also keep her safe. He shuddered. Who was he? An ex-boyfriend? Husband perhaps? Was he Sam's dad? They didn't look alike.

Matt peered out of the window. There was no sign of him. The street was quiet. He couldn't hear a thing, other than the few cars that passed by. He glanced at the clock. Not quite two yet.

Where are you Kate?

While he was stood cramming the crisps into his mouth, he had a sudden, awful thought. Had this guy found Kate? What if he knew what car she drove? Then there was Sam, she had Sam with her. Would he harm him? Matt put a stop to those thoughts. Thinking as he was would do no one any good. Although he didn't like the guy, he did not know him. He knew nothing about him, and practically nothing about Kate. But the feeling remained, one that the guy meant to hurt her in some way.

After thirty minutes of watching the empty street, he eventually saw Kate's battered old Mini pull up outside the house. He raced to the front door. It was only when his hand was on the door knob that he stopped. He needed to calm down. He didn't want to frighten her. Taking a deep breath, he forced himself to think clearly; he needed to help her, not scare her half to death. He opened the door.

Kate picked up the bulging shopping bags, closed the car door with her elbow, and staggered lopsidedly after Sam, who had

quickly bolted from the opened car door. Matt stood on the step, smiling as Sam jumped about on the adjacent front step, eager to get inside.

'Hi Sam, had a good time?' Matt asked, bending down to Sam's height.

Sam continued to jump up and down. 'Had chocolate cake,' he said, grinning at Matt with a chocolate covered mouth. Chocolate stains covered most of his top.

Matt turned his attention towards Kate, who looked at him cautiously, aware that his expression looked suddenly serious. He seemed nervous. Was this about inviting him out with them? Had she made him feel uncomfortable? Perhaps she shouldn't have asked him. Should she tell him about Jake? Perhaps it wasn't such a good idea.

'Can I come in for a bit?' Matt asked. 'There's something I need to tell you.'

Kate noticed the hesitant smile; it came out wrong, his eyes still looked worried.

'Yes, yes, can you just grab this?' She handed him a supermarket bag while she put the key in the lock. 'I'll make us a cup of tea.'

Kate followed Sam into the house and heard Matt close the door behind him.

'Sam, do you want a drink?' Kate asked as he walked into the living room.

'No, pyjamas,' Sam hollered from the couch.

Kate turned to Matt, who was hovering in the doorway. 'I'll just pop his pyjamas on and then we can talk. Is everything okay?' She carefully watched his expression, but he gave nothing away.

'I'm not sure. Sort Sam out and then we can talk.'

'Okay,' Kate swallowed down the fear that was threatening to rise within her. What was going on? She hurried up the stairs and

found Sam's pyjamas where she had left them, lying on his bed. She scooped them up and ran back downstairs. 'Come on Sam, pyjamas then drink.'

Sam reluctantly stood up and began to get undressed. Kate noticed that Matt looked away, and then moved towards the kitchen. She forgot that not everyone was used to children, and that he probably felt uncomfortable. Dressing Sam as quickly as she could, she gave him his iPad and then retracted into the safety of the kitchen where she found Matt sitting at the kitchen table, staring into space, his feet jiggling up and down.

'Look, I'll just get Sam his drink and then we'll talk, about whatever it is that's on your mind.' Kate's heart was pounding in her chest as she poured out Sam's juice, splashing some of the contents onto the kitchen counter. She had to slow herself down from running into the living room.

'There you are love. I just need to talk to Matt for a bit.' She ruffled his hair and watched him sip his juice.

'Yes Mum,' he replied between sips.

She sat and fidgeted with her hair while he drank his juice, then took the cup from him.

Sam had already found his Minecraft app and was busy building a new world.

She found Matt sat in the same position at the kitchen table.

'Whatever's wrong?' she blurted out as she dropped into the chair opposite him. 'Is it the fence? I'm so sorry, and if I made you feel uncomfortable about inviting you out with us then …'

Matt held up his hand to stop her.

She shook her head. What was going on here?

'Kate, you had a visitor today.'

Kate stared at him. 'A visitor? What do you mean?' She couldn't help it; she began to shake. She placed her shaking hands in her

lap, hoping that Matt wouldn't see them trembling.

Matt let out a deep breath and looked her in the eye. 'While you were out some bloke approached me as I was about to come inside. He asked me if you lived here.'

Panic clawed at her chest. It had to be Jake. She had been so stupid, thinking that he would simply go away, disappear in a puff of smoke.

'What did you say?' Kate's voice was small; she barely recognised it.

'I didn't tell him anything. To be honest he gave me the creeps. But he knew you lived here, I'm certain of that,' he paused, 'but he called you Holly. Who is he Kate?'

Kate could barely hear Matt's question as the blood was pounding in her ears, the *whooshing* sound blocking everything else out. It must have been him. No one else knew her real name. 'What did he look like?'

'Tall, dark, brown eyes, dark curly hair.'

Kate tried to swallow but her throat was too dry, her heart rate too quick. This couldn't be happening.

'Who is he Kate?' Matt asked more forcefully than before, but his eyes, Kate noted, still radiated kindness. She knew she was scaring him.

'His name is Jake.' Her hands started to tremble even more violently at the sound of his name on her lips. 'Can I have a drink of water, please?' Kate asked. She needed a moment to think. She needed to tell him *now*. The whole story. There was no escaping it. She'd feel better for it.

'Sure.' Matt jumped up from the table and retrieved a glass from the cupboard. Kate offered a wobbly smile; he must have remembered where to find them from the other night, when he had done pretty much the same thing, after *he* had called. Would it always be this way? Would Jake always be hiding in the shadows, destroying her happiness. More importantly, would he always have this hold over her little boy. She didn't care what happened to her anymore, but she would do everything in her power to protect her son. And if that meant hiding again, or creating a new identity, then she would.

Matt handed her the glass, sat back down, and placed his hands on the table. She took a few sips before placing the glass on the table. Then, with a deep breath, she began to tell him her story.

Part Two
The Truth

CHAPTER THIRTEEN

SEPTEMBER 2006

'Are you seriously going to wear that?'

I look down at the full-length dress with the capped sleeves and matching pretty pink pumps. *What's wrong with the way I look?*

'Seriously Holly, every man in a ten-mile radius will be looking at you dressed like that.' He shakes his head dismissively. 'Go change.' Jake picks up his newspaper, begins to read once more.

I stand there in disbelief. Should I go and change? I like this dress. I'm not even sure what else I have to wear. I very rarely go out with the girls. I'm always with Jake, in this house, this one room, surrounded by stuff that means absolutely nothing to me. I feel nothing, numb, the protective shell that I wear like armour has seen to that. If I don't go and change, he won't allow me to go out. I have no choice.

I head back upstairs to our bedroom and fling open the wardrobe door, to find what inspiration will strike me. But as I suspect, there is none. There's a long black skirt that I could wear with sandals, but all my other tops are t-shirts, nothing fancy. I opt for a bright blue long sleeved tee, as I think this will best please him. He surely can't find anything to complain about this outfit. I peer into the tiny compact mirror that I keep hidden in my bag. Although it has a slight crack in the corner, it allows me to look at myself in private, to see the real me, without him knowing, without prying eyes. My face free of makeup, I pinch my cheeks to add a bit of colour to my pale and drawn features. It will have to do. I run my hands over the skirt and absent-mindedly stroke my stomach. What will happen when he finds out? How will he react? I have absolutely no idea, but I'm going to keep it a secret for as long as I can. This way we will both be safe for that little bit longer. His betrayal towards me is through words, rather than violence; I can handle it. He loves me – this is why he's so protective of me. He wants to keep me safe. He tells me I am nothing without him. Worthless.

I glance at the clock. I'd better get a move on. They'll be waiting for me at the pub. I told them not to call round; I don't want to make a scene. It's better that I make my own way there. It's only a short walk.

'I'm off then,' I shout.

His eyes stay glued to the newspaper print.

He slowly places the newspaper onto the table and eases himself up from the kitchen table. I can smell the stale whisky on his breath.

'Remember the rules. No talking to other men and back by ten at the latest.'

I dare not look at him. He's letting me out, my chance for freedom. I rush for the door, my hand on the handle, when he spins me round, his hands tightly gripping my shoulders, his face inches from mine. 'Home … by … ten,' he annunciates every word as if I'm a little girl. 'Don't try anything funny, because I'll know about it.' He reaches forwards, swinging the door open for me. I squeeze through the gap. Don't turn back.

The cold evening air greets me like a long-lost friend. It's only as I walk down the road towards town that the thought strikes me. I

can go anywhere, do whatever I want. He would never know. But I also realise the foolishness of my thoughts. I have no money, only the fiver that he has given me for some drinks. The moment we had moved in together he had refused to let me go to work. Too many distractions and chances to mingle with the opposite sex, he had told me. He wanted to look after me. I needed to be at home. Nothing else. I have no phone and nowhere else to go. Should I tell my friends? But then what will I tell them? He doesn't hit me – there isn't a single mark on my body, but he abuses my mind, my self-confidence. Has all but ground it out of me. But I am still here. Holly is still buried somewhere deep inside of me. But now I have another problem, don't I? It isn't just me anymore. But how can I support myself, never mind a baby? No, it's hopeless. I love him, things will get better, they must. Perhaps the baby will change everything? Change him?

I am alone.

But am I?

My gran had always said that she would help me, if I ever needed her help. I haven't spoken to Mary since I moved in with Jake. She never liked him, and then when we had moved away from the area to make a fresh start – although now I know it was a ruse to get me away from my work, friends and Mary – Mary could no longer travel to see us, and I lost touch with her. I wonder if she still lives at her old address? Maybe Mary can help me after all? But how will I get there? I stop and look towards the pub, its warmth and laughter no longer inviting. I'll have to wear my mask for hours and I can no longer do so, I no longer have the energy. It is far too painful. With a heavy heart, I turn around and head back home.

CHAPTER FOURTEEN

She had to tell Matt the story. She had to protect her little boy. With a heavy heart, Kate realised that she desperately needed Matt's help. She hated to admit it, but she could no longer rely on herself. Jake was out there, and he was a dangerous man. She didn't want to be *that girl* again.

She took a sip of water, glancing fleetingly at Matt's pale blue eyes before averting her gaze back to the glass in her hand. Bracing herself for the words yet to come. 'He would tell me that I was ugly, that I was frigid, and that no one else would want me.' She swallowed, tried to compose her voice, to block the images of her past. 'My life was a living hell.'

Kate braced herself for the reprimand, *why didn't you leave him? Why stay with a man like that?* But Matt said nothing, just sat, his expression unreadable. Willing her to go on.

'I felt trapped, like I had nowhere to go. I believed him, believed in him. Everyone thought that the sun shone out of his arse. He was well respected in the neighbourhood; no one had a bad word to say about him. Who would have believed me? He'd never laid a finger on me, he was clever like that. Words were his weapon, not his fists.' Kate let out a deep sigh. 'You know what Matt, if he had hit me, things would have been very different.'

Matt raised an eyebrow, 'Would they have been?'

Kate's face blanched, feeling as if she had been struck. She swallowed down her curt reply. What would he know about her life with Jake? He had no idea, but a small part of her knew that he was right. She probably would have done the same things and made the same exact choices. But at least she had made the right choice in the end.

'So how old was Sam when you left him?' Matt asked, breaking the silence.

Kate smiled, remembering Sam as a new-born, the curve of his bow shaped mouth, his tiny fingers, downy hair. 'He was just a baby, a few weeks old.'

Matt stared straight into her eyes. 'You were very brave.'

Kate shook her head, dismissing him. 'No, I wasn't brave at all. It was just what I needed to do, to protect Sam. I couldn't let him hurt him. Jake's temper was becoming out of control … I couldn't risk him around the baby … he had never hit me, but the baby, I just wasn't sure …' Kate's voice trailed away, leaving them both with their thoughts.

'How did you survive Kate?' Matt eventually asked.

Kate swallowed down the hard lump in her throat, memories flooding in of her gran, the woman who had saved her. 'My gran,' she said, her voice barely a whisper. She blinked back unshed tears, looking down at her lap. She needed to tell Matt how wonderful her gran had been but not now. It was all too much; it could wait for another day. Now she had more pressing matters, and that was how to deal with Jake once he turned up on her doorstep. Because that *was* going to happen. She just didn't know when.

Matt slowly nodded, as if he understood, that no more words were needed.

'I'll tell you that story another time.'

'I'd like that,' Matt said the words slowly, gently, giving Kate the reassurance that she craved.

Kate sat and watched him, knowing that he wanted to say more; his left foot was jiggling up and down. What had she said to make him feel so nervous?

'Look, Kate, I'm just going to come out with this and don't take it the wrong way.' The words tumbled out of his mouth, he was unable to meet her eye.

Kate nodded.

'Sam is Jake's, isn't he?'

For a moment, Kate was rendered speechless. 'What, you don't believe me?' She had to stop herself from screeching at him.

'Of course, I do,' Matt quickly told her, 'it's just that if he is Jake's, then he does have a right to see his child, in a court of law.'

Kate could not believe her ears. After all she had told him, he was siding with the enemy.

Matt held up his hands, palms facing forwards, in an act of surrender. 'Kate, believe you me, I am not on his side,' he leaned towards her, lowering his voice, 'but in a court of law, he will be given rights. You have no evidence of how he treated you, and well, on paper it looks as if you just upped and left, changed your name.'

'I did,' Kate yelled, 'and you know why I had to do that.'

'*I* do,' Matt told her gently, 'but the court doesn't know the truth. They see things in black and white.'

Kate felt all her anger drain away. God damn it, he was right. She had no proof, just Jake's word against hers. She looked very much like a woman who had had enough and ran away.

With a looming sense of dread, she realised that when Jake next called at the house, she would have to let him in. She had no choice.

Once again, he had won.

Matt reached into his jeans back pocket and pulled out his phone. 'Give me your number and I'll text you mine. That way if he does show up, you can phone me and I can be here in a matter of minutes so that you aren't alone with him.'

'Oh Matt, you don't have to do that, honestly, I'll be fine,' Kate stammered. A part of her wanted to remain independent, but she also knew that having a man around when Jake showed up would help her. It wasn't just her safety she had to be concerned about.

'Well I think you should have someone here with you, the first time he calls around, and I'd feel better if you had my number. You never know when you may need me, you know … if there's an emergency.'

Kate thought she detected a slight blush creeping across his face and wondered why he felt embarrassed. She had just admitted to living in an abusive relationship and then taking a child away from his father. What must he think of her? If anything, she was the one who should be feeling embarrassed.

'All right then.' She reeled her number off to him.

He quickly keyed in the digits and sent the text. He looked up and grinned, 'There you go, you now have my number.'

'Thank you,' Kate told him. She couldn't help but feel the small tingle in the pit of her stomach. 'Do you want another drink?' she asked, heading for the living room; she needed to check on Sam. He had grown suddenly quiet, which was never a good sign.

'No thanks, I'd better be going. Got more boxes to unpack, that is unless you want me to stay? In case he comes back later'

Kate could hear his low chuckle as she found Sam sprawled fast asleep on the couch. Well that meant he would be going to sleep even later tonight, but she didn't have the heart to wake him. She bent down to retrieve the iPad that was perched perilously close

to the edge of the couch and kissed the top of his head. 'No, I'll be fine Matt, please don't worry about me.'

She turned to face him and took in the tight t-shirt that only made his physique that much more appealing. Her eyes travelled up to his sparkling blue eyes that radiated nothing but concern. How had he stumbled into her life, just now, when she needed him most? Was it a coincidence? Serendipity? She didn't believe in coincidences; he was meant to be a part of her life and if for now that meant being her friend, then she was happy with that. Now, all she could think about was Jake, and of how she needed to dig herself out of the mess she had found herself in.

'You did the right thing you know.' Matt's voice echoed quietly from the doorway.

Kate walked over to where Matt was stood, at the entrance to the kitchen. Without thinking, she gently kissed his cheek. His stubble tickled her nose and she breathed in his aromatic and slightly spicy aftershave. If he was surprised by her actions, he didn't show it. Instead he gave her a gentle hug and kissed the top of her head. 'I'll see myself out. Lock the doors, phone if you need me.' He arched his eyebrow and Kate gave a small smile. He was worried about her, and her guts twisted with the thought that she had made him feel this way.

'Just out of interest, what do you prefer? Holly or Kate?' Matt asked, as he stepped outside the front door.

'Kate. Holly died the moment I left him. I never want to be that woman again.'

Matt nodded, opened his mouth as if to say something, but then closed it, the thought unsaid.

Kate stood in the doorway, unable to move, as she watched him walk towards his front door. He waved before stepping inside.

She could still smell his aftershave long after he had gone.

CHAPTER FIFTEEN

MONDAY, SEPTEMBER 16TH, 2013

The cursor continued to blink on the screen, reminding Matt that he needed to type something, but his mind was completely blank. His eyes wandered to the pages of his open notebook, where he had painstakingly dictated notes about his current research, but the words made no sense to him, blurring on the page. He squeezed his eyes shut, pinched the bridge of his nose. It was hopeless. He pushed his chair away from the desk and wandered out of the lab, towards his office. He'd have a coffee; a change of scene, and then try again. He needed to get this work done today, as he was at the aquarium for most of tomorrow afternoon.

He swung the office door open and busied himself preparing coffee in his new coffee machine. In the end, he had opted for a very simple filter contraption. He just needed strong black coffee; he wasn't bothered about fancy lattes or cappuccinos. He never drank them. He sat and listened to the machine gurgling away, finding himself thinking of Kate yet again. He hadn't heard from her again over the weekend, but he had resisted the urge to text her. She knew where he was if she needed him. He had very nearly knocked on the door on his way to work, but he didn't want to upset Sam. He had seen her through the curtains; they were both home and safe. She had his number if she needed him.

He had to remind himself that he was nothing more than a neighbour. He was just a neighbour who just happened to care deeply about her and her little boy. He'd never forgive himself if something happened to her, or Sam.

The room grew suddenly quiet, the coffee now ready. He quickly found his mug atop a pile of papers, poured himself a generous cup and sat back down. He had forgotten to make a drink before he left home that morning. He sat and sipped the scalding coffee, not caring that it burned his mouth. What would happen when Jake turned up? He just hoped that he was at home and that she would phone him; he hated the idea of her being alone with him. The man was manipulative, obviously misogynistic and a bully, and Matt despised bullies. One thing that he had learned from his father was that you should always be respectful of women and that bullying was the lowest display of power.

He despised Jake.

While he was sat seething about Jake and wondering what he would do to him when they next met, he felt his phone vibrating in his pocket. Thinking that it might be Kate, he leapt up, sloshing hot coffee all over his thighs. Slamming down the coffee cup, he quickly wiped his coffee covered hands on his jeans – luckily they were black – before whipping his phone out of his pocket.

His heart sank; the display read, *Lisa*. If he hadn't put his phone on silent then he would have known it was his ex-wife from the rather appropriate ringtone, *Run Like Hell*.

His finger hovered over the end call icon for a fraction of a second before deciding that he really needed to answer the call; she would only call him back later.

'Hi Lisa,' he got in before she could speak. He forced his voice

to sound natural; he needed to prove that he was unaffected by her call, but he knew that she would recognise his nervousness and the fact that he was trying far too hard.

'Hi Matt, how are you?' Lisa's voice sounded light and breezy, as if she didn't have a care in the world, but Matt could detect the undercurrent of fragility, that she had summoned up courage to make the call. He heard the slight quiver.

He scratched his chin. Was she simply phoning up for a chat? He very much doubted it. 'Lisa, I'm at work, what do you want?' He knew he sounded pissed off, but he didn't care. He was past playing games with her. He was still puzzled about her behaviour from the other day.

'Can I meet you?' she asked.

'Meet me?' Matt's voice rose an octave, now more puzzled than ever. 'Why do you want to meet me?'

He waited for her reply, surprised at how nervous she sounded. He could hear her shallow breaths.

'I just ... I need to speak to you in person Matt, that's all, it's important.'

'Are you in trouble?' he asked.

'No, no nothing like that Matt. Listen, I didn't mean to scare you, it's just that, I really need to talk to you. Can I call around to yours tonight?'

Matt was momentarily caught off guard. He had no idea what game she was playing. She didn't even know where he lived, plus, she lived miles away. Or was she still on holiday? This was the first time she had phoned him since the divorce, and that was the way they had both wanted things to end. She had Dave, and he had his new life here. He should have changed his phone number. 'It'll take you hours to get here,' he finally told her.

'No, it won't,' she paused, 'I've rented a cottage in the village, just

for a month, as an extended holiday. I got a good deal, as it's out of season, you know …'

'What?' Matt rubbed his eyes. Nothing this woman was saying made any sense. What village was she talking about? 'Is Dave with you?'

'No, he's at home, I just needed a little break.'

A break? Now Matt got what was going on, everything was crystal clear. They'd had a fight and she wanted a shoulder to cry on. Well, she could forget about that, she'd made her bed and now she could lie in it. 'Listen Lisa, I can't do tonight. Just go and sort your differences out.'

He was surprised to hear her sudden sob echoing down the line and his resolve softened slightly. But he was determined that she would not set foot in his new home, no way, she wasn't going to taint his new life.

'Look,' he said, already regretting his words, 'I can meet you tomorrow at the café, on the uni campus, it's the only one in the central quad. I'll have an hour for lunch. I'll text you when I get there.'

Presumably Lisa realised that this was the best offer she was going to get and reluctantly agreed before ending the call.

Matt sat and stared at his phone, not entirely sure what he had just agreed to.

Kate was surprised to find the office so quiet for a Monday morning; even Bill wasn't in yet. Only a handful of journalists were sat at desks, hunched over laptops with phones pressed to their ears. Kate knew none of them. It had just gone 09:00 am. Usually the office was heaving by now. She had three people to interview today, all of them local she realised, as she glanced at the tatty note pinned to her desk. She could tell that Bill had written the

note quickly, as the ink was smudged. Kate touched the blurred words, smiling at the thought of Bill sat scrawling the note, letting her know that work was available. She shook her head, wondering why he had bothered to write it, when he had already sent her an email. Perhaps he wanted to save her a trip in, but she needed a change of scene. She hadn't slept well; images of Jake populated her dreams, and Sam had been up most of the night. Surprisingly though, he had been happy to go to school. She only had to wrestle his socks on.

When would he call her? Or more than likely, when would she see him? He'd track her down to the office, that was for sure, and she knew that was also the reason why she was here. It was a safe space. If he showed up at least she wouldn't be alone, well, that's what she had thought as she looked around the near empty building. She had nearly phoned Matt on Sunday evening, just to hear his friendly voice, but she couldn't bring herself to do it. He had already done enough, it wasn't fair. If she had phoned he would have been there in a flash, and then what? He was just a neighbour – she couldn't ask any more of him, even though she desperately wanted to.

She picked up the note and wondered what to do next. She wondered when Bill would turn up. Thankfully Veronica was nowhere to be seen, so that made her mind up. She plonked her bag on the desk and headed over to the staff room to make herself a quick cup of tea before phoning the people on her list. She'd give Bill half an hour.

Matt had to get out of the cloying lab, he needed air. He needed to clear his head, he couldn't think properly. Why the fuck had Lisa called him? He felt incredibly uneasy at the fact that she was so upset. He wondered if that smarmy Dave had hurt her in some

way; if he found out that he had, then god help him. Even though he was no longer married to her, he couldn't bear the thought of anyone hurting her. He knew that was why he had agreed to meet her; he had to check that she was okay, then he could finally let her go. If they had just had some silly argument, then well, he'd be pissed off, but at least she'd get over it, and they could sort it out between themselves. She was no longer his concern. What had gone on was between the two of them, nothing to do with him. Matt walked through the campus, nodding politely at the few members of staff who recognised him and headed over to *Burger Bill's* on the corner. He rarely ate cheese burgers, but he'd had a crap morning and a crap weekend and Bill's burgers were to die for.

As he reached into his wallet to pay for his greasy burger, his phone rang. He told himself that if it was Lisa, he would ignore her. He glanced at the screen and smiled. 'Hi Brian,' he answered cheerfully, 'how are things?'

'Good mate, good,' Brian shouted. He always shouted when on the telephone.

Matt smiled, heard the pause, and knew instinctively that something was wrong. 'What is it? Are the kids all right?' His mind was racing.

'Look, I'm not sure if I should be telling you this, and I only found out last night, but ...'

Matt closed his eyes and retreated to the closed walkway; he knew what Brian was about to tell him.

'It's Lisa ... well, look, there's no easy way to tell you this, but she's left *Smarmy Dave*.'

Matt rested his forehead on the cool brick, trying desperately to steady his breathing. He knew it, he knew that was why she had called. So, it was more than just a silly fight.

'Matt, mate, are you all right?' Brian's voice somehow sounded tiny and distant down the line.

'Yeah, I'm here,' Matt said quietly. 'She phoned earlier on.'

Now it was Brian's turn to be quiet; he obviously hadn't been expecting that. 'Matt, look, I know it's none of my business, but, if she wants to talk to you, well, just be careful, yeah?'

Matt swallowed, tried to clear his throat. He knew exactly what Brian was referring to, as he had been there the last time she had broken his heart. He did not want to go there again. He had to admit, that he loved this man just as a brother.

'Brian, it's fine, really, it is. She wants to meet me, but I'm meeting her here, on campus.'

'Okay,' Brian replied hesitantly.

'I'm not going back to her,' Matt said, his tone almost pleading, as if he was trying to convince himself, not Brian.

'I know mate, I know. Listen, do you want me to call down this weekend? Bethany is away with her parents and she's taking the kids, so I'm home alone.'

Matt grinned. 'Yeah, I'd like that. To be honest, I have a lot to tell you.' His thoughts drifted to Kate and Sam. He'd missed her the past few days. He wondered what Brian would make of it all?

'Well that sounds … intriguing,' Brian laughed.

'You could call it that.' Matt knew that Brian craved gossip; he was like an old woman.

'Look I'd better go, I'm on my break. I just wanted to let you know about what had happened. I didn't want you to be the last to know.'

Matt sighed, he *was* the last to know, nothing had changed on that score, but he didn't say so. 'Look, I won't tell her that you phoned me, I'll act stupid.'

'All right, I'll see you this weekend.'

'Yeah, see you then, give my love to Bethany.'

'Will do.'

Matt stood clutching the phone. So, Lisa had left perfect Dave. Where the hell did that leave him?

Bill arrived shortly after 09.30, just as Kate had put her coat back on, ready to leave.

'Where have you been?' she asked him, not quite hiding her disappointment. She was still hovering in the doorway, bag slung over her shoulder.

He sighed in response. 'Oh, you have no idea about the fun morning I've just had.' He had used the two fingers apostrophe for 'fun' so Kate knew that it was anything but fun. She stared at him with raised eyebrows.

'I'll just say one word,' Bill continued, '*Veronica.*'

Kate still didn't get it, but she wanted to hear the gossip. Anything that distracted her from Jake was good, very good indeed. 'I'll pop the kettle on, while you tell me all about it,' she called to him as she headed back to the staff room, shrugging off her coat along the way. She would tell him about Jake, she had to, but she needed a bit more time to prepare her words.

Bill trailed behind her, leaving a stack of papers on his desk as he walked past. He entered the staff room, grinning.

Kate turned to look at him while the kettle re-boiled, 'Go on then, what's happened?' She could barely contain her excitement. Something bad had happened, she just knew it.

'Well,' Bill beamed, 'all I can say is that Veronica has been temporarily … replaced …by me.'

Kate stared open-mouthed at him, slowly allowing the words to sink in. She opened her mouth several times before she could finally say anything. 'You mean … she's gone?'

Bill nodded while walking over to the kettle to make the tea. 'For now, yes, I am the acting editor-in-chief.'

'What on earth happened?' Kate blurted out, but then quickly covered her mouth with her hand. 'Oh, I suppose I'm not meant to ask you that,' she mumbled followed by a blush. Bill was a great friend, but he was also her boss. She had to be careful not to overstep the line. The two worlds sometimes became blurred.

Bill gave a low chuckle. 'No, it's fine to ask. She's taking some leave for ... personal reasons.'

Kate knew not to probe any further, so she left the matter where it was, for now.

'Well, I'm glad you got the job.'

'Me too,' Bill beamed.

Kate knew that this was the confidence boost that he needed. He'd do a great job. He might even help to launch the paper back into the twenty-first century.

Bill handed Kate her tea and took the chair opposite hers, placing his mug on the Formica table. 'Anyway, you had something to tell me?'

Kate slowly sipped her tea, gaining a few more precious seconds.

'Kate, is everything all right?' Bill reached over and touched her hand, patting it gently.

Kate swallowed her tea and took a deep breath.

'It's Jake, he's come back.' She could hear the tremble in her voice and hated herself for it. She looked up, noticing that Bill's face had drained of all colour.

'He's back, *here* in Muddletown?' he spluttered.

All Kate could do was nod.

He placed his cup down. 'Kate, has he threatened you?'

'No, nothing like that Bill.' Kate needed to explain, to make sense of what had happened to her without making him worry.

‘It’s hard to explain, I’ve seen him in town, but at a distance, I was in a coffee shop with a friend,’ Kate paused before adding, ‘and he has phoned me a couple of times.’

‘Shit Kate, why didn’t you tell me?’ Bill pushed himself away from the table and started to pace up and down the room. Kate knew that this would happen. Bill was so protective of her.

‘I didn’t want you to worry about me Bill. And I wasn’t sure that I had seen him. At first, I just thought that the man looked like him. You know, that my mind was playing tricks.’

‘But the phone calls Kate, you knew that was him?’

Kate sighed, ‘Yes, I knew it was him. But they were just phone calls. What could I do?’ She hesitated, not sure if she should mention Matt and his involvement, but she quickly made the decision that Bill had a right to know the full story.

‘My new next-door neighbour, Matt, well … he’s also spoken to him.’

‘You mean he phoned him too? How did he get the number?’ Bill asked, his brow creased in confusion.

Kate grimaced, waiting for the backlash that was about to erupt. ‘No, no not a phone call, in person.’

Bill’s face grew even whiter as he slowly sank into the chair. ‘In person? Where Kate? Please tell me that it was here in town or where this neighbour of yours works.’

‘No,’ Kate swallowed, wishing that her hands weren’t trembling so much so that she could pick up her cup and have a few more sips of calming tea. ‘He went to the house.’

‘Christ! This just gets worse. So, he knows where you live?’

Kate nodded.

‘That man now knows where you live, and where Sam lives. Kate, I am telling you now that he will want Sam back.’

Kate gulped. ‘I won’t let him. He has no right to see him, or

me.' She could see Bill visibly deflate before her eyes, all the anger replaced with anxiety.

'Kate, he will want to see his son and in a court of law there is no way you can stop him.'

'I know.'

'So, what are you going to do? He's found you, he knows where you live.'

Kate looked up at Bill's concerned eyes, wishing she had an answer. 'I have absolutely no idea.'

CHAPTER SIXTEEN

TUESDAY, SEPTEMBER 17TH, 2013

Matt had deliberately chosen a window seat with a perfect view across the campus. He wanted to see Lisa, before she saw him. He needed this advantage. He needed to be prepared. He was still wondering why the hell he had agreed to meet her. Nothing good would come from it. They'd talk, well, she would talk, he would nod, she would get upset, they'd row and then she would leave. But he had to see her, just this once, then he would never have to see her again. He needed to see her, just to know that she was safe in this world. He shifted in his seat. He'd sent the text fifteen minutes ago.

Any minute now.

He looked up and there she was, strolling across the campus grounds looking as beautiful as ever.

She wore heels, a powder blue that matched her skirt, or possibly dress. Matt couldn't tell as she was wearing a light sand-coloured coat that was buttoned up to her neck. Her blonde hair had been cut, he noted, from when he had last seen her. The shorter style suited her.

He continued to watch as she scurried across the grass, unsteady on her heels. He stifled a laugh. Always in heels. It would never cross her mind to wear jeans and trainers, heaven forbid. Her mother, now long dead, was to blame for her high heels obsession.

Lisa lifted her hand, shielding her eyes from the glare of the sun, and blinked as she stared towards him, through the window. Matt gave a polite wave, drained his cup, and took a deep breath. He could handle this.

Fifteen minutes to just check that she was okay, then he could leave.

He smelled her perfume the moment she entered the café; it hit his senses, taking him back to when they had first got together. She had always used the same perfume, he couldn't for the life of him remember the name.

Matt stood as she approached the table. Ever the gentleman. She offered him an air kiss, unbuttoned her coat, placed it on the back of the chair and then sat down opposite him. She was wearing a blue patterned dress, which Matt thought was too thin for September. She wore no cardigan.

'Can I get you a drink?' He made a sweeping gesture with his hand towards his empty cup and felt instantly foolish. Why was he so nervous?

'I'll grab it,' she said. 'Same again, filter.' It wasn't a question.

He smiled. 'Please.'

He watched as she sashayed her way across the café, moving as if she owned the place.

He glanced at his phone – fifteen minutes, he reminded himself, fifteen minutes then he'd walk away.

Lisa placed the two steaming cups down on the table then slowly lowered herself into the opposite chair. For a moment Matt glimpsed a fleeting look of insecurity. The slight tremble in her hand, there was a fragility about her that he hadn't seen before, buried under the expensive clothes and perfume.

'So, what do you want to talk about?' He couldn't be bothered with any pleasantries.

She didn't hide the fact that she was hurt at his bluntness, his apparent lack of concern. 'So, how are you Matt?' she asked sarcastically.

Matt tried to hide his sneer, as if she cared. 'Listen, you wanted to meet me here to chat ... so start talking.'

Lisa looked away. Stared out of the window. When she finally spoke, her voice sounded small. 'I've left Dave,' she said, after a moment's hesitation.

Matt raised an eyebrow. 'Really, you've left Dave? The perfect, charming and younger man you chose over me?'

'Don't be like that, Matt,' she snapped.

'What? Really? You come here and tell me that you have left your husband and for what? What do you want me to do about it?'

Lisa looked down at the table, shoulders slumped. 'I shouldn't have come here, I'm sorry to have wasted your time.' She pushed her coffee away and attempted to stand, but Matt placed his hand on hers. She was trembling. Was she frightened of him? Or of Dave? He wasn't sure, and he needed to know.

'I'm sorry Lisa, this is just difficult for me ... seeing you again after all this time, it's –'

'I know Matt, I'm sorry, I'll go.'

'No, you wanted to see me about something, not just about Dave leaving you, which I can't pretend to be sorry about,' he shrugged. He wouldn't lie to her; he had never lied to her, and he wasn't about to do so now. He took a deep breath. 'He hasn't ... you know ... hurt you in any way?' He couldn't look at her as he said the words. Kate's face appeared in his mind – had Dave done what Jake had done to Kate? The woman sat before him was not the woman to whom he had once been married. She was nervous,

her make-up not so perfect now that he could look at her more closely.

Had Dave hurt her?

'God Matt, where did you get that idea from? Dave, hurt me? Dave would never hurt me, never,' Lisa spat the words at him.

He had completely misread the situation, but she would eventually get over it. Dave leaving her was not his problem.

He picked up his cup, took a sip, and thought about what to say next. He had no idea.

Lisa beat him to it. 'So, you're wondering why I wanted to see you then?'

Matt couldn't help laughing, 'Well, it wasn't for a friendly chat, was it?'

Lisa smiled, 'No sadly not.'

'Why meet me then?' he asked. 'You need a loan for a new car? Rent money for the holiday let?'

'No, nothing like that Matt,' she scowled at him, 'I don't want your money.'

'Don't look all hurt, you could be wanting money. How would I know anyway?' He paused, scratched his chin. 'By the way, where are you living? Not here in Muddletown surely?'

Lisa offered him a shy smile and his heart sank. Dear god, she was living here. 'Why here?' he spluttered. She could live anywhere, yet she had chosen to live within walking distance of him. Christ!

'Is that really so awful Matt?' Lisa pouted at him.

'You have got to be joking? Can you not see how messed up this is?'

'Messed up? Is that what this is?'

Matt swallowed down his initial unpolite reply, 'Yes, Lisa, that is exactly what this is, and you still haven't told me why we are here?'

Lisa fiddled with the paper napkin, tearing off small scraps of paper. She wouldn't meet his eyes.

'Lisa?' Matt said softly. Despite all his reservations and the urge that he really needed to get the hell away from her, he couldn't leave her like this. Something was wrong.

'Isn't it obvious Matt?' her eyes bore into his.

Matt stared at those blue eyes; he felt sick to his stomach.

'Matt?'

'Lisa, just tell me what you want. I'm not in the mood for playing games here.' His gut twisted. Was she about to say what he thought she was going to say?

'You.'

Matt continued to stare at her, unable to look away. 'Me? What do you mean? You need help with the house? I'm sorry Lisa, but it's not such a good idea to have me helping out with stuff, people talk, you know, and what about Dave?' He knew he was rambling, making no sense, talking for talking sake, but this conversation had to stop, and it had to stop right now. He attempted to stand.

Lisa reached across the table and pulled his hand towards her. Forcing him to sit. 'No Matt, I want you back.

Matt's vision blurred. He blinked. He heard nothing but the buzzing inside his head.

'Matt?'

He felt fingers squeezing his hand; the rest of him felt numb. He suddenly felt sick.

Lisa's finger touched the gold band on the fourth finger of his left hand. 'You still have feelings for me, Matt.'

He jerked his hand away, suddenly coming to his senses, forming a fist, trying to erase her touch. He stood up, the chair screeching, wobbling.

'Matt are you okay?'

'No, nothing is *okay*, Lisa. What the fuck! You can't just tell me that you want me back like that. We're over Lisa, *over*, ancient history.' His voice was at the point of cracking. He could barely get the words out. 'I need to go.'

'Go?' Lisa stood, picking up her coat, attempting to put her arms in. 'We need to talk Matt. You're not over me.' She looked once again at his left hand.

'*Alone* Lisa, I need to think, get some air.' He shook his head; he should have taken the damn ring off before meeting her. He should never have agreed to see her again.

'You can't leave things as they are. We need to talk.'

'*No*, we *don't*, there's nothing to talk about.' He grabbed his phone from the table and stormed towards the door. The fresh air hit him like a slap to the face, it was just what he needed.

What had just happened? He staggered over to a bench, sat down and hung his head, sucking in the cold air.

He heard her footsteps, felt her warmth as she sat next to him.

'Just don't Lisa. I don't want to talk to you, not now, not ever. Just go.' He couldn't even look at her, it was just so painful. He had always wanted her back; she was the love of his life, but after all this time, he had grown used to the fact that she was never coming back to him. She was with Dave. But now here she was, offering herself up on a plate to him, and he didn't know what to do. He knew it would be wrong. What she was doing was simply a rebound reflex. She didn't want him. She just needed someone, a man in her life. She had never lived alone. She knew how he felt about her and she was using this weakness. He should hate her, but he couldn't bring himself to feel that way; he had loved her once, he still loved her. Life was never simple.

Then there was Kate. He couldn't stop thinking about her. It was her face that he saw in his mind as he went to sleep at night, not

Lisa's. That surely had to tell him something. But still, he yearned for the woman who sat quietly beside him.

'Please Matt, just think about it. Think about us. We could try again, be happy. I know we could.'

He heard the crack in her voice, knew that she was crying, but he did nothing to comfort her. The moment he did, that would be it, all his resolve would crumble away.

'I'm sorry Lisa, I'm so sorry. I need to go.'

'At least give me a call tomorrow, please,' she pleaded.

Matt nearly turned to look at her, but he gritted his teeth. No, this had to end, and it had to end now.

It was with a heavy heart that he stood up from that broken bench and walked away without looking back.

CHAPTER SEVENTEEN

WEDNESDAY, SEPTEMBER 18TH, 2013

The office was full of energy for a Wednesday morning. Kate sat watching her colleagues as they tapped away at their computers, instead of focusing on her own work. Through the vast goldfish bowl, she glimpsed Bill hunched behind the large imposing monitor, typing away. She grinned. He looked so at home sat there, as if he belonged. He *did* belong; that office should be his. It was such a shame that Veronica would be back in a few weeks' time. The atmosphere was a happy and relaxed one with Bill at the helm. Kate now enjoyed sitting at her desk, working, as she now felt part of the workplace, part of the team, which had never happened before. Veronica made her feel like a second-rate writer, not up to par with the qualified journalists. Bill caught her eye as she sat staring at him and she gave him a small wave. He waved back with a slight nod of the head, gesturing her into the office.

As she crossed the office floor, she wondered what he wanted. She worried that she had told him too much about Jake. She didn't want to worry him, but she knew he would. She had to tell him what was going on – not doing so would feel like a betrayal, and anyway, she hated lying. Bill of all people deserved to be told the truth. In addition, he always knew when something was wrong. He had an inbuilt radar for emotional type problems.

Bill flung open the door and then, taking her completely by surprise, pulled her into a warm hug. He gently patted her back before finally letting her go. Kate felt the slow blush creep across her cheeks and bent her head in the hope that Bill would not see.

'Take a seat Kate,' Bill gestured as he walked around the desk and sat down. 'How are you?' he asked after a moment's hesitation.

'I'm fine Bill, really I am,' she told him when she noticed the look of uncertainty cross his face. She shrugged. 'I've not heard from him.'

'Really, nothing? No more phone calls?' Bill shook his head, mumbling to himself. 'Now that is strange.'

'I know,' Kate agreed. 'But I can only take it as a good sign,' she crossed her arms across her chest, 'that's what I tell myself anyway.'

'Just be careful Kate,' Bill said, looking her directly in the eye to get his point across. 'What I mean is, don't underestimate him.'

'I'll never trust him again Bill,' Kate sighed. 'I just think that maybe all of this was a game to him, now that he's got bored … you know? I just –'

'But what about Sam?' Bill interrupted. 'He's found you, he's found Sam. I don't think he'd give up so easily. I think he's planning his next move.'

Kate carefully considered Bill's words. What he was saying made so much sense. Why would Jake give up on seeing his son?

'As I've already said, watch your back.' Bill continued, 'and don't go out late at night by yourself with Sam.'

Kate smiled, despite the cold shiver that ran down her back. 'That's exactly what Matt told me.'

'Well, he's a smart man, eh?' Bill grinned at her. 'You need to listen to him.'

‘I know, I know.’ Kate looked away; this was heading into uncomfortable territory. She didn’t want to talk about Matt with Bill. She hadn’t heard from Matt for days, and she knew that she should phone him, or just call round. She realised that she missed him. He had unwittingly become a part of her life.

‘Well, anyway, I just wanted to check how you were. I can’t help worrying you know.’

‘I know Bill, but honestly, I’m fine, please don’t worry.’

Bill stretched, arching his back, then slowly stood up. ‘Okay then, well, I’ll let you get back to work.’

Bill had assigned her the task of interviewing the winner of the Muddletown baking competition and a man who was petitioning for a local pizzeria. Kate wondered what the world had come to when the most important thing in life was to have a takeaway pizza. She knew that she should feel more enthusiastic, but she couldn’t muster up any enthusiasm whatsoever. No matter how hard she tried.

‘Do you want a cup of tea?’ she asked Bill from the safety of the doorway.

Bill chuckled to himself, ‘You’ll do anything to get out of phoning the winning baker, won’t you?’

Kate smiled, ‘What can I say? Anyway, I need to look after you now that you’re my editor-in-chief.’

Bill merely shook his head. ‘A tea would be lovely, then make those phone calls. Eleanor is a nice lady. See if she’ll give you her secret chocolate cake recipe.’

Now, that was something that would never happen.

It was after Kate put down the phone, thirty minutes after making the call to Eleanor, that the phone began to ring. Kate jumped to her feet and headed for the privacy of the stairwell.

‘Hello?’ she answered, in between gasps of breath.

'Hello, is that Mrs. Sullivan? This is Jane, Sam's teacher.'

Kate tried to compose her breathing as she slumped down to a crouching position, her back against the cold stone wall. She hadn't spoken to his new teacher, he had a new teacher every year. 'Yes, this is Kate, Sam's mum. What's happened?'

School only ever phoned when there had been an incident, either involving Sam, or another child. Kate wondered what he had done and prepared herself for the worst. Had he broken something? Hit another child? Hit a member of staff? She hoped it was none of those things. It was Wednesday, cooking day. She had sent him in with all his ingredients; they were making sponge cake. Sam loved cake.

'There's nothing to worry about,' Jane said gently, in that reassuring teacher type way.

'What's he done?' Kate asked, bracing herself for the truth.

'Well, Sam got a little upset when one of his friends left the classroom. And it sort of escalated from there. He did kick out and pull a member of staff's hair. We managed to calm him quickly down – he had a massage in his safe space and then went for a walk in the walled garden. He's settled now.'

Kate gasped while momentarily covering her mouth. 'Oh God! Is the teacher okay now?' Her face was burning; she was glad that this teacher couldn't see her.

'She's fine, please don't worry,' Jane said in a much gentler tone of voice, 'it's just that it's easier to talk to you about it on the phone than to write it all down in his chat book.'

'How was he when he first got to school?' Kate asked. He had been fine in the taxi.

'A little unsettled, we just think that the change that came about from the other child having to leave the classroom created more anxiety for him.'

'Thank you for letting me know. I'm glad he's settled again.' All Kate could think of was her little boy hitting and kicking out. She wanted to scream at this teacher that her little boy gave the tightest of cuddles, that he made her smile. She wanted to banish the image of him hurting others from her mind.

'He's fine now Kate. I just wanted to talk to you, rather than having to try and explain it in his chat book. I hope you don't mind me phoning you?'

'Yes of course it is, I don't mind you phoning me,' Kate told her honestly. 'I just know that you are incredibly busy.'

Jane gave a hearty laugh. 'Oh, always busy, but that's the way it should be. He's a lovely little boy.'

'Yes, he is,' Kate said, swallowing down the lump that was slowly forming in her throat. Perhaps they did know the real Sam after all.

'Well, I'll let you go, I'll write in his chat book about what he gets up to this afternoon. He's looking forward to making his cake,' Jane laughed. 'Most probably because he'll get a foot spa afterwards. Bye for now.'

Kate smiled; she was so lucky that Sam was in this school. 'Thanks for phoning Jane.'

'No problem. Chat soon.'

Kate ended the call and slowly made her way back to her desk.

Never a dull day.

Bill approached her desk as soon as she sat down. 'Everything okay Kate?' he asked as he perched on the end of her desk.

'It was just school. Sam had a meltdown when one of his friends left the classroom. He's fine now.' Kate forced a smile. Although she pretended that these episodes did not bother her, that they were just a part of life now, she still felt a little upset, in the fact that her little boy could hurt someone. She looked up and saw the

troubled expression on Bill's face. 'I'm fine, really I am.'

He gently patted her shoulder. 'I'll let you get on then,' he said, making his way back to the goldfish bowl.

Kate tried to continue with her writing, but it took her a few minutes to clear her head. Would she ever stop worrying about her little boy?

'Sam, stop it!' Kate yelled as she ducked to avoid a cushion that was heading in her direction. Sam picked up one of his Hot Wheels cars and flung it at his mother. It narrowly missed her cheek, thwacking loudly against the living room door.

'Sam, stop it!' she shouted again, lunging at him, attempting to pin his arms to his sides to prevent him from throwing anything else. As soon as she touched him, she knew that she had made the wrong decision.

Sam threw himself down onto the floor, meaning that Kate could not move him. He started to shout, his words incoherent. Kate slumped down on the floor next to him, knees hunched up, her back to the sofa, and waited for Sam to calm. Which she knew would eventually happen.

After fifteen minutes, Sam had calmed and crawled onto Kate's lap. She squeezed him tightly to her, rocking him gently. 'It's all okay Sam, everything is okay now.'

Kate was exhausted by the time she descended the stairs after showering and putting Sam to bed. She could hear him talking to himself. She stopped dead in the middle of the stairs, eavesdropping, trying to grab a glimpse into his day. But she only caught the odd word, what he was saying did not make sense to her.

Back in the living room, Kate found herself at a complete loss. She should really phone Matt. Tell him that Jake had not made any

contact with her. Instead, she decided to send a quick text as she didn't want to disturb him.

Hi Matt, just wanted to let you know that I've not heard from Jake. All good here, Hope you're ok? Kate.

She threw the phone onto the couch and plonked herself down next to it, then switched on the lamp. She sat slumped, staring at the phone screen, willing him to text back. It was a welcome surprise when the screen lit up displaying Matt's name.

'Hi Matt, you didn't have to phone,' Kate said quickly. She was so happy to hear his voice.

'I thought I'd call rather than text. I'm far too lazy,' Matt chuckled.

Kate smiled; there was no pretence with this man. She loved the sound of his voice; both comforting and sexy.

'Do you want to pop around? Sam has settled, *finally*. I think I have some leftover casserole in the freezer.'

Kate's heart sank when she heard his pause. She had obviously said the wrong thing.

'I'm a little tired actually, I was just off to bed, but wanted to check that everything was good.'

'Oh, okay, no problem, well yes, all good here,' Kate now felt foolish, 'thanks for phoning.'

'No problem, just glad you've not heard from him. But be careful Kate, I don't know, but I just don't think he will go quietly away.'

'I know,' Kate said, the old fear trying to rear its ugly head, 'I'll be careful.'

'I know you will.' Matt paused again, as if he was about to say something else, but instead he simply said goodnight.

Kate sat staring at the blank screen, suddenly sad. Something sounded off in his voice. He sounded different. She got up to close the curtains, a gnawing feeling of uneasiness brewing deep inside her. She had scared him off. He didn't want to get involved with a

woman whose ex-partner was stalking her, and who could blame him? She was damaged goods. The truth was staring her in the face. She suddenly felt old and tired, as she stood and looked out of the window, wondering what tomorrow would bring.

Matt's life was unravelling around him. He shouldn't have called Kate; he couldn't concentrate on what she had to tell him. He knew he sounded distracted, almost uncaring, and he hated himself for it. All he could think about was Lisa and what she had told him. He couldn't stop thinking about her.

He had spent the evening working on a presentation but had hardly got any work done. He couldn't carry on like this. He had moved here for a fresh start, to get away from her, but instead she had followed him, like a bloody lapdog. He cradled his head in his hands and closed his eyes. He couldn't think about her. Perhaps she would just go away? A bitter laugh erupted from his mouth. Isn't that just what Kate had been hoping for? That Jake would simply vanish. He was glad she had texted him; he wasn't sure if she needed his help, but she had reached out to him, and what had he done? Pretty much ignored her. He was a fool, when would he ever learn? He'd need to catch up with her tomorrow. Clear the air. Tell her about Lisa, she would understand.

He had no idea what to do about Lisa. He had ignored all her calls after she had phoned relentlessly all day. He nearly picked up once but had stopped himself. In the end, he had switched the bloody thing off.

He picked up his can of lager, now grown warm, and took a generous swig. Thankfully he had work to keep himself busy, he'd go mad with nothing to do.

He should have asked Kate about Sam as he had heard the commotion earlier on. He had never heard him making noise like

that before. He had had the perfect opportunity to do so when she mentioned that he had finally settled. He took another warm swig and grimaced – he shouldn't be drinking the stuff. He was a useless friend. He should have called round to see if she needed help, but to be honest he had felt embarrassed. It was almost as if he had been caught eavesdropping. Plus, he had absolutely no idea of how he could help them.

Maybe she thought he was pissed at her because of the noise. He toyed with the idea of texting her back, but then remembered that he had told her he was going to bed. It'd have to wait until tomorrow.

Admitting defeat, Matt switched the laptop off and the television on. He settled for the twenty-four-hour news channel. Learning about other people's misery would surely cheer him up; it would make his problems seem of little importance.

When the phone rang twenty minutes later his heart sank. He hadn't expected her to phone so late. He let the dulcet tones of *Run Like Hell* numb his senses before swiping the screen.

'I didn't think you'd answer,' Lisa breathed down the line.

'I nearly didn't,' Matt snapped. 'I told you not to phone.'

'I know, but I had to talk to you, to clear the air.'

'Lisa, there is no fucking air to clear. Go back to your husband. I've had it. Don't call me again, I mean it.'

Matt heard her gasp of surprise as he ended the call. It wasn't like him to lose his temper or to swear at her. He no longer wanted to be the nice guy. From now on, he was going to think about himself, do what he wanted to do. He took another gulp of lager and stared into the darkness. What frightened him most was the hold she had over him. Most frightening of all was that he had no idea how to move on without her. Move on and get on with the rest of his life. She was stood before him, arms outstretched,

inviting him in and blocking his path. She was his Achilles' heel.

Run Like Hell rung out once more. Matt counted to ten, then answered the phone.

CHAPTER EIGHTEEN

THURSDAY, SEPTEMBER 19TH, 2013

Kate sat at the kitchen table trying to collect her thoughts. She was so tired she could hardly think straight. Sam had been awake for most of the night, unsettled and not able to drift back to sleep; it was as if his brain was working too fast, that he could not process his thoughts. Eventually she had given up trying to coax him back to his own bed and had allowed him to watch the latest superhero cartoon on his iPad. The problem was she couldn't go to sleep while he was wide awake, so she had stayed up half the night with him, reading. Today she had phone interviews to catch up on, but at least she could do that from home. She felt like a walking zombie, even after three cups of strong coffee. But before she tackled any work, she needed to phone Bill, and then she would have to phone school and chat to them once again about Sam's recent behaviour.

Bill picked up on the first ring.

'Hi, Bill.'

'You okay Kate?' Bill asked.

'Yes, I'm fine, all's good,' she told him quickly, knowing that his first thought would be that Jake had contacted her. 'I'm just phoning to let you know that I'm working from home today.'

‘Okay, thanks for letting me know,’ he paused, ‘is everything really all right at home?’

‘Everything’s fine Bill, it’s Sam, he was awake most of the night.’

‘Ah,’ came Bill’s all-knowing reply. ‘I understand Kate, don’t worry. There’s no rush for those articles.’

‘No, I’ll get them done today for you, it’s just that it’ll be easier to do at home. I’m shattered. I need to phone school then I can get cracking on the phone interviews.’

‘Kate,’ Bill interrupted, ‘there really is no rush, they can wait until tomorrow if you like. Take the day off.’

For a fleeting second Kate considered this and then shook her head. ‘No Bill, I need to keep busy. Work is the best thing for me.’

‘I know Kate, just don’t overdo it.’

Kate smiled, ‘Thanks Bill.’

‘Yeah, now ring me if you need anything. Bye for now.’

‘Bye Bill.’

Kate ended the call and then immediately scrolled through her contact list to find the school phone number. She should really know it off by heart by now. The phone only rang twice before it was answered by the friendly receptionist.

‘Hi, I’m Kate Sullivan, Sam’s mum. Is it possible to speak to his teacher? If not, I can phone back later?’

‘Hi Kate, I’ll just see if she’s free to talk. I think she is already in class.’

Kate heard the click as the call was transferred and then Jane’s cheery voice echoed down the line.

‘Hi Kate, I’m glad you called as I was going to phone you later.’

‘Oh.’ Kate wondered why. ‘I was just phoning to say that Sam had an unsettled night. He just wouldn’t go to sleep, it’s not like him. He’ll wake up a few times in the night, but he always manages to settle back to sleep.’

'So, he'll be tired today then?' Jane enquired.

'Afraid so, I'm so sorry.'

'Listen, there's nothing to be sorry about. He'll be fine. We'll just have a low-key day with no demands placed upon him. As I mentioned, I was wanting to talk to you anyway, about yesterday. The trigger was another child leaving the classroom, but there have been lots of changes to his school day which may be contributing to more unsettled behaviour and may explain why he was so restless last night.'

'What changes?' Kate felt relieved that it was school and not her that was contributing towards Sam not sleeping. Half of her had wondered if he had picked up on how she was feeling about Jake. Sometimes he had a sixth sense about him; he picked up on feelings so easily.

'Well, we've had a new teaching assistant join the class, and as I mentioned we are doing new topics. The new art topic is not Sam's favourite subject I'm afraid. But we have been giving him the option of doing an extra maths work box instead, and he usually goes for this option.'

Kate laughed, 'He does love his numbers.'

'Yes, he does. Listen, he should re-settle, it's just a lot of changes at once, and unfortunately they couldn't be avoided.'

'I understand.' Kate really did, it was that sometimes life could not be planned and ordered – life was not like that. She now remembered the new targets that she had pinned to the noticeboard in the kitchen; she should have put two and two together but worrying about Jake had meant that she was not on top of things. She had to get her head together, for Sam's sake. 'Thank you, Jane. I'm so sorry to bother you.'

'Oh, don't be sorry,' Jane scolded, 'I needed to talk to you anyway, so you've saved me a phone call. I'll write how he has been

today for you in his chat book, but any concerns, please do phone. I'll always get back to you.'

'Thank you so much Jane.'

'No problem,' Jane paused for a beat, cleared her throat, 'listen, is everything okay at home? Any changes we should know about?'

'Yes, I mean no changes, everything is fine,' Kate replied, momentarily flustered. How could she tell this woman about Jake? Anyway, what was there to tell? Nothing had *actually* happened as yet.

'It's just that if Sam is struggling at home, in any way, please let us know as we can help. We can make more visual timetables for you or talk through coping mechanisms.'

'Thank you,' Kate replied. She so wished that she could confide in this woman.

'Okay, well, bye for now.'

'Bye.' Kate let out a long-held breath. Time for coffee and then to make a start on those interviews. The day could only get better.

Kate had a most interesting conversation with the local National Autistic Society group, who were setting up a Minecraft club for young people, so that they could interact with others on the platform, but in a safe and secure environment. Kate had sought comfort from the knowledge that there would be groups and activities in the local area when Sam was that little bit older. She remembered reading somewhere about a man in America who had set up a secure Minecraft server for his autistic son to use with others, and that it was now oversubscribed, but he never turned children away. Kate made a mental note to find out more about this.

She booted up her ancient laptop and then opened the Word application. She just needed to type up the interviews and then

she could have a rest. All things considered, she had had a pretty productive morning.

She still couldn't help worrying about Sam. She tried to empty her mind of all her worry, her doubts and the nagging feeling that Jake would show up at any moment, day or night. The cursor blinked at her, inviting her to start typing, but she couldn't concentrate. Sighing, she knew that she would get no more work done until she took a break. She needed fresh air. She decided that she would go to the shore; the wind would blow those stubborn cobwebs away. She hadn't been to the pier for a while.

On a complete whim, she grabbed her phone.

'Hi Emily, are you free for a walk?'

Matt nearly stumbled into Kate as he walked down the path, folders piled high, obscuring his view. 'Kate, I'm so sorry, I didn't see you.'

'I can see that,' Kate laughed. 'You have a lot of work to do then today?' she grinned, all thoughts of last night's awkwardness vanishing as she stood staring at him.

'Yes, you could say that. I forgot this lot this morning,' Matt's gaze lowered to the towering pile of papers he was balancing, using his chin, 'so I had to come back.'

Kate tugged her black beanie hat further down over her ears. The weather was growing colder, though the sun was bright today, not a cloud in sight.

'Off anywhere nice?' Matt asked.

'Just for a walk, I'm busy writing but need a breath of fresh air.'

'Well, you'll get that today.' Matt smiled once more, shifting his balance from one foot to the other, gripping the folders to his chest.

'Well, I won't keep you, I can see you're in a rush.' Kate headed off down the path, quickly followed by Matt on the way to his car.

He stopped at the end of the path and turned towards her. 'Listen, Kate, about last night. I was just so tired, and well, preoccupied …'

Kate gently touched his arm. 'Listen, no need to apologise. I just wanted to let you know that everything was okay, that was all.' She forced a tight smile. She had to remember that he wasn't interested in her and that that was fine. She should have known from the start that she was just too much trouble for anyone.

'No, just give me a minute,' Matt answered, his words tumbling out.

Kate pressed her lips together, looked at him more closely; his pale blue eyes almost seemed to be asking for some sort of forgiveness, but for what, she had no idea.

'I had a phone call.'

'From Jake? How did he get your number?' Kate shrieked in alarm.

'No, no, not from Jake, from Lisa, my ex-wife.' Matt vigorously shook his head.

Kate let the words sink in, his ex-wife? The woman he had left behind but whom he still had feelings for? 'Oh,' was all she could think to say.

'That's exactly what I thought as well, *oh*. Look, she's back on the scene, so to speak, and so I was just distracted when you phoned.'

'Look, Matt, this is none of my business, you don't need to explain anything to me.'

'But I do, Kate, I don't want you to get the wrong impression.'

Kate's eyebrows rose in confusion. 'Wrong impression? What do you mean by that?'

'Just that I'm not back with her. She's left her husband and moved here.'

'She wants you back?' Kate blurted out before her filter kicked in.

Matt shuffled from one foot to the other, looking anywhere but at Kate's face. 'It looks that way.'

It was now Kate's turn to feel uncomfortable. He shouldn't be telling her any of this. Why was he telling her anyway? What he got up to was no concern of hers. She had enough on her plate as it was.

She held her hand up, palm facing forwards. 'Matt, really, just stop, it's fine.'

'I had no idea that she would leave Dave. I was … getting used to being without her … and now, I just, well, I don't know what to do Kate.'

Her heart ached for him, it truly did, but this wasn't her problem. It was his. 'Look Matt, you need to have it out with her, tell her what you feel. Do you want her back? After everything she has done to you?'

'That's the problem Kate, I just don't know.'

Kate bit her bottom lip, told herself to say no more. He had to figure this out himself. But she knew that getting back with her would cause nothing but heartache for him.

'I wanted to catch you anyway,' Matt said, changing the subject and not quite meeting her eye, 'I should have asked about Sam last night.'

Kate's brow creased as she raised an eyebrow quizzically at him.

'I heard the noise, him shouting, but I didn't know what to do.' Matt told her as way of explanation.

Kate felt her face warm, knowing that she was slowly turning scarlet. She had wrongly assumed that Matt was out. 'I'm sorry about the noise –'

'No, no! You've got it wrong Kate, the noise didn't bother me, I'm not complaining, but I should have asked how you both were, and I didn't.'

'Matt, I'm used to it. Honestly, I am. He had a bad day at school, that's all, it happens.' Kate shrugged, deeply touched that he had been worrying about them. She wasn't used to it.

Matt nodded, not making a move to find his car key. Kate glanced at her phone, 'Sorry, I'm meeting a friend. I must go. I'll catch you later?'

Matt smiled, 'Yes you will. Are we still on for that trip to town on Saturday?'

Kate had completely forgotten about inviting him, but the idea that he wanted to go with them cheered her up. She still wondered about this ex-wife of his and why she was back on the scene. 'I look forward to it.' she grinned.

'Me too,' Matt grinned back.

Kate started to laugh; he had no idea what Sam could be like when out and about. He tried to walk everyone's dog. 'Enjoy the rest of your day, don't work too hard.'

'I won't, don't worry.' Matt lost his grin, his eyes hardened. 'Kate, be careful, I still think Jake is around here.'

Kate's happy mood vanished in an instant, *puff*, replaced by the usual growing sense of unease. A black cloud hung over her. She was trying to forget about him. She simply wanted to enjoy the rest of the day, have a coffee, a chat with Emily. *Be normal*. She had no room for Jake.

Kate walked away, leaving Matt rooting in his pocket for his car key as she headed toward the bottom of the road and towards the pier. Matt's car passed her just as she had stopped to cross the road. He gave her a wave and she waved back. Matt really had become a part of her life, and as selfish as it was, she didn't want to let him go.

As she walked her thoughts turned to him; something had been different, and as she pondered it suddenly came to her – it was the missing gold wedding band.

Kate spotted Emily huddled on a bench opposite the café. Behind her was the tall sea defence wall, its blocks of light grey stone helping her to shelter from the wind. Kate was thankful that she had chosen such a sheltered spot, as the wind had an icy nip to it. She scurried along the path, smiling as Emily rose to greet her.

'Darling, so lovely to see you.' Emily took her hand, gripping it tightly, as she gave two air kisses. 'Shall we go in for a warm drink? I fancy a hot chocolate today.'

Kate beamed at her friend, 'I love that idea, it's freezing.' She linked Emily's arm and they strolled towards the café. Kate sneaked a sideways glance at Emily, noting the flowery scarf that covered half her face and the oversized dark sunglasses that she had never seen her wear before. The sun was bright but not so bright as to need to wear sunglasses. Kate thought this an odd choice for such weather but decided to keep her thoughts to herself.

The old-fashioned bell tinkled as they entered the café. Kate was happy to see that the place had vacant tables by the windows that looked out over the pier. 'Grab a seat Emily, and I'll get us a hot chocolate each,' Kate said, taking off her hat and placing it on the table. 'In case they ask, do you want cream?'

'No thank you! I'm trying to watch my weight,' Emily said quickly.

Kate stifled a smile, thinking that a hot chocolate was not the best drink when on a diet. Plus, Emily was so thin that she looked like she would snap in a strong gust of wind.

Kate went to order and once she had the drinks firmly in her grasp, sat down on the worn wooden chair that had seen better days, opposite her friend.

'So, feeling any better?' Emily enquired, taking a slow sip of her drink.

It took Kate a moment to realise what she meant, remembering that the last time she had met Emily was when she had spied Jake through the café window. She sipped her drink to hide her embarrassment. She should have phoned Emily sooner. 'Yes, much better, thank you.' She couldn't for the life of her remember what she had told Emily. Had she told her that she had a cold? Or was it a vomiting bug? She decided to elaborate no further, as she would surely get caught up in the lie. She changed the subject. 'Anyway, how are you?'

Now that they were facing each other, Kate could clearly see that Emily looked exhausted. She still hadn't removed her sunglasses even though the café was dark, all dark wooden furniture and dim lights. Kate pondered this for a moment. 'Why don't you take your glasses off Emily? I bet you can hardly see a thing in here.' Kate kept her tone light, a suggestion, not a demand. She watched Emily squirm in her seat as she pretended to be engrossed in her drink, using the long-handled teaspoon to swirl the chocolate around and around the tall glass.

Kate put her own drink firmly down on the table. Her gut twisted. 'Emily, what's wrong?'

Emily continued to stare at her drink, as if she had not heard Kate's question.

When no answer was forthcoming, Kate reached across the table and touched her friend's hand, surprised when Emily grabbed her fingers.

'I can't take them off,' Emily said, her voice barely a whisper.

Kate's throat felt suddenly dry and she wished she had ordered coffee, not chocolate. She already knew the reason.

Emily looked up at her and slowly slid the glasses down her nose. Kate couldn't help the gasp that escaped from her mouth.

Emily's left eye was half closed and surrounding it was a large

purple bruise. A red scratch could be seen just under the eye. Even in the dim light of the café, the injury looked brutal.

'What happened?' Kate asked, as she watched Emily push the sunglasses back up her nose.

'Isaac had a bad day at school and when he got home he went into meltdown,' she paused to take a sip of her drink, 'you know what it's like when there's nothing you can do about it. You just have to let it run its course.'

Kate gave her friend a gentle smile encouraging her to continue.

'Well, when Gerald got home Isaac was still in full swing, you know, throwing stuff, shouting. It had been going on a good hour by the time Gerald got home from work, but I could see that Isaac was growing tired and that he would soon calm. I just sat and made sure he was safe.'

Kate nodded sympathetically. It was exactly what she would have done.

Gerald became angry, telling me that his behaviour was all my fault. I mean, how was I to blame? I had no idea what he was on about, and at that point I'd had just about enough, so I just laughed and told him so. Well, he became furious and told me that the way Isaac was, was all my fault, his autism I mean. He said that I caused it.' Emily paused for breath, her chin wobbling slightly.

'Oh, Emily, that's an awful thing to say. No one is to blame, you know that, right?' She swallowed down her tears. She had felt the same way to begin with, that she was to blame for Sam's autism, but she now knew it was nonsense to feel that way.

'Did you ever think that Kate?' Emily asked cautiously, 'you know, that it was your fault.'

'Yes, to begin with. I think every mother does, but then I realised that to do so was unhealthy. No one knows what causes autism. It just happens. No one is to blame.'

'I know,' Emily looked up, giving Kate another wobbly smile, 'but he has said it many times, and you get to believe it, don't you?'

'Well don't,' Kate told her sternly, 'you're a fantastic mum.'

Emily took a sip of her hot chocolate, not quite meeting Kate's gaze.

Kate looked once more at the dark sunglasses. Emily had not answered her question.

'Emily, how did you get a black eye?'

'Isaac threw one of his toy trucks at me, and as you can see, it caught my eye,' Emily replied quickly. Far too quickly for Kate's liking.

Kate inwardly sighed. She had hoped that Emily would trust her enough to tell the truth. She was still protecting that bastard. She knew it wasn't the first time that he had attacked his wife. Kate didn't know what to say. What could she say? *I know that you are lying, now tell me the truth.* If Emily had wanted to tell her the truth, then she would have done so.

Kate took a deep breath. She had to probe a little further – she couldn't give up on her friend. Kate thought about all the people who had let her down in the past. She had to be there for Emily. She had to be *that* friend who listened.

'Is that really what happened?' Kate finally asked.

Emily slammed her cup down on the table, causing hot chocolate to splash over it. 'What do you mean, is that what *really* happened? Of course, it is. Why would I lie to you?'

Kate braced herself for the reaction that she knew was to come. 'Did he hurt you?' she asked the question as gently as she could, but she still saw the look of absolute panic cross Emily's features before it was replaced with the mask that she wore so well.

'I'm not listening to any more accusations about my husband, not from *you*, not from anyone.' Emily stood up so abruptly that

she nearly knocked the chair over. After rooting in her handbag with shaking hands, Emily threw a five-pound note onto the table. Kate hastily did the same and then followed her friend through the café door, running after her, trying to keep pace.

'Emily, stop!' she shouted. She was out of breath and boiling hot. She swore as she remembered that she had left her hat behind, but she couldn't turn back now. She had to talk some sense into her, make her listen. Kate began to run faster and eventually caught up with Emily who had stopped by the end of the pier, propped up against the railings. She stood gazing into the grey waters below.

'I'm sorry,' Kate wheezed, hunched over, suddenly short of breath. 'I really am. I just want to help you.'

'Help!' Emily looked incredulous. 'Help me? *How?* Nobody can help me.'

'You don't have to put up with this. Nobody should. You don't have to live in fear.'

'And what should I do Kate? Leave him?' she gave a bitter laugh. 'Where would I go? I have Isaac, it's not that easy. You of all people should know that.'

Kate blushed. For a moment, she thought that Emily knew about her past, about Jake. She tried to cover her shock, looked down towards her feet, but it was too late. Emily had already taken in her startled expression.

'I meant about Sam, that you would understand having Sam,' her voice now gentle. She turned to face Kate, 'What did you think I meant?'

'Just that,' Kate answered too quickly, looking away, knowing that she would give the game away. Emily was very intuitive.

The two women stood in silence; only the squawking of the seagulls could be heard and the waves that lapped the shoreline.

‘This has happened to you, hasn’t it?’ Emily asked while looking at the waves.

Kate swallowed down the impulse to lie. She was asking Emily to tell the truth, so she had to be honest with her. She owed her that. She began to tell Emily her story.

Chapter Nineteen

Friday, September 20th, 2013

After a quick shower and a mouthful of coffee, Matt had jumped into his car and headed straight for the aquarium. A party of children was visiting today, so he wanted to make sure that he had everything organised and under control. He already knew that he did, but he wanted to double check things.

He enjoyed the relatively peaceful ride, with only a few other cars on the road. He knew that he would be the first to arrive, but that suited him just fine. He wasn't ready to talk to anyone just yet; he needed some time with his own thoughts and then he could start his day.

His last conversation with Lisa played out in his mind. She wanted him back and she would wait for him, however long that took. He cursed his weakness when it came to this woman. He should have just told her in no uncertain terms, to *go away*, and that was being polite, but he just couldn't do it. He needed time to think, to process what had happened and what *could* happen. If Kate hadn't walked into his life then he knew that things would be so much easier, but as things stood, she was one hell of a complication. He really liked her, and he wanted to get to know her more, but it wasn't fair to do anything about those feelings with Lisa back on the scene. He had to decide. Tell Lisa to stay, or to go.

He arrived at the aquarium at just past 7:00 am, so he had a good hour before Dan would show up. Ken might be in a bit earlier, perhaps to clean, but he couldn't remember his rota and what days he worked an early shift. He didn't mind Ken so much, a man who was lonely and liked the company of others. Matt reminded himself that he could be a *Ken* one day. It was a sobering thought.

Dan had given him a key, so once inside, he switched off the alarm, thankful that it was an easy code to remember, and turned on all the lights. He had only been here once before by himself and he liked the solitude of the place. Just him and the fish. He headed straight to the office, booted up his laptop and then made himself a coffee. He began to prepare for the school trip that was planned later that day. As he worked, all thoughts of Lisa faded, but he knew that they were there, lurking just under the surface. They would finally bubble up once more.

Kate had decided to take the day off, well more specifically, Bill had insisted that she do so. She had handed in her two phone interviews and there were no more jobs until Monday. So, she had the day to herself. Bill had told her that he would email her on Sunday night with any planned work, and that she should enjoy the long weekend ahead. He had said all this and then calmly told her to stay extra vigilant. As if she needed reminding.

This was why she now found herself sat once more on the bench outside the café, on the pier, but this time with a cone of chips in her hand. She licked the salt from her fingers and welcomed the sharp wind blowing through the strands of her hair.

She closed her eyes, trying to empty her mind of all thoughts, all worries, but it was useless. She had sat with her back against

the wall, allowing herself a clear view of anyone approaching her along the pier. She couldn't truly relax, not even here, sat on a bench eating chips. Kate sighed, would she ever be free of him? It had been a week since she had seen him outside the café. Did that mean she was safe? Was he playing mind games with her? Kate already knew the answer. Men like Jake loved the thrill of the chase, the hunt; it was all about control and he was slowly gaining control over her once more, even though he was not back in her life. Kate had a nagging feeling that he would soon show up, unannounced and as charming as ever. She scrunched her eyes up against the glare of the sun and threw the empty paper cone into the dustbin at the side of the bench. She'd go for a walk to the end of the pier and then head back home to clean. She heaved herself up, slinging her bag over her shoulder, then strolled quickly along the empty pier.

Ken never showed up for work and Matt felt a little sad that he couldn't have a chat with him; he liked the old fella. It was only later on that morning, when chatting to Dan, that he was told that Ken was going into hospital the following week for a knee replacement. This meant that Dan had had to hire someone else for the short term and he wasn't happy about it. Matt supposed that even though Ken liked to talk an awful lot and had to be reminded not to overfeed the fish, he was reliable and ultimately likeable.

'I was lucky to get someone so quickly. I'd only put the advert online yesterday and he replied straight away. He's just moved to the area and needs the money. He's younger than Ken too,' Dan smirked.

'I'll miss Ken,' Matt said as he closed his laptop, 'he's a nice bloke.'

'Yes, he is, and after the op, well, he can come back when all is well and good.'

Matt grinned, 'I bet he'll be right fed up at home. Those poor nurses, they'll get an ear bashing.'

Dan grinned and nodded. 'I'm just off out to the wholesalers, I'll only be an hour. Will you be okay managing the tour?'

Matt nodded, 'No problem at all, everything's set up.'

'Right then, I'll catch you later.' Dan picked up the van keys from the desk and quietly shut the office door behind him.

Matt glanced at the clock. He had an hour before the kids arrived, so he'd get some of his own work done first. He loved days like this.

He had just settled into writing his report when his phone rang. He deliberated whether to answer or not, but knew he had no choice. 'Lisa, I'm at work. I told you not to phone me.'

'Can you meet me for dinner tonight?' she quickly asked, ignoring him.

'You what? Are you for real? Did you not just hear what I said?'

'Of course, I heard you,' she snapped, 'I'm just choosing to ignore you.'

Matt nearly ended the call but instead started to count slowly to ten; he needed to calm down.

'Well? Dinner … tonight?' Lisa asked impatiently.

'It's not a good idea Lisa.'

'Why ever not?'

Matt let out a shallow laugh; there was no humour to it. 'Seriously? Do you want me to list the reasons?'

'There's no need to use that tone.'

'A, you are married,' Matt blurted out, ignoring her, 'B, I don't want to have dinner with you, and C, you need to talk to Dave.'

'For heaven's sake Matt, we've been over all of this. I have nothing

left to say to Dave. It's ended, over. I made a stupid mistake. One that I'll regret for the rest of my life.'

Matt pinched the bridge of his nose, wishing the conversation to be over. 'Lisa, I'm busy, I need to go.'

'Don't hang up on me …'

Matt ended the call and switched the phone off. He'd had enough. He needed to work. He needed to forget.

When Kate got home she curled up on the sofa and sat staring into space. Five minutes she told herself, before she would start the ironing. She thought about Matt, and how he had seemed yesterday. He had looked tired, dark circles under his eyes, and he needed a shave. His life was a mess too. Kate couldn't believe the cheek of his ex-wife. The woman sounded mad. How could she treat him in such a way? Just because she had broken up with her husband, she assumed she had an automatic right to waltz back into her ex-husband's life. But then Kate reminded herself, that she barely knew Matt, and she knew absolutely nothing about his wife. She shouldn't judge. People had judged her based on lies and appearances. It was just that she felt an attraction to Matt; it had been there yesterday as she stood talking to him. She had felt that spark of electricity and she was sure that he had felt it too. But with Jake lurking in the shadows, and Matt's ex back on the scene, there was nothing they could do about it.

Then there was Emily. Kate was worried sick about her friend. She had tried phoning her after she had spoken to Bill, but she hadn't texted back. Kate forced herself up off the couch, her legs stiff as she had been sat with them curled upwards and retrieved her phone from the kitchen. Still no message. Kate began to type a quick text, asking if everything was all right at home. If she hadn't heard back from her in an hour, then she would phone

her. Kate just hoped that Gerald was at work and that her friend was safe.

Matt watched the last of the school group leaving and heaved a sigh of relief. The tour had gone well. The children had all been on their best behaviour, most probably due to the strict nature of their teacher and had seemed to take in what Matt had told them. He loved inquisitive children and didn't mind the many educated questions that they had fired at him. One little boy had reminded him of how he used to be as a little boy. All long-limbed, pale and slightly geeky. He would go far.

Matt made a coffee once he had tidied up after them and then contemplated making an early dart. He had earned it. There was nothing more for him to do anyway. He gathered all his papers and shoved them into his briefcase. Dan was busy preparing feeds behind the tanks, so Matt shouted his goodbyes to him as he made his way into the foyer. When he got to the front desk he remembered he had forgotten his phone – he'd left it charging on the shelf by the window. Sighing wearily, Matt turned on his heels and retraced his steps. He unplugged his phone, shoved the charger into his briefcase and his phone into his jeans back pocket. Making his way once more down the corridor, he pushed open the heavy door into the large foyer and came face to face with a man that he faintly recognized. The man sneered at him for a moment before pushing past him. Matt turned in astonishment to watch the man hurrying away as he heard him shout Dan's name. It was only then that Matt remembered who the man was. Matt shuddered; Dan had hired Jake.

CHAPTER TWENTY

Matt had not enjoyed his so-called *romantic dinner*. The food had stuck in his throat and he had cursed himself for ever agreeing to the stupid meal out in the first place. What was he thinking? He should have called straight round to Kate's as soon as he got home from the aquarium, but he didn't want to frighten her, and that is exactly what he would have done. So instead he now found himself racing back home, the letter burning a hole in his pocket. He had to tell Kate about Jake, he had no choice.

Lisa hadn't been best pleased with his lack of enthusiasm. He had barely uttered a word all evening, as he sat picking at his food. His appetite deserted him. Kate was no longer safe. It just didn't feel right that he was sat in a warm and expensive restaurant, while Jake could turn up at Kate's house, unannounced, at any moment. He had to get back to her.

In the end he had blamed his lacklustre performance on a viral bug. She had accepted his excuse, but of course had not believed him. He'd kissed her on the cheek as she bent down to get into the taxi and made a promise that he would call her in the morning. She had assumed that he would stay the night, of course she had. He had to tell Kate what had happened. He had half-wondered about telling Lisa, but he chose not to. It was not her problem, but then again, really, it wasn't his.

When Jake had caught up with him outside the aquarium, shoving the letter roughly into his jacket pocket, Matt had nearly shoved him out of the way and told him to fuck the hell off, but something had stopped him. It was better that Jake was harassing him and not Kate. 'Give it to Holly,' he had growled at Matt, before storming back inside the building.

Matt had contemplated throwing the letter away, but what would that accomplish? It would only delay the inevitable. Jake was obviously living in the area now, so there was no way she could escape him. Anyway, it wasn't his decision to make.

Matt slowed to a crawl and parked outside his house, the place he now called home. He turned off the engine and sat staring into space. Whatever was in that letter was bad news, and he was about to deliver it to a woman who deserved far better in her life. He pulled the scrap of paper from his pocket and read the name that was scrawled upon it. *Holly*. Her past had eventually caught up with her and Matt had absolutely no idea how he could help her.

'Another rub Mum,' Sam demanded. He grabbed Kate's hand and placed it on the top of his leg that was slung across her lap. She began to gently stroke his leg, her palm moving in rhythmic circles as she watched him playing a noisy platform game on his Nintendo DS. There had been no problems when he had returned home from school. He had only asked for his pyjamas and then after a five-minute run around the house, had happily bounced onto the couch to play on his iPad. That was once she had found the charger, as it was displaying the twenty percent battery left sign. She had forgotten to charge it that morning. Sam always checked the battery sign once he switched the iPad on. It always

had to be over twenty percent, as anything less could mean that the iPad could suddenly turn itself off. It was unpredictable; the game could stop working at any moment, and that was not good, not good at all.

Kate bit into her microwave pizza, plain cheese and tomato, that was now stone cold, and thought about Emily. She hadn't heard from her all day and she was worried, especially as she hadn't returned any of her texts. Was Gerald away this weekend? Kate couldn't remember. She fumbled with her phone and sent another quick message, just asking if she was free to meet on Monday for a coffee. It would appear as a completely innocent text if Gerald was screening her calls; Kate had a horrible feeling that that was exactly what he was doing.

'Mum, scratchies,' Sam demanded as he grabbed Kate's hand once more, this time placing it on his back.

'Just gentle scratchies Sam,' Kate told him, as she gently rubbed his skin with her fingernails as he continued to be mesmerised by cartoon characters jumping over lakes and swinging from trees. She was worried sick about her friend but felt powerless to do anything about those concerns. What could she do? Other than be there for her?

What did worry her was Isaac's safety. Would Gerald hurt him? Men like him craved power, so it was a possibility. Kate shuddered at the thought. She needed to talk some sense into Emily, make her see that she needed to leave him, but the only person who could make that decision was Emily herself.

Kate took another bite of pizza and wondered what to do for the rest of the evening. She felt like re-watching the *Gilmore Girls* – doing so always cheered her up. She'd try and settle Sam first and then she could have a glass of wine and try and forget about Jake, about Emily's worries and about why Matt had been wearing a

suit and tie when she had spied him leaving the house a few hours earlier.

It was completely irrational, to question where he was going. He was free to come and go as he pleased. They were just friends. But seeing him dressed up like that had stirred something deep within her. She wanted to be the woman linking his arm, the woman who he would tenderly kiss on the cheek, and the woman who he would take to bed. Because he was most definitely on a date, and the lucky woman had to be Lisa. She tried to banish these thoughts, but they kept resurfacing, refusing to be sunk. She had no right to think this way. But she knew the reason. The *green-eyed monster*. It was only a matter of time before they were back together, but it was bound to end badly.

Kate looked around the small living room. All her worldly possessions shoved onto shelves, as well as hidden in the dark recesses of her mind. She was content with her life. She had Sam. She should be happy, she was happy, but that spark of longing, of sharing her life with someone else would always be lurking within her. And it was this that saddened her the most.

'I want a drink,' Sam piped up, as his fingers deftly handled the small device's controllers.

'How do we ask Sam?'

'Please,' he replied without looking up or stopping his game.

Kate dragged herself up from the couch and once in the kitchen, flicked the switch for the kettle. She might as well make a coffee at the same time.

'I want drink!' Sam bellowed over the sound of the boiling kettle. Kate muttered to herself, he could be so very impatient at times. Not his fault; she knew and understood why he became impatient, but it still annoyed the hell out of her.

She poured some apple juice into his cup and quickly made the

instant coffee, nearly splashing her hand with boiling water. *Slow down Kate.* Would she hear from Jake again? She looked towards Sam, engrossed in his game, and prayed to whoever would listen that Jake was well and truly out of their lives.

Kate jumped at the sound of her phone's ringtone.

'Too loud Mum,' Sam shouted at her while covering his ears. 'Turn it off, off, off.'

Kate dashed back into the kitchen where she had thrown the phone onto the table, and quickly answered the call. To her immense relief it was Emily. 'It's okay now Sam, I've turned it off,' Kate shouted before turning her attention to Emily.

'Hi Emily, sorry, I forgot to turn my phone onto silent. How are you?'

Kate heard the hesitation in Emily's voice, before she finally told her that she was fine.

'I just didn't want you worrying about me, you have enough on your plate. I wish that you'd told me about Jake earlier. I could have helped you,' she paused, clearing her throat before she continued, 'well, okay, I'm not too sure how I could have helped, but I'm a good listener.'

Kate smiled; she should have trusted Emily more as a friend. She'd have to make amends for that.

'I know Emily, but I'm worried about you. Is it safe for you to talk?'

Kate heard Emily exhale; she sounded relieved, 'He's not here, he's away for a long weekend, thank god. If I could up and leave him, I would.'

Kate knew she meant this, but why not just leave him? She had, so Emily could. 'Why not go this weekend?'

'Oh Kate, where would I go?'

'A friend's house? Your mum's? She lives far enough away.'

'Kate,' Emily snapped, 'I have no other close friends and besides, my mum would tell me to go back to him, telling me that I don't know how good my life is ...'

Kate couldn't hide her surprise, her hand covering her mouth as it gaped open. She had assumed that Emily's mum would know what was going on in her daughter's life. She finally managed to reply. 'You haven't told her?'

'She's old Kate, I can't cause her this type of worry. She knows we aren't getting on but that's all.'

'You have to tell her,' Kate urged.

'No, I don't Kate, it would kill her. I can't cause that kind of stress.'

'Where will you go then?'

Emily laughed, 'Where is there to go, especially when I have Isaac? Nowhere, I'm trapped Kate, and the worst of it is … he knows it.'

Kate swallowed, her throat dry. She couldn't help her friend; Emily was as stuck as she was. Then she had an idea. 'What about the women's refuge, out of town? I forget the name, but I could find out for you.'

'A refuge, with an autistic child Kate! For god's sake! It would be a disaster.'

'You'd be safe,' Kate snapped back. 'At least let me find out about where they are and how you can get a place, it may not be so bad.'

'Oh, all right then,' Emily eventually replied, sounding resigned.

'I'll do that then for you and call you tomorrow when I have news.'

'Thanks Kate, I just need to be brave, and I feel, I feel ...'

'I know,' Kate reassured her friend. 'I'll call tomorrow, but I'm here if you need anything.'

'Thanks. I need to go, Isaac is shouting for me, he doesn't like me chatting on the phone.'

‘Oh, I know that feeling,’ Kate chuckled. It was only then that she realised she could not hear the DS or Sam’s running commentary from the other room. ‘I need to go to, I need to check on Sam, but remember to call if you need me.’

Kate hung up and strolled back into the living room. Sam was sprawled on the sofa, the DS closed. He was fast asleep. Kate retrieved the crocheted rainbow blanket from the basket in the corner of the room and draped it over his sleeping body. She stroked his blonde curls and gently kissed his cheek. No matter what had happened in her life, she had kept him safe, and that was all that mattered.

She eased herself down onto the end of the sofa and pulled the remaining blanket over her lap. It was as she closed her eyes that she heard the gentle knock at the front door. Kate’s heart started to hammer in her chest as she made a frantic dash to see who was there. She didn’t want whoever it was to wake Sam, but that was the least of her worries. What should she do if it was Jake?

As she peered through the frosted glass a sigh escaped her lips. Why was Matt here? She fumbled with the locks and the door swung open to reveal a stoical looking Matt.

‘Whatever’s wrong?’

‘Can I come in?’ Matt pleaded. ‘We need to talk.’

Kate took in Matt’s suit, the dark blue tie and his freshly washed hair. He’d had a shave and she could smell his aftershave, that blend of wood and spices that was now so incredibly familiar. She looked behind him to see if Lisa was in the car or hovering out of sight down the path, but it was just Matt. A million thoughts raced round in her head.

Why was he here?

She stood aside to let him in.

‘Sam’s asleep, I was just about to take him upstairs,’ she told Matt as he hovered in the living room doorway.

Matt shoved his hands into his pockets and cleared his throat. 'Listen, I need to tell you something.' He pulled the letter from his pocket. 'It's about Jake. He gave me this, to give to you.'

'You've talked to him? Met him?' Kate's eyes clouded over; her hands had formed into tight fists by her side and she was shaking. Matt had met with him. How could he have kept this from her?

Matt took a step towards her. 'No, it's not like that Kate. I don't know the guy, he just turned up at work today, at the aquarium.' He shrugged apologetically. 'He's the new cleaner.'

The new cleaner? Kate's head was whirling, what was he talking about? Jake was working there?

She stood and looked at the letter that Matt was holding out towards her. She didn't want to touch it, never mind open it. She looked down at where Sam was sleeping, glad that he was unaware of the drama that was about to unfold around him and she wished that she could press pause. To forever stay in this moment. She didn't want to read what Jake had to say to her – she already knew.

'I'll just take Sam up to bed,' Kate said, stalling for time.

'Let me carry him up for you,' Matt offered, as he placed the letter on the table. Kate nodded and then silently watched as Matt bent to lift her little boy up, ever so gently. She walked up the stairs ahead of them and opened Sam's bedroom door, pulling back the duvet. She watched as Matt slowly lowered him onto the bed before taking a step back. Kate covered her son in his cartoon themed duvet cover, making him appear even smaller, and then gently kissed his forehead.

When Kate entered the living room, Matt held the letter out to her once more.

'Tell me what happened?' Kate asked as she lowered herself onto the couch, patting the seat next to her. She needed to know what happened before she could read the letter.

Matt sat down and told her how Jake had turned up, completely out of the blue, and that he had given the letter to him. That was all. They hadn't had a conversation.

'I have no idea how he found out where I work Kate. It's just as much of a shock to me as it is to you.'

'I doubt that.' Kate instantly regretted her sarcastic tone. 'I'm sorry, I know it must have been a shock to you, but nothing about that man surprises me anymore.' She stared at the letter in Matt's hand. 'I need to read it don't I.' It wasn't a question.

'He knows where you live and where I work,' Matt answered.

Kate continued to stare at the letter. She was finding it hard to breathe.

'Would you like me to stay while you read it?' He shuffled in his seat, looking at the door, 'Or I could go?'

'I'm sure you have better things to do of a Friday night,' she said as she glanced at his smart suit, his now loosened tie. Where was Lisa? 'Did you go out to dinner?'

Matt offered her a sheepish grin. 'Yes, we went out for dinner.' He pressed the letter into her hand. 'Now stop changing the subject, you need to read this. I really will go if you want me to.'

'No, stay ... Please,' Kate urged him quickly, 'if you don't mind.'

'I don't mind at all,' Matt told her gently. 'I'll go and make us a cuppa, give you a bit of space.'

Kate was about to object, to tell him that he could sit next to her. She needed to feel his solid presence, his stability, that somehow, he would make everything right again. But she realised how foolish this sounded, even to her own ears. So it was with trembling fingers that she tore open the envelope.

Kate began to read:

"Holly,

I've changed, I've been in therapy, I no longer drink like I did. You

need to give me a second chance. You took my son away from me, and I can never forget, nor forgive, what you did. I lost six years of his life and he has no idea who his father is. I need to be a part of his life, no matter what happened between you and me. If you refuse me access I will go to the police and tell them that you abducted my son. You have no choice. I'll be at the Bookshop Café tomorrow at 11 am. I know you go there every Saturday and sit in the exact same window seat, so don't play games with me. Make this happen or I won't be responsible for what happens next."

Kate hadn't noticed that Matt had crept quietly back into the living room and had placed a cup of tea on the floor by her feet. 'May I?' he asked her gently, gesturing towards the letter in her trembling hands.

Kate passed him the piece of paper, picked up her tea, numb with shock, and took a scalding sip. She watched Matt read, waiting for a change in his expression, but she saw none. He hid his feelings well.

'I have no choice,' she eventually told him, as he passed the letter back to her.

'You always have a choice,' he began, but stopped when Kate began to shake her head.

'Not this time. What he says is true, I did abduct his son.'

'But for a very good reason, this is nothing but blackmail!'

'But it's true,' Kate shouted. Silencing them both.

Matt picked up his cup and took a sip. It was only when he placed the cup back on the floor, that he began to speak. He kept his voice even, soft.

'That's all very well, but you did it to keep your baby safe, to keep you both safe. What else could you have done?' He stood and started to pace the room, in front of the couch, his hand raking

through his short blond hair. 'What I don't understand is why it has taken him six years to get in touch?'

Kate looked at him, completely bewildered. 'What do you mean, why? He's obviously only just found out where I live.'

'No, Kate,' Matt said quickly, sitting back down next to her, his face so close to hers that she could see the pale intensity of the blue of his eyes, the furrow of his brow. 'No, I don't believe that for a second. His life carried on the same, in one way or another. Something has happened recently to change all of that, to make him need to contact you. That's what worries me.'

Kate tore her gaze from his eyes and thought about this for a moment. What Matt said could be true, but couldn't Jake just want to see his son? That was the obvious reason, wasn't it?

'Kate, look at me,' Matt urged her, 'I'm telling you, something doesn't add up here. Meeting him is a bad idea. I'd honestly seek some professional help.'

Kate let out a bitter laugh. 'Where from Matt? Where would I get help? The way it looks from everyone else's viewpoint is that I upped and left my boyfriend with a new baby, denying him all rights to see his child. As you've already told me, I have no proof of what happened to me. None at all, so I have to meet him.'

'I'll come with you then,' Matt said quickly.

'What,' Kate gasped, 'no, I can't ask you to do that.'

'You're not asking. I'm offering,' Matt offered a lopsided smile, and despite everything, Kate's heart lurched at the sight.

'That's incredibly kind of you, but, this is just something I must do myself,' she mumbled.

'Does Sam need to be with you?' Matt gently asked.

Kate gave him a weary look, 'That's the whole point, Matt, he'll expect him to be there. Look, we'll be in a public space that Sam knows well, he'll be happy and we'll both be safe.'

'How about I travel with you and hang about nearby, just in case. It would make me feel better.'

Once again Kate thought how lucky she was to have this man in her life, who asked for nothing in return. 'Thank you, that sounds like a good idea.'

Matt laughed, lightening the mood. 'I am full of good ideas,' he beamed at her.

Kate couldn't help but stare at him, his pale blue eyes that were far too serious for a Friday night. Why wasn't he with Lisa? She was desperate to ask him, but now was not the right time. He'd tell her if he wanted to. She picked up her cup of tea and took a calming sip. Everything would work out. It had to.

'Maybe he has changed,' Kate suggested with a weak smile.

Matt shook his head, remembering the menacing way that Jake had looked at him, the deliberate shove as he had sauntered past him. 'No Kate, men like that never change.'

CHAPTER TWENTY-ONE

SATURDAY, SEPTEMBER 21ST, 2013

He rubbed at his temple using his thumb, trying to ease the throbbing ache behind his eyes. Sadly, this was not from the effects of alcohol but from the lack of a good night's sleep. Matt almost wished that he had a hangover. Sam's repetitive questions weren't helping matters.

'We go to the museum, then to the Bookshop Café,' he told Matt for what felt like the hundredth time. Matt nodded, but gently, as too much movement felt like a load of stones rolling around inside his skull. He wondered if he was brewing a migraine. He hoped not.

Sam sat with his ear defenders clamped to his head, huge pale blue domes that gave him an alien like appearance. He rocked backwards and forwards, humming a tune that Matt did not recognise, in between telling him about their itinerary.

Sat in Kate's too-small car, Matt felt slightly claustrophobic and very nervous. Not at Kate's driving ability, but at what would happen once they got to the café. Before that they had to trundle around the museum. Sam was completely unaware of the tension in the car, but Matt could feel it, and he knew Kate could feel it too. She had explained to Matt, that Sam knew they were meeting a friend of Mummy's and that he was to be a kind and polite boy. Kate told Matt that if Sam could sit in his usual seat, with his usual apple juice and chocolate cake, then he would be fine. Sam wasn't the worry, Kate had told him in hushed whispers when he had knocked on the door that morning. Jake was.

The rain had been relentless since the early morning, and there was no sign that it would stop any time soon. The city took on an almost sombre appearance when the skies were dull, Matt thought that this echoed the day perfectly. It wasn't a day for sunshine.

'Nearly there Sam,' Kate hollered over her shoulder to where Sam was sat in the back, on his blue booster seat. He sat staring out of the car window, watching the familiar buildings whizz by.

Matt had reassured Kate that once they left the museum he would circle the streets around the café. He had instructed her to call if something were to happen. He would only be a matter of minutes away.

'It'll be fine, you know,' Kate tried to reassure him. But he had detected the tense muscles in her jaw, the way she was holding the steering wheel far too tightly, and the overly optimistic tone of voice. Nothing was right about what she was going to do. But he also knew that she had to do it.

Run like Hell began to blast out of Matt's phone. Startled, he fumbled in his jacket pocket. It wasn't there.

Kate gave him a wry smile.

'Too noisy, stop it, stop it! Turn it off!' Sam shouted above the tinny ringtone.

Matt thought that he could make one hell of a noise for such a little boy.

He eventually rooted the phone out of his jeans back pocket, and reluctantly hit the green button.

'Can you meet me for brunch tomorrow?' Lisa asked all in one breath. 'I really enjoyed last night.'

Matt's head throbbed. He closed his eyes, willing her to go away. 'Listen, now's not a good time. Can I phone you later?' he grimaced, glad that Lisa couldn't see him. He heard the huff of annoyance echo down the line.

'Just give me an answer Matt, we need to talk, and properly this time.'

Matt had an excuse all lined up, as Brian was calling round tonight. He knew that Lisa could not stand the sight of Brian, those two in the same room was not a good idea.

'I can't Lisa, I completely forgot that Brian's down this weekend.'

'Oh.'

Matt braced himself for the torrent of abuse that would surely follow, but the line remained silent. 'Lisa, I'll phone you later, I'm in the car.'

'You've got hands-free,' Lisa began to protest.

Sam started to hum loudly.

'Listen, I need to go. I'll call you later.' Matt hung up before she could say anything else.

He shoved the phone back into his pocket, remembering first to switch it to silent. The rain continued to stream down the windscreen, the sky growing darker.

'Lisa?' Kate tried in vain to hide her smirk.

'Oh, you have no idea.' Matt turned to look out of the window. He didn't want to talk about Lisa. That was a discussion for another day.

The car lurched to the left as it approached the one-way system and the familiar rows of shops whizzed by. Everything seemed oppressive in the low light and drizzle that continued to coat the streets. Kate indicated to turn into the multi-storey car park

located under the huge Boots in the centre of the small city. The car was plunged into darkness.

Sam started to flap his hands, frantically, up and down. Matt wondered if he was okay; he seemed happy enough, but the movement seemed unnatural for a boy of his age.

'Here we are Sam.' Kate parked the car, on the ground floor, right next to the lifts. She turned to face Matt. 'He loves this car park.'

'Just wait for me to open the door Sam,' Kate instructed. Matt stepped out of the car and suddenly felt redundant. To the casual observer they looked like any other family enjoying a trip out to the shops. But Matt knew different. He waited for Kate to open the passenger door and smiled as Sam jumped out, immediately reaching for Kate's hand.

'Right, well, the museum it is then,' Kate told Sam, forcing a smile that made her cheeks ache. Matt walked on her other side. The smell of her perfume was now diluted with the fumes of the cars, the musty smell of the underground, he missed it already. He gently touched her arm.

'It'll all work out you know,' he offered with a smile.

Kate carried on walking towards the lifts, propelled along by an over-enthusiastic Sam.

'It has to,' Kate whispered, as they stood in front of the lift. Matt watched Sam press the up button without being prompted.

'The alternative doesn't bear thinking about,' Kate added as they stepped into the lift. Once again, Matt had no words. She was completely right.

The museum had just opened, and Sam was the first person to step through the door. Or rather to run through the open door, while Kate screeched for him to slow down. The lady on the desk gave

Sam a polite wave as he whizzed by, already climbing the steps to the top floor.

'You come here a lot then?' Matt tilted his head towards the smart looking woman who couldn't stop smiling at Sam.

'Oh, yes, every Saturday, for as long as I can remember,' Kate said, striding ahead to catch up with Sam.

They caught up with him at the large painted mural of the American Civil War. Sam stood and stroked the wall, marvelling at the bright colours, the action that had been captured, like a still life painting.

'Doesn't he get bored?' Matt asked, curious as to why this little boy loved the museum so much. 'You know, seeing the same things again and again, week after week.'

Kate glared at him. 'Says the man who knows nothing about autism.'

Kate instantly regretted her sharpness, as she watched his cheeks redden. She must remember that this was all new to him, whereas it was second nature to her. He had wanted to be with them, to support them, to help them. She must remember that. She knew it was Lisa who was the reason for her sharpness, her irritability. Not Matt. 'Sorry, I forget sometimes ...'

'It's okay,' Matt shrugged, 'so he likes *sameness*?'

Kate nodded, 'It's soothing, it reassures him ... it's hard to explain.' Kate's voice faded as she followed Sam around the corner to where the swords and bayonets were kept. Safely deposited in glass boxes.

Sam stood transfixed admiring them, his boyish face pressed to the glass.

'We just need to follow him around, he always walks the same route,' Kate whispered.

Sam, now apparently bored with the weapons, headed off to

look at the medals and a display showing the trenches.

'This is the house,' Sam proudly told Matt.

'That's right Sam, this is where the soldiers lived,' Kate said, as she stood next to him, trying to imagine the horrors that these men must have lived through.

Bored once more, Sam headed off around the corner to explore the next part of the museum. This was the section about the Victorian era, where his favourite model was situated, that of the man in the stocks.

'He loves this, ever since he was two it has fascinated him,' Kate whispered in Matt's ear.

Matt stood and watched as a curious looking Sam scrutinised the model of the man in the stocks. He was stood so close to the mannequin, as if drinking in every detail, his hand stretched out to touch the face, and then, as if the spell was broken, he headed off to look at the local Roman statues.

'So, every Saturday then?' Matt couldn't contain his smirk.

Kate smiled, 'You're welcome to come out with us again.'

Matt stiffened, forming a tight smile; everything was about to change between them. He knew it and Kate knew it.

As if reading his mind, Kate glanced at her phone.

'How long have we got?' Matt asked.

'Fifteen minutes,' Kate replied as she caught up with Sam.

Matt sighed. He only wished they had longer.

Kate quickened her step as they approached the café, gripping Sam's hand even tighter. She noticed that Matt was walking closer to her little boy, as if shielding him. He was just as protective as she was. What was she doing, she wondered? Was she doing the right thing? What if Jake tried to grab Sam? Did he have some type of trick up his sleeve? What then? She considered what Matt had told

her earlier on, that Jake must really have some other reason for meeting her, another reason other than seeing his son. Why had he waited six years? Surely, he would have found a way? So why now? What kind of trouble was he in? She had no money to give him if that was his thinking.

Sam's step quickened as they trod the familiar pavements, his little boy excitement growing for the anticipated chocolate cake that he loved so much. She hoped that they would arrive first. Let Jake find them, not the other way around. She needed to get Sam settled and happy before she could talk to him. It was going to be awkward. Everything about the man made her skin crawl, but she couldn't show this to Sam as he'd pick up on it and be frightened and she didn't want to scare him.

'I'll be around the corner, if you need me,' Matt whispered into her ear as they reached the café entrance. All she could do was nod; she couldn't let her voice betray how nervous she was feeling.

After a gentle stroke of her arm, Matt turned and carried on walking down the street, clutching his phone. With a trembling hand, Kate pushed open the café door.

Kate followed Sam over to their usual table, allowing him to lead the way, and quickly scanned the room. There was no sign of Jake.

'Take off coat Mum!' Sam demanded, as he attempted to shrug his arms out of his bright blue Puma jacket. Kate helped him and placed it on the back of his chair. He sat, removed his ear defenders and gratefully took the phone that his mother offered him, eager to start playing his beloved Minecraft. It was only then, as Kate handed him the phone that she realised her mistake. She had no discreet way of contacting Matt, as she would now have to grab the phone off Sam, creating a scene. She just hoped that she didn't need to use it.

There were only a handful of people in the café, huddled over their phones, and staring at newspapers, so Kate knew that they would be served quickly. She told Sam she was going to order and headed towards the counter, upon which sat an array of cakes, scones and biscuits, all stacked high.

'Hi love,' said the friendly lady behind the counter, as she wiped her hands on the front of her apron. 'The usual, is it?' she smiled.

Kate returned the smile, 'Yes please, the gluten free chocolate cake and apple juice for Sam, and just a filter coffee for me please.'

The woman's brow creased, 'No chocolate cake for you love?'

Kate's smile faded. The woman seemed genuinely worried – if only she knew the real reason why. Kate's stomach was a mass of knots; she'd just about manage a few sips of her coffee. She quickly thought of an excuse.

'I'm not feeling that great this morning,' she offered apologetically, and was glad when the lady merely nodded and dropped the subject.

Kate paid and was told that they'd bring the cake and drinks over to them.

Sam was still glued to the phone screen.

Luckily, Sam's favourite chair faced away from the door so with Kate sitting opposite him, she got a fantastic view of the café entrance. She would see Jake as soon as he set foot through the door.

Kate twirled a strand of hair around her fingers, wishing she had scraped her hair back into a ponytail. She placed her hands onto the Formica table. She didn't want to appear nervous, even though her stomach felt like there was a bunch of butterflies in it.

It was gone 11:00 am. Where was he? Kate knew he was playing mind games with her, it was always about power. She was the sitting prey.

She grabbed the laminated menu that was on the table and held it in front of her, not reading the words. She knew the menu off by heart, she just needed something to do with her hands. She couldn't sit and stare at the door. Anyway, she'd hear the jingling bell.

Fifteen minutes passed before he made his appearance. Sam had eaten his chocolate cake, most of which was now smeared across his face, and he was halfway through his apple juice. Kate calculated that they had ten minutes tops, before he wanted to go. That was Jake's fault, not her little boy's.

Jake strode into the café as if he owned it, of course he did, he was always so sure of his presence, of his importance. Kate realised that he hadn't changed one little bit in the last six years. She felt as if she had been sucked back in time; she felt weightless, as if time had stopped. But he continued to walk towards them, as if nothing had happened, nothing had changed. His eyes were still those dark, brooding pools that Kate had loved. She forced herself not to look away, although she desperately wanted to. Looking at him caused too much pain as she was transported back in time once more, to a time when he was at the centre of her universe.

Kate did not stand. She would not give him the satisfaction.

She watched him hesitate for a fraction of a second, his eyes flickering away from hers, before he continued towards their table.

She could not take her eyes off him as she watched him slowly lowering himself into the wooden chair. Sam continued to play on the phone. Kate would not say the first word, that was down to Jake. He wanted this, not her.

'Well, it's been a long time, *Holly*,' he sneered, as he attempted to drag Kate back to her former self. She was not about to let him do that.

'It's Kate, not Holly,' she told him, not quite hiding the tremble in her voice. She clasped her hands in her lap.

'You'll always be Holly to me,' he said with a glint in his eye and a small smirk.

Kate inwardly shivered. She would not rise to the bait. That was, after all, what he wanted, to get a reaction. He wanted to create a scene. It was now all too obvious, he had his public space.

'What do you want Jake?' she asked, suddenly tired of it all. The games. The hiding. The chase.

Sam was still immersed in his Minecraft world, totally oblivious to the man sat with them, the man who called himself Dad.

Jake let out a bitter laugh. 'Oh, for God's sake, really?' he looked pointedly at Sam and then back at her, 'what do you think I want?'

Kate's blood ran cold. So, he really did want to see Sam, no ulterior motive? She wasn't so sure. She'd only spent less than two minutes with him; she couldn't read him properly, not yet.

'Well, we're here,' she offered with a sweep of her hand.

'Clearly,' his sarcasm echoed across the table.

'Why wait six years?' she hissed at him. She couldn't help it, she had to know. 'Six years, I thought we were, that we ...'

'Oh, I know what you thought all right,' His brown eyes bored into hers. 'You thought you'd got away with it, but you haven't, no way. There's no way you can keep him from me.'

Kate bristled at Jake's choice of word, *him*. 'It's been six years.'

'I'm well aware of that. It's taken me that long to track you down. Just be glad I never alerted the police.'

Why didn't he call the police?

Kate let out a snort. The police, there was no way he would have contacted them, not with how he had treated her. That conversation would have opened a whole can of worms. 'Aren't you even curious as to how I did it? How I got away from you, started a new life?'

His mask slipped for a second. Kate caught the hard glint in his eye before he composed himself.

'No, I'm here now, that's all that matters.'

Kate watched as his shoulders tensed, the slight flicker in his eye that gave him away.

Matt's words rung once more in her ears. Something didn't add up here. What did he really want? It wasn't Sam, he had barely looked at him.

'Mum,' Sam asked, his eyes raised from the glare of the phone screen, 'we go now?' He handed Kate the phone.

Kate took it from him as if it was no big deal, but her heart was pounding, thankful to have it in her grasp once more; if she wanted to call Matt, now she could.

'In a few minutes love,' she tried to sound as normal as possible, but she knew her voice sounded strained, awkward. She hoped that Sam did not pick up on it.

Sam reached towards his cup of apple juice and started to slurp the remains.

'Are you not going to introduce us?' Jake asked.

Kate tried to swallow down her rising fear – this was the moment she had been dreading most. 'Sam,' she said softly, touching his arm so that he'd look at her, 'this man is Jake, he's a … he's a friend of mine.'

Jake shot daggers at her, but she chose to ignore them; there was no way that she was going to try and explain that this man was his father, not in the middle of a café, busy or not, walls had ears after all.

'Okay,' was all Sam replied. 'Can we go now?'

'I've only been here a minute,' Jake interrupted.

'Five actually,' Kate snapped, 'and that's your fault for being late.'

Jake lunged across the table and grabbed her wrist in a vice-like hold. Kate flinched. At both the unpermitted touch of his skin on her flesh, and at his strength. She shot him a warning look, but

also cursed the fact that he would see the fear in her eyes. She had moved on, but she could never forget.

'Let go of me,' she said, trying to pull her arm free.

Jake sneered once more before finally letting go of her arm. 'We need to talk properly,' he told her.

Kate rubbed at her arm. 'What about Jake? About us? There is no us.'

'About Sam, I have rights.'

Kate drew in a deep breath, then slowly stood, pulling at Sam's coat from the back of his chair. 'Let's get your coat on Sam.'

Sam obediently stood up, glad at the prospect of leaving, and allowed his mother to gently ease his arms into the sleeves of the coat. She scooped his ear defenders off the table and put them on.

'What's wrong with him?' Jake asked, as he pointed to the ear defenders.

'Nothing, *nothing* is wrong, he's perfect.' Kate checked that the ear defenders were on securely and gave Sam the thumbs up sign.

Jake shook his head, standing up, blocking their escape route. 'Don't think that I haven't seen you with him,' he snarled.

Kate froze. So, he *had* been watching her. She thought about denying it, but what was the point? She'd only get caught up in the lie.

'He's a friend,' she snapped.

'A very protective one.' Jake leaned in closer towards her, whispering into her ear. 'I know what he is, and I'm watching him. I saw him walking around outside before I got here. He didn't even see me. He's not so good *now*, is he?'

Kate reached for Sam's hand, she wouldn't rise to the bait. She tried to push past him, but Jake placed his arm around her waist, leaning in close to her ear. To anyone walking past it would look like they were lovers saying goodbye.

'I'll give you until tomorrow night to get in touch, you have my number. If I don't hear from you, I will go to the police … *Holly*.'

'Sam, let's go.' Kate placed her shaking hand on Sam's shoulder, guiding him towards the door. The phone was to her ear even before the door had swung shut behind them.

CHAPTER TWENTY-TWO

SUNDAY, SEPTEMBER 22ND, 2013

Matt woke to the sound of the radio blasting from the kitchen downstairs. It had taken him a few moments to register where the sound was coming from, and who was responsible for such a racket at six in the morning.

Only someone who was used to getting up at the crack of dawn with small children could possibly be up cooking breakfast at such an ungodly hour on a Sunday morning. Matt could smell the bacon wafting up the stairs, luring him out of bed.

'You're up early,' Brian said, without taking his eyes from the frying pan. 'You want some?'

Matt greedily eyed the bacon, instantly forgetting that he was exhausted. 'Sure.' He pulled out a kitchen chair and sank down heavily upon it. He'd had another restless night. He rubbed his eyes. 'Do you want a hand?' he asked half-heartedly.

'No, you're fine mate,' Brian responded cheerfully, still busy at the stove. He gestured towards the kitchen counter with the spatula, 'Help yourself to coffee.' It was only then that Matt registered the full cafetiere on the counter top.

He pushed himself up from the chair and grabbed a chipped mug from the cupboard, tuning in as he did so to the sound of

Little Angels – at least Brian had the decency to tune into Rock FM. It was far too early for dreary Radio Four.

Matt looked through the kitchen window, angling his head slightly, to see if the garden next door was bathed in illuminated light. Everything was dark. No lights on. Hopefully, Kate was still asleep.

He poured his coffee and sat back at the table. 'What time did you wake up?' he asked.

'Not long ago,' Brian turned and gave Matt an apologetic smile, 'Sorry if I woke you.'

'No, it's fine.' Matt meant it. 'Lisa will be here soon, so …'

Brian stopped mid-stir, spatula frozen mid-air, abandoning the frying pan. He turned to face him. 'She's coming *here? Today?*' he spluttered.

His expression said everything.

'She phoned yesterday, and I was, well … distracted … so when she suggested brunch here … I sort of said yes.'

'Brunch!' Brian shouted. 'This gets worse.'

Matt slithered down into his chair and placed his head on the table. It was far too early for a Brian lecture.

'Listen mate, I know you don't want to hear this,' Brian said as he sat down next to his friend.

'Too right I don't,' came Matt's quick reply.

Brian barely suppressed a grin and placed his hands palm down on the table, marking his territory. 'She's no good for you mate. Phone her back, tell her you have plans or something.'

'Yes, plans for brunch with her,' Matt answered sarcastically. 'She'd know I was lying.'

'So? Does that really matter?' Brian shrugged.

'She already knows that you're here.'

'*Really.*' Brian made the word sound like it had a thousand

consonants; he was enjoying making his friend feel uncomfortable. 'And she *still* wants to come over?' he added.

Matt nodded, suppressing his own grin this time.

'To grill me, I suppose,' Brian sighed as he pushed his chair back. He went back over to the stove. 'Well, I'll let her have her bit of fun, but I'm not going to hide my feelings about her.'

'I wouldn't want you to, I should have told you yesterday.'

'But you were *distracted*,' Brian chuckled, then gave him a wink.

Matt sat bolt upright once more, 'What's that supposed to mean?'

'Oh, you know,' Brian wiggled his eyebrows, 'the woman next door.'

Matt made a half-hearted attempt to be absorbed with his coffee cup.

'It's Kate, isn't it?' Brian asked tentatively.

Matt smiled. 'Well, that's her name *now*. You're right, I can't stop thinking about her,' he said sheepishly.

With raised eyebrows, Brian handed him a plate of bacon and scrambled eggs. It smelled divine.

'What's that supposed to mean?'

Matt suppressed a sigh, 'It's a long story.'

Brian plonked his own plate on the table and sat down. 'Believe you me, with two small kids at home, I need a bit of excitement,' he flashed one of his famous grins, 'now, dish the dirt.'

Brian listened intently to what Matt had to tell him, recalling his version of events.

When he had finished, Matt felt as though a huge weight had been lifted from his shoulders. 'So, what do you think?'

'What do you mean?' Brian asked before biting into his second bacon butty, brown sauce dripping down his chin.

Matt hated the stuff but he bought a bottle especially for his friend. '… of the situation, of Jake … stalking her, and me,' he exclaimed, 'come to think of it.'

'Stalking?' Brian said the word slowly, as if confronting and then examining its full meaning, 'I think that *stalking* is a bit of a strong word to use.'

'Too strong! You haven't met him.'

'I know, I know,' Brian held up his hands in a 'don't shoot the messenger' type of way. 'It's just that, well, she did run away from him and take his kid. I'd be kinda pissed off too.'

'You'd have a good reason.'

'Okay, okay, it's just that as a father, I'd do anything for my kids.' Brian gave a knowing look which Matt knew only too well, the unsaid, *if you had kids you would know what I'm talking about.* But he would never say those words to him. He knew that they would hurt.

'She had a damn good reason though,' Matt said through gritted teeth. He could feel himself getting angry and he knew his anger was being directed at the wrong person. 'He's a manipulative bastard, and he's come back into Kate's life for a reason which has nothing to do with his son.'

'So, he has an ulterior motive? Which is?' Brian took a final bite of his butty and licked his fingers.

Matt shook his head, 'I don't know, and that's what worries me. He's dangerous. I know it.'

'Have you thought that he could be in trouble? You know, like he owes money to someone or something? He could be hiding out here.'

Matt scratched his chin, and although he didn't like to admit it, it was exactly what he thought. He believed that Jake had got in with the wrong crowd and that Kate was caught in the middle of it all. Sam too.

'Do you think he could hurt her?' Brian eventually asked.

'Yes,' Matt replied without hesitation, 'I think that he will and that's what frightens me. I tried to talk to her yesterday, about what happened with Jake in the café, but she refused to talk about it in front of Sam.'

'Understandably so,' Brian stated.

'I know, I get that. But I have no idea of what she is going to do next. I asked her if she was planning on seeing him again, and she just gave me this look. I just know that she will. It's as if she feels that she owes him something, for taking Sam away.'

'This is all fucked up.' Brian pushed his plate away and drained his coffee, all in one fluid movement. His beanie hat was pulled down low over his ears. Matt wondered if he had slept in it.

'Kate's past has finally caught up with her, it always does,' Brian mumbled as he began to clear the table.

Matt thought about Lisa and their impending brunch. Yes, the past never stayed buried, he was living proof of that.

Matt texted Kate while Brian was in the shower. She'd replied quickly, telling him that she was thinking about what Jake had said and told Matt about Jake's ultimatum, to which he swore under his breath. The bastard still had control over her. Matt sent her a quick reply, telling her to think carefully about phoning him, and that Jake wouldn't go to the police, as he had too much to lose. Plus, Matt was almost certain that Jake was hiding something. He once again reminded Kate to be careful to which she replied she would. After wishing each other a happy Sunday, and that Matt would pop round that evening if that was okay, he put his phone on silent and began to clean and tidy the house in preparation for Lisa's arrival.

He knew that he had no reason to feel nervous. He also knew that he didn't need to clean his house like a man possessed. It was

his home – he could live as he pleased. It was just that he felt this great need to prove himself to her. That he was doing well without her, and a clean, tidy home would show her that. Well that was his thinking anyway.

As he was pushing his Henry hoover over the laminated living room floor, headphones clamped to his ears, singing along to the latest album by *Elbow*, Brian jumped in front of him, waving his arms about.

Matt bent down, turned Henry off and pulled the headphones down to rest around his neck.

'Shit! You nearly gave me a heart attack,' Matt laughed.

Brian just stood there grinning at him. 'What are you doing?'

'What does it look like I'm doing? I thought you were meant to be domesticated?'

'And what's with all the potpourri shit? And the lighted candles?' Brian asked, as he looked around him, ignoring Matt's sarcasm, swinging his arm around the room. 'It smells like a florist in here.'

Matt shrugged, 'They make the place look homely.'

'Homely? What are you on? It's not you. Matt, she'll know a mile off that it is all for her, and you don't want that. You don't need to impress her.'

'I'm not trying to impress her.'

'Says the man with shares in Laura Ashley,' Brian smirked, 'just chill.'

'Okay, okay,' Matt huffed before unplugging Henry and then wheeling him back into the downstairs cupboard.

'I'll sort out the brunch for you guys, then I'll make tracks,' Brian shouted from the kitchen.

Matt stood up too quickly, forgetting about the low sloping ceiling, whacking his head in the process. 'Shit, that hurt,' he rubbed the top of his head, sure he could feel a lump. 'No, Brian, please stay.'

Matt backed out of the cupboard and headed into the kitchen.

'Won't it be a little awkward? You know that she hates me,' Brian asked as he began to measure out the coffee grounds.

'I know,' Matt said. There was no need to lie, both Lisa and Brian hated each other. 'It's just that I could use your company, you know, someone on my side.'

'Someone to make sure that she doesn't worm her way back into your life again, you mean,' Brian asked with arched eyebrows.

'Matt smiled, 'Something like that, yes.'

Shaking his head, Brian turned to the countertop where he had piled an assortment of croissants and other fancy looking rolls. 'Okay then, I'll stay.'

'Thanks, I owe you one.'

'You most certainly do.'

'The house is lovely Matt, it really is.' Lisa stood in the middle of the living room, looking around her. She wandered into the kitchen, her cream high heels *click click clicking* on the laminate floor. As always, she looked immaculate. The tired-looking Lisa from a few days ago had all but vanished. Now in front of Matt stood the confident and radiant looking woman he had fallen in love with. His heart lurched. Why was she doing this to him? She wore the same provocative perfume, its floral scent drifting towards him, and no amount of breathing through his mouth could dampen its aroma, or memories. Lisa poked her head out of the kitchen window.

Matt lurked behind her, unsure of what to say, of what to do. To him it was a house, where he put his stuff, slept and ate, nothing more. *They* had had a home, but she had torn it apart. *She* had a home, but it now looked like she was on the same path as him to singlehood.

'Where's Dave today then?' Brian entered the kitchen on the pretence of making coffee. But as the percolator was full to the brim on the small table in the living room, surrounded by what looked like a bakery, it was obvious that he was there just to wind Lisa up. So far, he had been remarkably quiet.

She turned to face him, a barely strained smile plastered on her face. 'Well, obviously, he's not here.'

'*Obviously,*' Brian repeated slowly with a flash of a smile and then he was gone, back into the living room.

'Does he always wear that ridiculous hat?'

Despite himself, Matt laughed.

'Leave him alone, he's been a good friend to me.'

Lisa ignored his remark and turned back to the garden. 'It's a lovely garden Matt.'

Matt knew exactly what she was thinking. He had thought the same. It was the perfect size for children to play in, for *their* children to play in, if there had been any. He thought about the time when Sam had got in through the broken fence. It was only a week ago, but he felt as if he now knew the little boy. He felt as though he knew Kate, when in reality he knew very little about her.

'So, is Dave not coming up here then? You know, to try and work things out …' Matt asked gently, no accusation, as Lisa slowly turned away from the window.

For a moment, Matt thought that she was going to ignore his question, but she pulled out the kitchen chair and sat down. She placed her immaculately manicured hands onto the kitchen table. 'He's at home, well *his* home.'

'But why hasn't he followed you here? Has he just given up too? Can't he be bothered?'

'Given up? You think I've given up?' she shrieked.

'Well, yes.'

Lisa's face turned scarlet, she bit her lower lip. 'It's over, you know, me and Dave. I should never have married him,' Lisa finally told him, her words tumbling out in her haste to say them.

'Like you never should have married me?' Matt snapped. He recalled with a bitter taste in his mouth that she had used the same exact line on him, minutes after she walked out on their marriage, slamming the door as she escaped into the night.

'I should never have said that to you. I was angry, upset, a whole lot of things. But I never regretted being married to you.'

Her blue eyes held his gaze for a fraction longer than was comfortable. Matt had to force himself to look away. He took a deep breath. 'Look, me and you, again, it's never going to work. We just need to leave what happened in the past. We both need to move on with our lives.' Matt couldn't believe he had said those words. Did he mean them? Hell no, but he wanted her to believe them. He needed to believe them. That was all that mattered. They could never go back to how they were before. And anyway, what about drippy Dave? He surely wouldn't just sit back and let her walk away?

'So, you don't love me?' Lisa's words were barely audible.

'I loved you,' Matt nearly choked on his words as he forced them out. 'I still have feelings for you. But …' he held his hand up when she opened her mouth to speak. 'But, we can never go back. Never, Lisa, we'll only get hurt again.'

Lisa's shoulders slumped and for a horrible moment Matt thought that she was either going to lash out at him or start sobbing.

'Go back to him for God's sake, go back to Dave,' Matt finally told her. 'Try and make things work out.'

'I don't love him Matt,' Lisa shouted, her eyes wide. 'When are you going to get that through your thick skull? I love you and I always will.'

Matt squeezed his eyes shut. He couldn't look at her. He could not have this conversation with her now.

'It's *her*, isn't it?' Lisa's eyes flashed to his, warning him to tell the truth.

Matt's head whipped up. 'What do you mean? Who are you talking about?'

Lisa let out a bitter laugh, 'Seriously? You're asking me who I am on about? You know full well, that woman next door.'

Matt began to protest but she cut him off. 'You were in the car with her yesterday. I could tell. You sounded different.'

Matt let out a long breath, not knowing if he should try to deny it.

'Don't lie to me. You were with her, weren't you?'

What was the point of denying it? She could read him so well. 'So what Lisa. We're divorced, I can see who I like.' He saw the flash of pain in her eyes, that she quickly tried to hide by looking away, but he saw it. He needed to tread carefully; no matter what had gone on in the past, he didn't want to hurt her. 'Listen, we are just friends and the situation is … well, it's complicated.'

'Complicated? Really? Take a look at us Matt. It can't be any more complicated than us surely?'

Matt wasn't sure if he should tell her the truth, about Jake and Kate's past. He could leave things as they were, but that would mean Lisa thinking the absolute worst of him, or he could try and explain how difficult things were for Kate, and that was why he was helping her. She was a single woman living alone with a small child. What else was he supposed to do? Sit back and do nothing? He went with option two.

Matt told her exactly what he had told Brian a few hours

earlier, and to her credit, Lisa sat and listened to him, not once interrupting.

'So, you see what I mean when I say that the situation is complicated. There really is nothing going on, nothing romantic anyway.'

'Always the knight in shining armour,' Lisa said. But there was no irony, no sarcasm; she meant it. That was the thing about her husband, *ex*-husband, he was a gentleman, and he couldn't bear to see anyone in trouble. He always had to do the noble thing. That was what had first attracted her to him.

Matt stood, no longer wanting to have this conversation. He was bone tired and knew that they would just go around in circles. He also knew that with time, Lisa would grind him down, meaning that he would agree to them trying again. 'Look, let's go and sit and have some coffee, eat some croissants and just forget about the past ten minutes. Okay?'

For a moment Lisa looked as if she was about to protest, but then she nodded and pushed herself up from the kitchen table. 'Okay, we'll play happy families,' she whispered, as she walked past him towards the living room, 'but I want you to know that I want you back. I want us to try again. I mean what I say Matt. Just think about it. For me.'

She gently took his hand and led him from the room.

Like a lamb to the slaughter, he followed.

CHAPTER TWENTY-THREE

'Sam, please, just try a pea for me,' Kate urged.

'No! Take them off plate!' Sam demanded, his face now the colour of a tomato. Kate had a feeling that her blonde-haired, blue-eyed boy was about to blow.

'Okay, okay.' Kate jumped up from the table and stormed over to the kitchen cupboard to fetch a plate.

She quickly returned to the table and popped each of his cut-up nuggets and potato smiley faces onto the new plate. 'Look Sam, no peas.' She moved the plate towards him.

Sam screwed up his face in frustration. 'No! Take them away! Take them away!' he screamed. He pushed the offending plate of peas towards Kate, who caught it just before it would have bounced off the table and onto the floor. The peas would have rolled into all the nooks and crannies.

Kate sighed, 'All right Sam.' She grabbed the plate and, fighting the horrible urge to fling it at the wall instead threw it into the sink, the tiny green balls floating on the surface of the water. She wondered why every single tea time had to be so bloody difficult. Why couldn't he just try the peas? Just this once? He ate no veg and he couldn't survive on bananas alone, although, come to think of it, he was doing a pretty good job of it.

She'd make him a smoothie later. It was better than nothing. She counted slowly to ten and sat back down. She idly moved the beans around her plate. Beans on toast was all she could stomach, but she'd hardly eaten any of it.

She pushed the plate away.

Kate glanced at the home screen of her phone, where it sat between them on the table. She hadn't let it out of her sight for fear that Jake would ring. He hadn't phoned. But then again, he wasn't going to, was he?

It was her who needed to phone him. She needed to tell him that he could see Sam, but she kept putting it off. She wasn't even sure if she could say the words. *Of course, you can see your son, Jake*, as if nothing had happened. That nothing was different after six years. She'd wait until Sam was in bed and then she would have to phone him.

Kate's mood had brightened briefly when she received a text from Emily, alerting her to the fact that both she and Isaac were safe and that she had 'done what they had talked about.'

Kate had very nearly replied, her natural instinct to support her friend, that she understood, but then had decided not to. Emily had deliberately sent an ambiguous text because she did not want Gerald to be able to trace her. Emily was safe, that was all that mattered. Kate was happy for her friend, wherever she was. She hoped that she would get in touch again once it was safe to do so. She would like to meet her. Her only concern was Isaac. What about school? She'd need to find another specialist school for him, and that would prove very difficult, given the circumstances. But she supposed that that was the very least of Emily's worries, as he too was safe.

'Finished Mum,' Sam beamed. All innocence, the pea fiasco long forgotten.

'Good, have your drink love.'

He obediently picked up his cup and drained his apple juice in one long gulp.

Sam's chair scraped back as he ran off into the living room; soon to follow were the sounds of cows mooing and villagers echoing their mumbled cries.

Kate plonked herself down next to him, cradling a small glass of red wine. She didn't feel guilty; she deserved it after what Jake had put them through. She was just glad that Sam had not once mentioned the strange man in the café. She had been on tenterhooks ever since they got back yesterday lunchtime. She wasn't sure if she should even mention Jake to her little boy, but she knew that she would have to at some point. It was just, did she really have to tell him that Jake was his father? She wasn't even sure if he would understand. Kate took a large gulp of wine and closed her eyes. This could wait until Sam was in bed. She'd phone Jake and then decide what to do.

She drained the glass.

'Righto mister, you ready for your shower?'

Sam jumped up from the couch, his iPad bouncing on the floor. Thank goodness for that protective case. She leaned down to pick it up, saving it from being trodden on, and then followed Sam upstairs to the bathroom.

Kate gently closed Sam's bedroom door and tiptoed down the hall. Her phone had buzzed while she had been dressing him and so she grabbed it from her bed. It was a text message from Matt.

Can I call round this evening? Need to catch up.

Kate grinned. She needed to talk through things with him. He would understand. She sent him a quick text.

Sure, Sam's now in bed, so any time.

She quickly glanced in the dressing table mirror and gasped out loud. She hadn't realised just how tired she looked. Her skin had that greyish tinge that only the truly exhausted had. Her hair had grown frizzy because of the humidity of the shower, and her top was covered in splatters of tomato juice. She couldn't greet Matt like this. Grabbing her phone once more, she frantically sent a new text.

Just give me ten minutes.

She removed her jumper, tossing it onto the floor. She then rummaged through her to-be-ironed pile, managing to find a clean blue long-sleeved top. There weren't that many creases, so it would have to do. She ran a comb through her hair and then, when she realised that she was only making her hair even more frizzy, found a stray hair band and gathered her hair into a scruffy ponytail. She then ran into the bathroom and washed her face, applied some tinted moisturiser and liberally sprayed some perfume over herself. Even if she didn't look much better, she felt it.

Kate wondered what Matt would say when she told him that she had decided to let Jake back into her life, well *their* lives. She knew that she would have to be careful, and she wasn't prepared for Jake to see Sam alone. That would happen much later, and only when he had gained her trust, that's if he ever did. She just had no idea of how to go about this. What were his rights in seeing his own child? They weren't a couple, had never even been married, and Sam had no idea who he was. She was completely lost on where to start with it all. Would Citizens Advice be able to help her? She really needed to find out the people who could help her with the legalities of the situation. With a heavy heart, she knew that she should have already contacted those people. Perhaps Matt could help her?

Kate began to pile up the plates and cups that had accumulated on the draining board and was so absorbed in the mundane task that the knock at the door made her jump. Although she knew it would be Matt, she still peeked through the frosted glass and shouted '*who is it?*' before opening the door.

'Hi,' Matt grinned.

Kate took a step back and crossed her arms to stop herself from launching herself at him. His aftershave was the same musty odour, reminding Kate of comfort, of home. She hadn't realised how much she had missed him and how glad she would be to see him again.

'Come in.' She closed the door behind him, sliding the lock across, then followed him into the living room. 'Drink?'

'No, I'm fine thanks,' he told her as he settled himself onto the couch.

Kate's smile slipped a little. Did that mean he wasn't going to stay long? But maybe he had just had a drink? She shouldn't read anything into it.

'So, has Brian gone back home now?' Kate was a little disappointed that she hadn't had the chance to meet him. She'd glimpsed him from the car yesterday when they had got back home, but Sam was desperate to get inside the house and Kate's nerves were a little on edge, so it hadn't been the time for introductions. Instead she had settled for a wave and a smile. She had noted that he had kind eyes.

'Yes, he left about an hour ago,' Matt hesitated, 'he'd like to meet you next time he visits.'

Kate beamed at him, 'I'd love that, then I can get him to dish all the dirt on you.'

Matt playfully swatted her arm, 'Oi, there's no dirt to dish,' he held out his hands, 'honestly, I'm as interesting as watching paint dry.'

‘I doubt that’s true,’ chuckled Kate. She had to force herself to ask the next question. ‘Did you get back to Lisa?’ Kate had been wondering if she had turned up next door. She hadn’t noticed another car parked outside.

Matt shifted in his seat and cleared his throat, ‘Yes, she called round for brunch.’

‘Brunch, really? How sophisticated,’ Kate smiled.

‘Well, I wouldn’t go that far. Brian had basically raided the local bakery.’

‘Oh, that’s funny,’ Kate laughed.

‘They actually hate each other, so it was an entertaining few hours but with very few laughs.’

‘Oh dear,’ was all Kate could say. She had no idea what to say when it came to talking about his ex-wife. She needed a drink; she needed something to occupy her hands. ‘I’m just going to pop the kettle on, you sure you don’t fancy a brew?’

Matt smiled, ‘Oh go on then.’

Kate relaxed – he was going to stay after all.

‘I’m a little uncertain on where we stand, even though I know allowing her back into my life is entirely the wrong thing, I think that perhaps she is right, we should give it another go. Brian of course thinks I’m mad,’ Matt’s voice trailed off as he gave Kate a half-hearted shrug.

Kate stared at her cup. He was mad, completely and utterly mad, if he was considering taking his ex back. He’d moved hundreds of miles to get away from her, but she had followed him. Although Kate had never met the woman, she knew the type oh so well. Married for a long time, grows complacent, has a midlife crisis, an affair, then realises her huge mistake and wants to go back to how things were. Life was not like that. Matt was trying to move

on, even Kate could see that, so why couldn't Lisa? Or did she? Perhaps she just didn't want to see what was staring her in the face. She was probably one of those women who could not stand the thought of living alone, without a man. Kate had never had that luxury. She was happy in her own skin, with her own stuff, making her own decisions. Not once had she ever wished that she was married.

It was now nearly ten and Kate knew that she couldn't put off phoning Jake for much longer. She was glad that Matt was here and that he suggested she phone Jake with him in the house for some moral support, just in case Jake decided to get nasty. She had a feeling he would.

'So, what are you going to do then?' Matt eyed the phone that she was now clutching for dear life.

'I'll have to let him see Sam,' Kate finally answered.

'Kate, you don't need to do any such thing. He's blackmailing you. He won't go to the police. If he really wanted to do so, then he would have gone to them years ago. He's hiding *something*, I just don't know what it is.'

'Perhaps he is, perhaps he isn't,' Kate said, 'I just know that he has a right to see his son, and I can't stop him.'

Matt's jaw clenched as he sat forward, willing Kate to look at him. 'Kate, for the hundredth time, I do not trust him.'

'Neither do I, but what can I do Matt? You tell me?' Kate's voice grew louder, breaking on the last word.

He sat back, looked up at the ceiling, his head resting on the cushion. 'I'm sorry, I'm not having a go, it's just that he's trapped you.' Matt's eyes clouded over as he looked around the living room, at the photographs, the picture symbols for Sam, that represented family life and love. 'You made this fabulous new life for yourself and for Sam, and with all of his … difficulties … you've survived,

you're happy, and now he turns up and has all of this control over you. It's just not right.'

Kate stared at Matt with new eyes. What he had just said was the most honest and beautiful thing that anyone had ever said to her, and for the second time that night she wanted to hug him, to reach across and take his hand in hers, but of course she couldn't. He was taken, and she was damaged. There was no chance of anything ever happening between them. But she felt it, that spark that was there the first time that they had met.

'He deserves another chance Matt,' was the only answer Kate could give him.

'What did you say?' Matt's cool blue eyes turned a darker shade and she did not like the frown that he wore. 'Seriously? You think he deserves another chance? After what he did to you?'

'Not with me,' Kate snapped, 'with Sam, he deserves a chance with Sam.'

Matt continued to stare at her, his expression unreadable, before looking away.

'Perhaps it is the time to forgive, to move on, to pick up the pieces and try and rebuild what went wrong, for Sam's sake,' Kate offered quietly as a silent prayer, hoping that Matt wouldn't tell her she was mad. She just needed his support, for him to be on her side. She didn't need his criticism.

'What he *smashed* you mean Kate. There's no going back from that.'

There was an edge to Matt's voice that Kate had never heard before. She folded her arms in front of her chest, suddenly feeling unsure of herself for the first time in his company.

'Isn't that what you are trying to do with Lisa?' she said without thinking through her words first. Her cheeks flushed red, she

hadn't meant to say that thought out loud. He'd caught her off guard, weakened her defences.

Matt stood and headed into the kitchen.

Kate wasn't sure if she should follow, even though it was her house. She'd upset him. She had no idea what to say to him now, she wished those words could be taken back. Taking a deep breath, she followed him. Her heart lurched when she saw him perched at the table, head bowed. Ever so quietly she pulled out the opposite chair and sat down.

She'd wait for him.

'I'm sorry,' Matt said as he finally looked up, acknowledging her presence, 'you're right, the idea of me and Lisa trying again is completely ludicrous.'

'Matt, I'm sorry, I should never have said that to you. I know nothing about your marriage, or Lisa. I should learn to keep my stupid mouth shut.'

Matt smiled, 'Perhaps I should learn to do the same?'

'Oh no,' Kate said quickly, 'no, always tell me what you are thinking. I admire the honesty.' And she did. She knew with a solidness that Matt would never intentionally lie to her. He would always tell her the truth, and there was a lot to be said for that.

He grinned, the smile that lit up his face. This time it reached his eyes. He slapped the table with the palm of his right hand. 'Right then, you'd better make that phone call.'

'I'll phone him now,' Kate said with determination that she did not feel. She didn't want to show Matt just how nervous she was. 'Will you stay while I talk to him?' she asked from the doorway.

He frowned, 'I said I would, didn't I?'

'I know, it's just that …'

'Kate, it's fine, we're fine. Go talk to him, I'm here if you need me.'

Kate swiped the screen on her phone, located Jake's number and then finally hit the call button.

Kate shakily placed the phone onto the table. On unsteady legs, that no longer felt like her own, she headed back to the kitchen where Matt was still sat.

'Drink?' he asked, looking up from a newspaper that was spread out on the table.

Kate always bought the local paper but rarely read it. She found this ironic and suppressed a giggle. She swallowed, nodded. She needed a drink. 'I think that there's some wine left.' She sank down onto the kitchen chair and watched while Matt poured a generous amount of red wine into her waiting glass.

'So, what's the plan?' he asked as he slowly sat down opposite her.

Kate swallowed down a huge gulp of much needed wine. 'He's calling round tomorrow after school to see Sam and then we'll take things from there.' She said all this while staring at her glass, unable to bring herself to look at Matt. She felt so ashamed.

'Do you want me here?' Matt asked.

Kate detected a slight tremble in his voice. She thought about this but shook her head. She so desperately wanted to say yes. 'No, I think it'll be better if it's just the three of us. Seeing you might ... antagonize him.'

Matt nodded, 'Okay, but I'll make sure that you can contact me at any time while he is here, just in case.'

'Thank you, I appreciate that.' Kate still couldn't meet his eye. He'd already done so much to support her and Sam. She took another gulp of wine. She did need his help though, and she knew that he wanted to help. 'I meant to ask you actually, who could I contact about getting support, or just finding out what my rights are as his mother, you know for Jake seeking access to Sam?'

Matt scratched his chin, closed his eyes for a second. 'I have no idea, Citizens Advice?'

Kate smiled, 'That was my first thought, I'll give them a phone first thing. I'll chat to Bill as well, let him know the score. He may know what to do.'

'Who's Bill?' Matt's eyes grew wide.

'My oldest friend here, well, actually, he's my boss, but he's more like a father figure to me.' Kate felt a sudden tightness in her throat and her eyes stung. She really did need to speak to Bill, to tell him what was going on. 'He knows the full story, about what happened to me.'

Matt's jaw tightened; she watched his Adam's apple bob up and down as he carefully folded the paper, putting it to one side. 'That's good you have a friend Kate.'

This time it was Matt who couldn't quite meet her eye, and he continued to stare at the paper.

But Kate saw a flicker of disappointment flash across his eyes. She knew she had made a big mistake. She had referred to Bill as a friend who knew her whole back story, and Matt, who was also a friend, only knew half of what had happened. She hadn't told him about how she ended up here, in this house, alone with a new baby. 'I haven't told you, have I? The full story I mean.'

'No, but that's okay Kate. You don't have to.' Matt made as if to stand.

'Matt.' Kate reached over the table, her fingers gently brushing his. She couldn't bear to see him look so hurt. She felt a zing of electricity rush up her arm and her mouth tingled. She had never felt anything like it. As panic seized her, without thinking, she let go of his fingers. She looked to Matt, to try and gauge if he had felt it too. By the looks of it, he had.

They sat and gazed in bewilderment at each other, neither

knowing what to say.

It was Kate who broke the spell with a nervous smile.

'Would you like to hear what happened to me? How I got here with no money, no friends and a new baby.'

Matt nodded and smiled, his eyes crinkling in what Kate thought was a most delicious way.

'I'd love to hear your story Kate.'

It was her gran who saved her life. Everything changed with just one phone call.

Part Three
The Idea

CHAPTER TWENTY-FOUR

MAY 2007

I gaze at my new-born son, only a few days old, and wonder why Jake can't love his own flesh and blood. He calls me ugly, fat, and that now at least, no other man will want to touch me. I long more than ever to get away from him, but I have no means of doing so. I am stuck.

Jake is working on a building site; he was lucky enough to get the job after losing the last one. It isn't well paid, and it is hard manual labour which he constantly complains about, and it is apparently now all my fault that he must work extra shifts as he has an extra mouth to feed.

I finish feeding Sam and place him gently back down into his Moses basket, right next to the couch so that I can peer down at him, making sure that he is safe, that he is still breathing. I have constant panic attacks that his little body will just stop breathing. Although irrational, I can't help worrying. I think that most new mothers must feel the same way.

The phone call comes as such a surprise.

No one ever phones the house. Not even cold callers. I sit paralysed for several seconds before hobbling to the hallway to answer it, scared that the constant ringing will wake my son.

'Hello?' I say breathlessly, barely recognising my own voice. I can't remember the last time I have spoken out loud. Not to Jake. I try to avoid all conversation with him if possible.

'Holly? Is that you dear?' the frail voice echoes down the line.

I grip the handset, thinking that the lady sounds just like my gran, Mary, but much older. But it couldn't be.

'Gran?' I whisper.

'Yes, dear it's me, Mary. Oh, my goodness. I've found you at long last dear. I'd nearly given up hope of ever finding you.'

A series of sobs echoes down the line before Mary manages to compose herself. I sit quietly, not knowing what to say. My gran has finally tracked me down.

'Oh, Gran,' I finally find my voice, 'I've missed you so much, I've so much to tell you.'

'Me too dear,' she says between sobs, 'How are you? Are you still with him?'

I cringe – even my gran can't bear to say his name after what must be, well, over two years. 'Yes, but …'

'Holly, are you happy with him? You don't sound happy love. I can hear it in your voice. I never told you this, but I spoke to him once, before you moved … and well … I can't repeat what he said to me … but he was vile, and I was so worried, and then, when I eventually managed to travel to your house, you were gone,' Mary's voice cracks on the last word as she lets out another series of heart-wrenching sobs.

'I'm not happy Gran,' To my shame I find myself crying; hot fat tears tumble down my cheeks.

'Oh love, let me come see you. Can I do that? Give me your address. I only managed to get your number by sheer chance. It's a long story, but what I will say is that I found a lovely young man to help me, a private detective no less.'

Despite the ache in my chest, I laugh. My gran always has a way with men, charming them with her good looks and witty repertoire. She obviously hasn't lost her magic touch with her advancing years. I quickly rattle off my address and to my surprise, I find that my gran only lives thirty miles away. She moved to her new bungalow a year ago, so we have been living so close to each other but never knew it.

'Jake's not home until 7:00 pm, so you can come around later, or tomorrow, he's gone by eight and won't be back until late.' I gush, desperate to see my beloved gran once again. I can tell her anything. Maybe she can help me get away.

'Holly, I'll come around tomorrow love. I can't drive anymore, not with my bad eyes, but I'll get the train and then a taxi love.'

'Oh Gran, that's far too much trouble. I don't want to put you out.' I can't bear the thought of my gran struggling on and off trains.

'It's no bother love. I haven't gone to all this trouble just to chat to you on the phone. I want to see you,' she pauses, 'I want to know that you're safe love.'

'I'm ...' I begin but stop myself. I can't lie to my gran. 'I need to get away, but I don't know where to go, or what to do, and things are complicated ...'

'Nothing's ever that complicated Holly. There's always a way.'

I can tell my gran is smiling, ever the optimist. 'But Gran, I have a baby.'

I hear the sharp intake of breath.

'Oh, my goodness, *a baby?*' Mary gasps out loud.

'Yes, a son, he's only four days old.'

'*Four days old!* A little boy? Oh, I can't wait to see him love. Listen, I'll be at yours first thing in the morning and we'll make a plan. You and me.'

'Thank you, thank you so much.' I can't help the tears that begin to flow once more down my cheeks.

'Don't you thank me Holly, it's what grans are here for, I'll see you and that baby of yours bright and early tomorrow morning.'

After saying our goodbyes, I hang up and for the first time in a long while, I have hope. Hope that my future can indeed be so different than the life that I am currently living.

I cannot take my eyes off my aging gran. Although it's only been a few years since I last saw her, she seems so much older. Her hair is now completely white and her face is lined with wrinkles. I wonder if I am partly responsible for her rapid ageing. I know that she must have worried about me, not knowing where I was. I should have tried harder to find her. But then what else could I have done? It wasn't my fault, but that doesn't stop me from feeling guilty.

Mary can't take her eyes from a sleeping Sam, who is now cradled in her arms. I observe my gran's face, a look of pure joy, and bite back a tear, a hard lump like granite, that I swallow down, for all the time that has been lost.

'So, what are you going to do love?' Mary asks, her eyes quickly scanning the room before landing back on Sam. I notice that my gran's eyes linger on my long, unwashed hair, too thin body, and the dark circles under my eyes.

I want to get away from here, to just run away cradling Sam, but how can I? 'I have no idea Gran.'

To my surprise, Mary smiles. 'Well I do … I have a plan.'

I stiffen. A plan? Now she has my full attention.

'I've had a lot of time to sit and think, about what I would do if I ever found you.' Mary smiles and reaches across to hand Sam to me. 'Here, you take him, I need to get my bag.'

I kiss the downy hair on Sam's head, a pale yellow colour that is a mass of small curls. I inhale the magical smell that is all baby, and marvel at the fact that this small bundle is all mine. No matter what happens now between me and Jake, and all the crap that has gone before, I still have this beautiful baby. Not everything in my life has turned rotten.

I watch Mary shuffle through the contents of her bag, or rather, her large oversized shoulder bag. She gives the impression of being her very own Mary Poppins, and I wonder what she will pull out next.

'Ah, here we go,' Mary says with relief, 'I made a list for you, with a contact number, address and so on. Have a read. Here, I'll hold Sam for you.'

I hand Sam back over and take the folded pieces of paper. I start to read.

My gran has written the name and address of a house that is located in the sleepy village of Muddletown, Lancashire. I have never ventured further from the Dorset border and wonder what the area looks like.

Puzzlement creases my features. 'Why have you given me this?' I have an inkling of what it means, but it doesn't make sense.

'Now, just listen to me, okay,' Mary says, giving a stern look.

I nod, my eyes resting on Sam's sleeping body.

'Well, you see, as I've been saying, I've had a lot of time to think. I never trusted Jake, never, I always thought you were too good for him and that he was a controlling bugger.'

I just stare, I daren't speak, my gran has hit the nail on the head.

'Well,' Mary continues, 'I knew that if I ever did find you and you weren't happy, that I wanted to provide you with an escape route. A means of getting away from him, from here, without him ever knowing or being able to find you.'

My head starts to swim and I'm glad that I'm not holding Sam. I feel woozy.

'Gran, what exactly is this?' I shakily push the papers towards her.

Mary breaks out in a huge grin, 'It's your escape plan.'

'My escape plan?' I hardly get the words out, shaking my head. 'I don't understand.'

'What's to understand? I have a friend living up north who has this friend who rents out several houses in the area. I gave him a phone yesterday and he told me that this house in Muddletown has just become available. So, I put down a deposit for you.'

I am rendered speechless; it is all too much to take in. A new home, away from here. A deposit paid. Life is never this easy.

'I can't just up sticks and move to Lancashire Gran,' I stutter, 'I have commitments here, besides, I have no money and with Sam ...'

'Shhh Holly,' Mary soothes, 'you've just had a baby, and that in itself is a big upheaval, I remember it well. But for your own safety and for your baby's safety, you need to get away from here, do you understand?'

Once again, I nod. I do understand. I do need to get away, but the logistics of doing so are just so complicated. There is no way I can do it.

'Holly,' Mary says gently, 'do you trust me?'

My head shoots up and I meet Mary's eyes. 'Of course I do Gran, you are about the only person in the world who I do trust.' I stifle a sob, blinking; it's true, I trust Mary with my life.

'Well then, what I have for you is a lifeline. A new start in life as I've already said, I've had time to plan, to figure things out, unlike you. Here, grab my bag and you'll find a clear folder. Look inside it. I'll just pop Sam down and make us a brew.'

I slowly bend down to pick up the bag, my insides slightly protesting as I am mindful of the episiotomy scar and sensitive

stitches. I quickly locate the folder and place it on my knee. It feels heavy. I unzip the fastening and tip the contents out onto the couch beside me.

Inside is an information booklet with the words '**Deed Pole**' written at the top. My gran wants me to change my name? Slowly it begins to sink in. The only way I can get away from Jake and be truly free from him, with him never being able to find me, is by changing my identity. My gran has given me a lifeline and I know that I need to grab it with both hands.

I quickly scan the pages, reading the process that is involved and the time that it will take. I can apply to change my name via phone, internet or post. I read through the various options and realise that my quickest and best chance is to do so via phone. I can be fast-tracked the following day. When approved, I can then change all my documentation – bank details, passport, everything. I will simply vanish. I wonder how my gran has secured the house for me, and then realise that the house must be in my gran's name, not my own, as I am not my new version yet. I'll ask her when she brings in the tea.

I put the form to one side and then go back to the stack of papers that Gran has given me. I sit and read everything carefully, learning that the house is a two-up two-down in Muddletown, Lancashire, not far from Morecambe. I have heard of Morecambe, of course I have, but I have never been there. The house is rented out by a Mr Jenkins, and Gran has provided me with his contact details. In total he has eight properties; I'm not sure if this is a good or bad thing.

'Here we are,' Mary breezes into the room, bearing two steaming cups of tea. She places them both onto the coffee table. Drink yours before the baby wakes up.'

I take a tentative sip but it's far too hot, so I place it back onto the coaster.

'Gran,' I begin, 'I don't know what to say. It's all too much, in a good way,' I add, when I see the worried look on her face. 'It's just, how can all of this be possible? Is it really that easy?'

'If you want to get away from him and start afresh, then yes, it is that easy. I've got a home for you, a deposit has been put down, we'll set up a bank account in your new name, I already have savings put away that will tide you over, and there is enough money there to pay the rent for the next year.'

I can't hide my gasp, 'That much money?'

'Oh Holly, I'm an old woman with money to spare. What do I need money for? I have everything I need. It's just sat there, so I popped it into a savings account and you shall have it.'

I start to protest but Mary shushes me. 'No, listen. This is my gift to you. I should have stopped that man, stopped what happened, but I didn't.'

'There's nothing you could have done Gran,' I tell her, tears once more starting to stream down my cheeks.

'I know dear, but I still feel guilty. So this is my way of saying sorry, making amends.'

'Oh, Gran, there is nothing to be sorry for,' I choke on my words.

'Well be that as it may, this makes me feel better about what happened. I am in a position to help you now.'

'So, everything is ready?' I tentatively ask. 'I mean, the house is ready for me?'

'It's all ready for you and baby Sam. It's in my name now, but once we get your name changed, then it will revert over to you. Don't look so worried, Stan knows the score.'

'Stan?'

'Mr Jenkins, as long as he gets his money, which he will and has, he won't ask any questions.'

'But what about Sam, does he know about him?'

'Yes, I explained about the baby. It doesn't change anything.' Mary reaches over and takes my hand in hers. 'I have money put aside for you, you just need to change your name and then we can move.'

I nod, I still can't believe that any of this is real.

'I take it that the baby has Jake's name?' Mary asks with a knowing look.

I nod.

'Well there's nothing we can do about that I'm afraid.'

'What do you mean? Surely I can just change Sam's name when I change mine.'

I already know the answer before my gran shakes her head.

'You need both parents to sign the paperwork for a child, so Sam will have to keep his name. Hopefully, he won't be able to trace him.'

I swallow, my throat dry. This is a big gamble, and I know that my gran is thinking the exact same thing. But what else can I do? It's safer to go than to stay.

I swallow down a fleeting feeling of guilt. I'll be taking his son away – is that the right thing to do? But then I think about his increasing temper, his mood swings. What if he loses his temper with Sam? What then? I can't risk it. I will do whatever it takes to protect my son, and it is in that moment that I know what I must do.

'I've had a look at the forms, and the fastest way to change my name is by phoning them up.'

Mary grins. 'Right then, there's no time like the present.' She pulls her mobile from her never-ending Mary Poppins bag.

CHAPTER TWENTY-FIVE

MONDAY, SEPTEMBER 23, 2013

Kate looked out into the open plan office from the safety of the goldfish bowl. Bill sat and listened intently as she spoke. She needed to tell him; he had a right to know about what was going on in her life. He had been there from the very beginning.

'Kate, I know you've heard this a thousand times, but you can't trust him.'

Kate rolled her eyes at him, biting the urge to tell him that *yes, she had.* 'Bill, my hands are tied. He has a right to see his son. I can't stop him.' She fiddled with her pen, clicking it on and off. What else could she say? It was only when Bill reached over to take the pen from her that she realised how nervous she was.

'Kate,' he slowly said her name, gaining her attention. 'Take the day off, the stories I have planned for you can wait a few more days.'

She was tempted to simply pack up her things and go home, to wallow in her thoughts while waiting in the house for Jake to make an appearance. But there was no good in that plan. Plus, Veronica was still on leave and would be for a few more weeks. Bill was far too accommodating, and she didn't want to take advantage of their friendship; Veronica would use it against him. Not to mention the rest of the staff. She didn't want any special treatment.

'No, I need to keep busy. I'll do the phone calls and make notes today, and then I'll write them up tomorrow.' She offered him a weak smile. It was a compromise and she knew that he would take it.

'I still think you're making a mistake,' Bill told her as he reluctantly handed her the list of names she needed to contact.

'I know,' Kate said, rising, 'but what can I do?'

She heard Bill's sigh of resignation as she left the room.

Kate had managed to contact three of the names on the list. The last person, a Mrs Cruickshank, had won a local award for adopting cats and Kate just knew that it would be a *long* conversation. Kate was and had never been a cat person. She just didn't get why people were so enthusiastic about them and why they were treated almost like babies. When she was growing up, a lady down the road used to walk her cat on a *lead*. Even as a little girl she had thought that this was ridiculous. Thankfully, she could use the phone supplied by the paper, but still, she needed to sound professional and enthusiastic, and she just didn't have it in her today. Her mind was obviously elsewhere. She had told Sam that morning, over a bowl of Cheerios, that the man from the café would be in the house when he got home from school. But Sam had just shrugged, humming his inner tune while he ate his breakfast. Kate wasn't sure if he had understood her, or if he simply wasn't bothered. Either way, she didn't want to press the matter too much. She had warned him, so at least he wouldn't be shocked to see him in the house on his arrival home. She didn't have a picture of Jake to add to the visual timetable; all photos of him had been left behind when she moved to Lancashire, and she hadn't owned a camera phone at the time. She couldn't bring herself to add the visual image of 'Dad'. That word conjured up so

many meanings, a man who was kind, who was present and who was a role model. Jake was none of those things.

But could he be?

She had half-expected to hear from Emily. She hoped her friend was safe. She remembered her gran's saying, that no news was good news, so she hoped that all was well. Someone had to have luck on their side. She would resist calling her. Emily would call when she had the opportunity to do so. Hopefully, it would be soon.

She picked up the phone, bracing herself for a long conversation with Mrs Cruickshank.

Matt watched the retreating backs of the party of thirty school children and breathed a huge sigh of relief. Dan spun round, a huge grin plastered on his face. 'Well that went really well.'

Matt couldn't help laughing. The tour had been hugely successful, the children eager and full of questions, but Matt knew that Dan was not referring to those facts. 'You are unbelievable you know,' Matt told him, giving him a pat on the back.

'Well, what could I do? She slipped me her phone number, I couldn't refuse. Actually, where is it?' Dan frantically rummaged around his jeans pockets until he found the crumpled piece of paper. 'I'm adding this in my phone now, before I lose it,' he grinned.

Matt shook his head but couldn't help smiling. 'She was very pretty.'

'Now, now,' tutted Dan, 'you have your missus.'

Matt cringed. Dan had no idea of what was going on his life. He had wrongly assumed that Matt was married, and then when he had pointed out that he was divorced but still wore his wedding ring, Dan pointed out the obvious, that it was merely a separation and they would be back together. *He'd seen it happen a million*

times. Matt cursed, he was proving to be right, even though the wedding ring was now hidden in his bedside drawer. They were slowly drifting back together, with only one conclusion possible. But strangely, this made him uneasy. It wasn't the ending he wanted. 'Well, that's a whole other story for another day,' Matt told Dan as he strode towards the office.

End of conversation.

Dan held his hands up. 'Well, I'll leave it for now. You want a coffee?' he asked as he followed Matt into the office.

Matt sunk down into his chair, shaking his head. 'No, I'm fine thanks, I'm just going to get what I need before I head back to the uni.'

Dan busied himself boiling the kettle while rooting for the teabags. Matt shoved papers and his laptop into his bag. It was only as he stood that he asked the question that had been burning inside of him all morning. He cleared his throat, 'So, what do you think of the new cleaner then? You miss Ken?' He tried to sound indifferent, as if he was asking a casual question.

'Yeah, he's okay, I mean he seems all right,' Dan shrugged.

Matt nodded, not sure of what to say next.

Dan scooped his teabag from his cup with a pen and dropped it into the waste paper basket. 'Sad story though, you know.'

Matt's ears pricked up. *Sad story?* What lies had Jake been spreading?

'Oh?'

'Well, he told me that he had been searching for his wife and son for the past *six* years. Can you believe that?' Dan paused dramatically to sip at his tea.

Matt could barely breathe.

'He told me, the reason he was here was because he'd finally found her living under a false name. He had to use a private

investigator, said it nearly bankrupted him.'

Matt's body went rigid. What other shit had Jake spread? He didn't want to hear any more, but at the same time he didn't want Dan to stop talking. Jake was digging his own grave.

'He told me that he's here to get his son back, and that no one and nothing will stop him.'

Matt was glad that he wasn't holding a cup of tea. He placed his hands on his bag to steady them. 'Can you believe what this man says? I mean, you've only just met him,' he asked.

'Eh?' Dan scowled. 'Why would he lie?' he asked, shaking his head. 'No, he was telling me the truth.'

'It just sounds a little far-fetched, don't you think?' Matt said, while shoving papers into his bag. Dan believed what Jake had told him. Matt knew he should just tell Dan the truth, but it wasn't his story to tell. Kate trusted him, and he couldn't betray that trust. He remembered the look in Jake's eyes that night in the lobby, his aggression. He was a calculating bastard, and besides, Jake had never been married to Kate.

'Well, I feel sorry for the fella. He's hoping to get back together with them, start afresh. He wants to forgive and forget. I couldn't do that. Not if my missus ran out on me with my kid.'

Matt stood up on shaky legs. He couldn't look at Dan, couldn't listen to any more of this shit. Forgive and forget? He had abused Kate until she had no other option but to run from him. What cover story had he told other people? Jake really was the charming bastard that Kate had described, able to pull the wool over everybody's eyes. But the charm didn't work on Matt. And as for the *trying to get back together*? Did Kate know of his plan? She had told him that she was willing to give Jake the benefit of the doubt for Sam's sake. He'd have to talk to her. Tell her what Dan had just told him. *Shit, shit, shit*. Why was he always the bearer of bad

news when it came to this woman? His gut still told him that Jake had an ulterior motive, and it had nothing to do with Sam, or his supposed love for Kate. He didn't love either of them, that much was obvious. This was all about Jake, and he had a feeling it was to do with money.

Matt waved goodbye to Dan, telling him he would be back on Wednesday. He felt in his pocket for his phone and made sure that the ringer was on and at full volume. If Kate needed him then he would be there for her in a flash. He wouldn't get a chance to speak to her before Jake arrived, but he would phone her tonight, fill her in on what he knew and check that she was okay. He wondered how the two of them would get on, what they would talk about, and a stab of jealousy hit him like a punch to the gut. She had her life and he had his, and whether he liked it or not, Lisa was a part of his life now.

Kate sat drumming her fingers on her knee, her phone face down on the bookshelf. She was resisting all temptation to glance at the clock on the screen. Sam was due home in half an hour, so that meant Jake could arrive at any moment. Her pulse quickened, her palms slick with sweat. She was sure that she was having a panic attack. Kate told herself to breathe, that she was being stupid. She leaned forward, placed her head between her knees and gulped in a huge lungful of air.

Jake just wanted to meet Sam, to become acquainted with him, to be his dad, that was all. There was no *ulterior motive* as Matt had suggested. But she would not leave him alone with her son. They would stay in this one room.

What would they talk about? They had six years to catch up on, but Kate was not interested in what he had been up to. As far as she was concerned, his life had ended the moment she had stepped

on the train and out of his life. She had been careful, covered her tracks, she was so sure that there was no way for Jake to trace her, but she should have known. Jake was far too clever, he'd have been one step ahead. He would never have given up. He hated to lose at anything. But he was here now, and would soon be standing in her home, invading her space, her possessions, her thoughts, her air. What was once new, untouched, would be tarnished. Everything would feel different.

Kate shuddered, pushing these morbid thoughts to the back of her mind. Thinking like that would do her no good. She had to focus on the here and now. Sam was her priority. She would be polite, she would be civil, but that was all. She owed Jake nothing.

The heavy pounding of the front door made Kate jump. She picked up her phone and glanced at the screen; Sam would be home in twenty minutes. She had to fill twenty long minutes with this man. She prayed that the taxi would not be late.

The door slowly opened to reveal a grinning Jake. He stood there, blocking out the sunlight, clean shaven, pressed shirt and tie. Already the air felt different.

He thrust the large bouquet of flowers towards her. Irises dominated the bouquet that also featured ferns and daisies. They were her favourite flowers.

Kate's shoulders tensed. The smile she had been forcing slowly slipped. She wasn't sure if she should take them or not. He was here for Sam, not her. Once again, she heard the warning bells ringing loud and clear in her mind.

He has an ulterior motive. Be careful.

Reluctantly, she took the flowers and motioned for him to step inside. Turning her back on him, she walked quickly into the kitchen, clutching the large bouquet. She opened the cupboard under the sink with the pretence of looking for a non-existent

vase. The action gave her those much-needed seconds in which to think. But she now realised her mistake. She didn't want him in her home.

'Sit down Jake, I won't be a minute,' she called out from under the sink.

'I'm fine here.' Jake's voice was loud and controlled with that all-knowing air of authority that Kate loathed.

'No vase,' she shrugged, as she dipped out of the cupboard, banging her head. She stood, running her fingers over her scalp. No bump. Her voice shook slightly and she dry swallowed, summoning up the courage that was buried deep within her. Being so close to him didn't help. She could smell the aftershave that he used to wear. His posture was the same, she could remember those cruel dark eyes, taunting her, telling her that she was an *ugly bitch*. She squeezed her eyes shut. She had to remember that image. His face contorted, mocking her. She needed to remember the man that he used to be. The man that he might be now. She would not be fooled by him. Not for a second.

She reached into the drainer and found a small measuring jug, then filling it quickly with water, she placed the bouquet inside. It would do for now. Once he had gone she would dump the flowers in the bin. But right now, she didn't want to make a scene. She wanted everything to be calm for when Sam came home.

'Tea?' Kate asked, as she reached for the kettle. She swore that she heard Jake mumble something but she wasn't sure.

'Yeah sure.'

As she opened the cupboard, searching for some decent cups that weren't chipped, tea bags and teaspoons, she was aware that Jake had not moved from where he was propped against the kitchen door. He remained silent while she made the tea. For once she wished he would talk.

Kate handed Jake the tea and suggested they sit in the living room. That way she would see the taxi when it pulled up outside. More importantly, she had left her phone on the living room table. She needed to be near it.

Kate stood awkwardly while Jake sat at one end of the couch. She then slowly sat down on the wooden chair opposite him. She cradled her tea, not knowing what to say. She wanted to pretend that what was happening was not real, it couldn't be.

'So, you not going to ask me how I've been? What I've been up to?' Jake sneered. 'I mean, for all you know I could have topped myself when you did your midnight flit.'

Kate bit back the urge to tell him that it wasn't a midnight flit, *you stupid man*, as she had left him in the morning, and that she couldn't care less about what he had been up to in the past six years. But of course, she said none of these things.

'Cat got your tongue?' Jake locked his eyes on hers, 'It's not like you to be so quiet.' His lips curled into a cruel smile.

'For God's sake Jake, what do you want me to say?' Kate spat. She had wanted to remain calm, composed, but his mere presence was making that incredibly difficult. 'You were ... I had to get away.' Her words then started to tumble out; all her pent-up rage suddenly had an outlet. 'Let's get this out in the open now, before Sam gets here. I left you and started a new life. I wanted nothing more to do with you and I still want nothing more to do with you,' she paused to catch her breath, 'but you are Sam's dad, and you have rights, which is why you are here. That's all this is, so you can wipe that smile off your face.'

Jake grinned, then slowly slurped his tea. 'Let me just ask, *Holly*,' he said after wiping the back of his hand against his mouth, 'how is the old cow?'

The colour drained from Kate's face. How dare he! How dare he

talk about her gran like that. Tears stung her eyes and her pulse quickened. He was doing it to rile her, to get a reaction. But he would not win. Instead, Kate stood and walked over to the window, arms crossed against her chest, against him, searching the street outside for the taxi, knowing that it was still far too early for Sam to arrive home. But she could not force herself to look at him.

'She died, not long after I settled here.' Kate closed her eyes. She could still see her gran, as clearly as if she was stood in front of her. She could smell her vanilla perfume, and hear her laugh, that beautiful laugh that could chase the blues so effortlessly away. She missed her so much. She would not talk about her gran with Jake. Her gran was her secret, he had no right to disrespect her memory.

Kate peered through the window. She would stay like this until the taxi pulled up. At least this way he couldn't read her expression. If he could, she would give the game away.

But she could not stand the silence; it unnerved her more than Jake's hurtful words. 'Do you want to stay for tea?' she asked, even though she wanted him gone as soon as possible. She couldn't help the way she had been raised. Always be polite, be kind. It had been drummed into her.

'No, I'm working in a few hours.' He ran his hand through his hair. Kate had noticed that his hair was longer than he used to have it.

He smirked, 'But then you should know that. Surely your boyfriend has told you?'

Kate was glad that she was still facing away from him, as he couldn't see her reddening cheeks, 'He's not my boyfriend, he's my neighbour, and why would he tell me that you are working at the aquarium?'

There was a brief pause before Jake replied. Kate cursed her stupid mistake.

'So, he *has* told you then, of course he has. I gave him the note while he was there, so why wouldn't he tell you that I now work there?'

Kate closed her eyes, choosing to remain silent. It was no good arguing with him, he wouldn't listen.

'You seem very cosy together.'

Kate remained silent. He wanted a response and he wasn't going to get one.

The seconds ticked by.

Sam flew into the house, coat dropped onto the floor and shoes kicked aside. With a flying jump, he landed on the couch in one full sweep. Dragging his iPad up from the floor by the side of the couch, he gave Jake a cursory glance before asking for a drink.

Kate forced herself to slow down as she opened the fridge and located the apple juice. She sloshed the juice all over the worktop in her haste to get back to Sam. She felt anxious at the thought of them being alone together.

She handed Sam the drink, which he took with a polite *thank you*.

Jake watched as Sam gulped down his drink, and then as he thrust the empty cup back at Kate, before bowing his head to look at the illuminated screen once more, the room echoing with the noise of cows, sheep and villagers.

Jake threw Kate a quizzical look. 'You not going to introduce us then?' His tone was brisk with a touch of annoyance.

Kate bristled as she knew what was coming next.

She tapped Sam gently on the shoulder as she crouched in front of him. 'Sam, love, this man is Jake. Do you remember him from the café?'

Sam continued to tap away at the screen.

'Sam,' Kate continued, her voice now strained, 'Sam, can you put the iPad down and say hello to Jake?'

Sam gave a momentary flicker of the eyes, as they met Kate's, a brief acknowledgment, before landing back on the screen.

'Okay, Sam, I'll get the sand timer, five minutes and then we will switch the iPad off, okay?' Kate pulled herself up from the floor and went to fetch the sand timer from the wicker basket in the corner of the room.

'Sam, turn that thing off, I want to chat to you,' Jake demanded.

Kate's head whipped round to find Jake reaching forward to take the iPad from Sam's tight fists.

But it was too late.

Sam let out an anguished howl, that was both pitiful and sharp. He heaved himself backwards onto the couch, taking both the iPad and Jake with him. 'No, no, no, no, it's mine, not yours,' he growled.

Jake let go and stood up abruptly, visibly shaken. 'What the fuck's the matter with him?' he shrieked at Kate.

Kate felt the colour rising to her cheeks. Firstly, because he had used foul language in front of her son, secondly because he had insulted her son, no correction, *their* son, and thirdly he had ignored her instruction, to wait for five bloody minutes. Is this how it was going to be?

'Jake,' Kate hissed while rubbing Sam's back in rhythmical circles, 'let me get the timer for him, and then you can talk.'

Jake raised his hands in defeat and slowly lowered himself back onto the couch, sitting at the very edge. Kate turned to the wicker basket once more to retrieve the timer and missed Jake's look of utter contempt.

'You haven't answered my question,' he said slowly, as Kate once more crouched on the floor in front of Sam.

Kate sighed, 'He's autistic, Jake, it's just how things are.' She realised how fed up she sounded, but she didn't care, he wouldn't understand anyway, no matter how she tried to explain things. 'He needs to be warned about things, you can't just snatch his iPad from him, it's not how it works.'

'He's rude,' Jake pointed towards Sam's bent head with his index finger, 'he's not even acknowledged that I'm here, has he?'

Kate noted his sneer this time and bristled at his choice of words; her son was not rude, far from it. She also didn't like talking about Sam's condition with Sam in the room. He took everything in.

Kate struggled to keep her temper under control, so she spoke slowly, trying to soften what she said. 'He is autistic, Jake. It means he has difficulties with communication, in understanding the world around him, it's just his way.' She bit her lip, struggling to find the words to describe the difficulties her little boy had to cope with every day, while trying to convey that she wouldn't change any of it, it was just how he was. He was her little boy, and she wanted Jake to love him as much as she did. But Kate knew that this would never happen. She could see it in his eyes, the way he looked at the little boy. He would never understand him, and this filled her with a sadness she hadn't been expecting.

Jake's eyes flickered to the sand timer that was now perched on the bookshelf. Sam's eyes were still rooted to the iPad. Kate had no idea where to look.

The three sat in silence until the last grain of sand filtered through. Kate rose and brought it over to Sam, placing it in front of his face, obscuring the iPad screen. 'Sam, five minutes have finished now. Put the iPad down please.'

Sam mumbled a grunt of complaint but did reluctantly relinquish the iPad, much to her relief.

Sam sat with his head still bowed, as if looking at an imaginary

screen, not sure of what to do next. Jake shifted uncomfortably in his seat. Kate watched him squirming, enjoying the fact that it was now his turn to feel uncomfortable. See how he liked it.

Jake opened his mouth to speak but shut it again. Kate thought he resembled a goldfish. He turned to Kate, obviously wanting her to start the conversation.

She sighed, 'Sam, this man is Jake, we met him at the café on Saturday. He is a friend of mine, and he wants to be your friend.'

'Friend?' Jake spat, 'friend? Are you joking?' He turned to Sam and placed his hands on his shoulders. Kate flinched as Sam's posture stiffened and wondered if Jake had felt the tensing of her son's muscles, the fight or flight response, or if he had simply chosen to ignore the fact.

'Sam, I'm your dad. I've been looking for you for so long, and now I've found you.' He stared at the boy, waiting for a response.

There was none.

'Look at me when I'm talking to you,' Jake's grip tightened, '*look at me*.'

Kate lunged forward and tried to pry Jake's hands from Sam's bony shoulders. After a moment of deliberation, he let go.

'Fuck this,' he growled, pushing himself up from the couch. 'What's the point? I may as well be talking to the fucking wall.'

His words were like a slap to the face. Kate cringed at his foul words, his lack of empathy, and total lack of understanding for their son. She blinked back her tears, she would not cry in front of him. Never again.

'Jake, please, this isn't the way,' she urged, 'and please stop swearing.'

She was prepared for a fight, an argument, but instead, Jake merely raised his eyes to the ceiling and let out a deep breath.

'I'm not very good at this, I need time to adjust, to figure things

out.' He strode towards her. 'Can we try again tomorrow?'

Kate was suddenly too tired to argue. She just wanted him to go, to be alone with her thoughts and her little boy. She would agree to anything. 'Yes, that's fine Jake, we'll try again tomorrow.'

Inside she was screaming at him that *they* didn't need to try again, *he* did. She never wanted to see him again.

As Kate closed the door behind him, his words finally sunk in. He was the same selfish man, telling her that *he* needed to consider his own feelings, how *he* needed to adjust. Not once had he asked about Sam, or how he might be feeling. Kate also thought about the fact that he had not brought a gift with him for Sam.

Matt was right, he wasn't interested in Sam at all.

CHAPTER TWENTY-SIX

TUESDAY, 24 SEPTEMBER 2013

The radio blared out a range of classic rock anthems. Matt was certain that the university café never played Rock FM, but today he was glad that they had chosen his favourite station. He ripped open his fourth packet of brown sugar and stirred the tiny crystals into his milky mug of tea. Today was one of those days. He felt sick to his stomach with the decision that he had made. He knew he should be feeling euphoric, content even, in the knowledge that he now had a second chance with the only love of his life. So why was he feeling so deflated? Perhaps it was the thrill of the chase? That he had been wishing for this for so long, that now it was here, it no longer held the same allure. But that was both cruel and ridiculous. This was his ex-wife, a woman he had loved nearly all his adult life. Did he still love her? Or was he in love with the idea of being in love with her? He honestly didn't know. What he did know was that he had been given a second chance and he was going to grab it with both hands.

He had to make this work.

Kate had finally texted him late last night. He had been so relieved to hear from her, that he had phoned her straight back. She had told him that her meeting with Jake had gone pretty much as she had expected, terribly, but that Jake was going to call around again the following evening. Matt had told her that he would be there in an instant if she needed him, Lisa or no Lisa, to which she had sounded grateful. However, he could tell that she was hiding something from him. He knew this from what she did not tell him. He would bet anything that Jake had acted like a complete arse, as well as being completely ignorant towards Sam. Matt secretly hoped that Sam had ignored him, either that or had bopped him over the head with his iPad. He suppressed a smile at the thought of it. He just hoped that Jake hadn't upset Kate in any way. She deserved so much better in life, so much better than allowing that scumbag back into it. He just wished that he knew what his ulterior motives were – not Sam, and not Kate, there was no love lost there. He had a feeling that Jake finding them after all these years was all about the money, or his lack of it. Matt hoped that Jake would quickly figure out that there was no money to be had; Kate was a single part-time working mum, so where was the money coming from? Jake would soon figure this out and then just disappear, back to the hole he had crawled from. He just hoped that the vile man would leave no debris, nor a trail of destruction behind him. He had phoned with the intention of telling Kate about his conversation with Dan, but the words had stuck in his throat. He'd leave telling her for now.

Matt's thoughts were all about Kate as he gazed out of the large, panoramic window, onto the university lawns. Frowning, he wondered what Lisa would say if she could read his thoughts right now. He needed to update Lisa about Kate, the fact that Jake was now back in her life. He had already explained that they were simply friends, but he had a feeling that Lisa didn't like Kate for some reason. Right now, he could do with a woman's input on what was going on. He'd just explain that he was worried for her and Sam's safety, that was all.

'Hello, you look lost in thought.'

Matt looked behind him to find Lisa standing there, smiling, her hand laid gently on his shoulder. He hadn't felt her hand, nor registered the fact that she had entered the café. He offered her a sheepish grin.

'Hi, you look lovely.' He rose and gently kissed her cheek. The aroma of her familiar perfume filled his nostrils. His eyes lingered over her clothes and hair, aware that he had told the truth, she really did look stunning. She wore a pair of cream linen trousers, a fitted floral blouse and pale blue cardigan, all of which were teamed with a pair of pale blue kitten heels. Her hair was immaculately styled, not a strand out of place. How did women do that?

Lisa gave him a knowing look.

Matt had slipped up on his obvious appraisal of her appearance. She knew she looked good, all done to impress him. She didn't yet know of his decision.

What was strange was that as Matt glanced at the immaculate clothes, the perfect make-up and the practiced pose, it all seemed a little too perfect. Was that even possible? He thought of Kate, the way in which her wardrobe comprised of casual jeans, t-shirts and practical dresses, worn with boots or tatty Converse. Oh, he had noticed what she wore. She looked natural, lived in, without the effort, and Matt preferred this look to the manicured and coiffed woman before him. He coughed, shook his head slightly, clearing his thoughts. He shouldn't be thinking this way about another woman, not when he was having coffee with his wife, well ex-wife, who was soon to become his girlfriend. His life was growing more complicated by the second.

Lisa pulled her chair out; it made a loud screeching noise against the parquet floor. She gestured towards his coffee. 'Started without me?'

'You are late,' Matt responded with a smile. 'I'll go and grab you one now, latte?' he asked as he stood.

'Please,' Lisa smiled.

Matt needed the time to think, to get his thoughts back on track, back on Lisa. He needed to focus. What the hell was wrong with him today? Kate was off-limits, a friend, the future was staring right at him. So why did it still feel like his past?

'Here you go,' Matt forced himself to sound normal as he placed the two coffees down on the table. 'I needed a refill,' he added as he watched Lisa eyeing his extra cup.

'So, how are things?' Lisa asked after taking a sip of her coffee.

Matt knew what this was, that she was asking him if he had decided about *them*, their future. He cleared his throat. 'Listen, I've been thinking … about what we talked about,' he swallowed, now not sure if he would get the words out, 'I think we should try again, you know, me and you, give it another go'

Lisa's expression changed from that of obvious anxiety to that of pure joy in less than a nanosecond.

Matt just hoped that he had made the right decision, he really didn't want to lead her on. But what really tugged at him was that he already felt that he had made a massive mistake, and if he could take those words back, he would.

'Really? *Us*, as in you and me?' Her breath was raspy.

Matt could barely hear the words.

'Yes, why not eh?' his voice trembled slightly, betraying how nervous he felt despite his outward nonchalance. He also knew that this was probably not the romantic response she was expecting, but they were well past that stage by now, they knew each other too well, warts and all.

'Oh,' she beamed, 'for once I'm speechless.'

Matt laughed; he'd never known her to be lost for words.

Without any warning, she leapt up and threw her arms tightly around his neck. 'Sod the coffee, we should be drinking champagne.'

Matt slowly unfurled her arms from around his neck, acutely aware that they had drawn the attention of several customers who were sat nearby. Luckily, none he recognised. 'Okay, okay, we'll celebrate tonight.'

'I'd love that,' Lisa gushed. 'How about you cook me a romantic meal Dr Harper?'

Matt nearly spat his coffee out, as A, he was the world's worst cook, and B, he was thinking more along the lines of a restaurant. 'I meant taking you out somewhere.'

'Oh no,' Lisa shook her head playfully, 'it'll be more romantic at your place.'

Matt raised his eyebrows. He wasn't so sure about that, but he supposed it would save him money so he agreed.

For the next half an hour, they sat in companionable silence, sipping coffee and devouring croissants with strawberry jam.

As the time neared for him to go back to the lab, he cautiously broached the subject of Kate. He was so worried about her; he needed a woman's take on what was happening.

'Well, he is the father Matt,' Lisa said grimly, 'he has rights, all you can do is be there as a friend.' She paused. Matt noted the tension in her jaw, the firm set of her mouth. It was clearly killing her to say those words. 'But just don't get too involved.'

Matt blanched at her words – so she still felt that he had feelings for Kate. He could never hide his feelings. But then why lie? Kate was a friend, and he was worried about her and Sam. There was nothing wrong in admitting that. Plus, he could tell that Lisa cared too.

'You don't want to cause friction, or upset between Sam and his dad,' Lisa continued sternly, 'you just need to leave them to it.'

'He has a history of violence Lisa.' Matt said, his words clipped. 'That was why she left him, he was verbally abusive to her, *cruel*. God knows what would have happened if she had stayed.'

Lisa's cheeks reddened. She began to stutter a reply but stopped, lowering her gaze as she began to swirl the remains of her coffee around in the cup. 'It's the little boy you're worried about, isn't it?' she eventually said. 'Could he harm him?'

'I honestly don't know Lisa, but I couldn't stop thinking about them all last night.'

As soon as the words were out of his mouth, he wanted to take them back. To chew them up and swallow them down.

Lisa all but dropped her coffee cup onto the table, sloshing the remains onto the pristine white surface. She crossed her arms and stared out of the window with unseeing eyes. Matt noted the red tinge to her cheeks.

'You really do care about her, don't you?' Lisa asked quietly.

'Yes, yes I do,' Matt replied without thinking, 'but not how you think.' He raked his hand through his short blonde hair and took a deep breath. 'She's living by herself with her little boy, who's autistic, she's just, no, *they*, are just so ... well, with Jake back in their lives, I worry about them.'

Lisa pursed her lips and finally turned to face him. 'I get it Matt, I really do. I hope that she's okay, and that this Jim, doesn't hurt either of them.' She looked away towards the window once more. 'It's just that they aren't your problem. You can't save everyone.'

'Jake,' Matt corrected her, 'and I also hope that he doesn't hurt them, physically or mentally.' He chose to ignore her last comment.

He'd make sure from now on that he'd never bring up Kate's name in conversation ever again. He picked up his own coffee and

slowly sipped, whiling away the few minutes until it was time to leave.

Standing on the busy pavement outside the uni cafe, Matt kissed her gently on the lips, inhaling the scent of her flowery perfume. He needed to do better, much better. It was only after they had said their goodbyes that he worked out what had been bothering him during their time spent together. Not once had she mentioned what she had been up to recently. The entire conversation had been about him. He also felt a steadily growing feeling of unease as he realised that he had no idea where she lived. She had made no mention of him going to her house. He stood outside the café, motionless, as students swarmed past him on their way to lectures, wondering how well he knew his ex-wife, and if he even knew her at all.

Kate had finally got around to writing the final copy of her interviews from the previous day. She had found it hard to concentrate, but it had done her the world of good. She hadn't thought about Jake for the past few hours.

She pushed her chair back from the desk; it groaned in complaint, while she slowly stretched and flexed her muscles. Her neck and shoulders ached with a lack of sleep and built up tension. She closed her eyes and prayed that Sam would have a better night's sleep, that he would be a little more interested in Jake when they met later, although she doubted it. Jake needed to accept Sam, the way he was, but with a sinking feeling in the pit of her stomach, she knew that he never would.

'Why don't you make an early dart Kate?' Bill said softly, rubbing his neck as he stood behind her, coffee cup in hand. Had he not been sleeping well? Perhaps the strain of being in charge

was too much for him. Kate wondered if he had started drinking again, but she had smelled no tell-tale alcohol on his breath, no tell-tale odour of mints, and he seemed his usual happy self, just tired. She had just been so absorbed in her own life that she had neglected those around her, including Bill. She needed to keep an eye on him.

Kate turned to face him and smiled, 'Well, I'm all done here, so I might as well go. I need to grab a few things for tea and then I'll head home.'

Bill nodded, started to step away from her chair, but then hesitated. 'So, how did it go yesterday, with Jake?' His eyes radiated such kindness that Kate had to look away. More than anything she wanted to tell him that it had been a huge success, that they had got along like a house on fire, but he would see through the lies. She had to tell him the truth and that would hurt more than lying to him.

'Not good, but I'm hopeful about later on,' she said, trying to soften the impact.

'Later on? He's calling around again?' Bill asked, looking completely horrified at the thought.

'Well, yes, it wasn't a one-off, he has a right to see his son.'

'I know, I know,' Bill said raising his hands, 'but, it didn't go well, you said?' He raised an enquiring eyebrow; it wasn't really a question at all.

Kate sighed and stood up, then perched on the edge of her desk, now resigned to tell the truth. 'No, it was awful. Sam just wasn't interested and ignored him.'

'Well that's Sam, but surely he understands why?'

Kate shrugged, 'He knows about his autism, but he has made no attempt to find out more about it. He hasn't accepted that that is the way things are.'

Now it was Bill's turn to shrug, 'Well stuff him Kate. If he won't understand, nor accept Sam for who he is, well, I hate to say this, but what's the point? He found you to reconnect with his son.'

There was a moment's silence while Kate registered the words, and once more she knew that Jake had a completely different reason for wanting to reconnect with them. It wasn't about Sam at all, but she couldn't say any of this to Bill. He would only worry more.

'I'm sure it was just a shock, that's all. I think that the more he gets to know Sam, then the better things will be. It'll just take time.'

'If you say so,' Bill said dismissively. 'Just be careful, I know I've said it a thousand times, but if you need me, call. I don't trust the guy.'

'You've told me that a thousand times too,' she smirked.

'Aye and with very good reason,' Bill said before turning and striding back to his office.

Kate had the horrible feeling that she had just managed to both insult and disappoint her best friend. Jake's poison blemished everything.

She should have been more careful, more observant, but now that Jake was back in her life, Kate had let her guard down. That was why she walked slap bang into him outside the doors to the *Muddletown Muse*. His arms tightly gripped her shoulders as she tried to flee, not knowing who the stranger was. It was only as she looked up that she finally saw his face. Fear had paralysed her, stopping her from screaming. Although she was momentarily glad of this, the fact that she hadn't managed to humiliate herself in public, it also terrified her, as Jake was strong, and he had easily shown that he could overpower her if need be.

She stepped back and wriggled free from his hold.

‘You scared me,’ she said, her voice trembling slightly. She willed her breathing to slow and her hands to stop shaking.

‘You should be more careful,’ he smirked, cocking his head to one side.

Kate pulled the strap of her bag up over her shoulder and glanced at her phone that she was clutching for dear life. The display read just after 1:00 pm. ‘What are you doing here anyway?’ she asked him in a tone that told him she was finished playing games.

‘Meeting you,’ he said, like it was the most natural thing to do in the world.

‘We agreed that you would call round at the house, after Sam finished school,’ she hissed at him, puzzled as to why he was stood in the doorway to her workplace. It shouldn’t have surprised her really, the fact that he knew where she worked. He had, after all, tracked down her home address and where Matt worked.

‘I just thought we could have some lunch as I’m here, that’s all, thought it would be a nice thing to do.’

‘But how did you know I would be finishing work now? I’m not here all the time. I work odd hours.’

He just stared at her.

‘I know, I just thought that I would hover around, and wait,’ he shrugged.

Kate shook her head, there was no point saying anything else. He had obviously followed her here this morning and had taken a chance on her finishing early. Either that or he had bugged her office. Could he have done such a thing? No, that was such a ridiculous thought, Kate chided herself for even thinking it. ‘Well, I need to do a bit of grocery shopping but then I suppose we could go on to the café.’ What was the point in trying to suggest anything else or refusing him? She didn’t want him in her house just yet, a public space was much better.

'Okay. I don't mind tagging along with you.'

'Okay then,' Kate sighed. She turned to head towards the minimart at the bottom of the road, but Jake stopped her with his hand on her shoulder, forcing her to turn back towards him.

'Listen, I messed up. But, I'm clean now. It's just that, well, I can forgive you for what you did, so you should forget about what I did, about who I was back then.'

Kate looked into his eyes properly for the first time. There was no trace of irony or mockery to be found within them. He meant what he said. The problem was that Jake had nothing to forgive and she could never forget.

She turned without uttering a word and continued walking down the street.

CHAPTER TWENTY-SEVEN

Sam picked up the car from the scattered pile on the car mat and began to move it forwards and backwards, while making the occasional *brum brum* noise of the engines. Each model of car had its own unique sound. Surrounding him were cars, trains and various cartoon characters from popular preschool television programmes. Kate stepped over her son and the mess of cars, as she made her way through to sit on the edge of the couch. She smiled stiffly at Jake, who continued to stare at Sam.

'Do you want another cup of tea?' Kate asked, trying to keep the desperation out of her voice, hoping he would not make a scene. For a change, the problem wasn't her son, but the man grimacing next to her.

Sam had come home from school happy; he'd spent time in the sensory room and had enjoyed the science lesson all about sound, this was what his chat book told her. Jake had been uninterested when she had told him about Sam's day. He'd just nodded. Why was he here, sitting in her house? What was the real reason?

'Is he going to talk to me or what?' Jake asked, sitting forward slightly and pointing at Sam, as if Kate had no idea who he was talking about.

'Let him play for a bit, he's happy,' Kate urged, wishing to keep the peace.

Jake huffed and reluctantly sat back. 'He's just rude,' he finally said, like a sulky school boy. Kate thought that he should know all about that but bit her tongue.

'He needs time to wind down after school,' Kate told him, her words forced. She had already explained this to him, the fact that Sam needed winding down time, no pressure, no tasks, no rules, as he'd had a day of it at school.

'He's been playing with those same cars for over half an hour now, how do you put up with this?'

'Put up with what?'

'This … this ignoring you!'

'Oh, for God's sake Jake, he's not ignoring you, or me, he's playing.'

'Oh, so we're back to blaming everything on his autism then are we?' he spat out his words, 'there's no such thing.'

Kate flinched, 'What did you say?'

'You heard me.'

Kate could swear that she saw a smirk flitter across his face. She had obviously heard him but refused to acknowledge those hateful words. 'Of course autism exists, Jake. How can you say such a thing?'

Jake stretched back on the couch. 'It's just an excuse for naughty children.'

Was he trying to goad her, trying to start a fight? 'What? I can't believe you just said that, and about your own son.'

'Doesn't change the facts,' he said as he jabbed a finger towards her face, 'and it's all your fault.'

He had fired the words at Kate; they felt like bullets. How many times had she sat there and thought those very same words? Back

when Sam was tiny and a whirlwind of energy, throwing things, ignoring instructions, apparently locked in his own little world. But now she knew different. Back then she hadn't a clue about what was going on with her son, but now she did, now she knew that Sam's autism was not her fault. What was her fault was the situation that she now found herself in, and once again, it was all down to Jake. All of it.

She looked him straight in the eyes, refusing to flinch at the words that were bound to come spewing out of his mouth. 'How can I be to blame?' she stammered. 'What absolute nonsense.'

'You took him away from me, that does something to a child that does. It changes them, does something to their brain. It's obviously affected Sam.'

Kate stared at her ex-partner, father to her child, in absolute astonishment. She knew that he believed every single word that he had just said.

'Jake, he was a few weeks old, he couldn't understand what had happened between us, nothing.'

'But he's had no father figure in his life, that's what I'm talking about.'

Kate shook her head, completely bemused that he would think such a thing.

'He needs discipline,' Jake continued, pointing his finger once more at Sam, 'he needs to learn how to behave, not some fucking special school that'll mollycoddle him. It's a tough world out there.'

Kate's blood ran cold at the word *discipline*. She had seen that side of Jake far too many times. What had she been thinking allowing Jake into her home, thinking he was a changed man? He hadn't changed at all. He was still the same spiteful, conceited and controlling man of the past, and she had now given him access to her son.

Kate pushed herself up off the floor and stood protectively in front of Sam, hands on hips, her voice quivering slightly, but she managed to get the words out, 'I think you should leave.'

'What?' Jake slowly stood up from the couch, locking his eyes on hers. 'What do you mean, go? I've just got here.'

Kate's heart thumped madly in her chest. She had to get him out of the house. She didn't trust him in the state he was in, particularly after his last remark. Plus, Sam had no intention of talking to him today.

'We'll try again tomorrow.' She didn't want him back in her house, with her son, but what else could she do? Tomorrow she would be better prepared.

'This is ridiculous. I come here, I sit and drink tea, while he sits and plays with his cars, trains or whatever ...'

'*He* is your son,' Kate snapped. She couldn't help it.

'I fucking know that, but he has no idea that I'm his dad.'

'Dad?' Sam's blue eyes met Kate's at the sound of the word *Dad*. 'That man is Dad?' he asked, pointing to Jake.

Kate felt her blood run cold; her hands shook as she bent down next to her son.

'Yes, love, Jake, that man, is your dad.'

Holding a blue Ford Escort in his tiny fist, Sam scrutinised the strange man standing before him. He blinked several times before turning his attention back to his toy cars.

'*Fucking great! Fantastic!*' Jake roared, while raising his hands in the air. 'This is a complete waste of time.' He turned and headed for the front door.

Kate's shoulders slumped, the tension slipping away, but her relief was replaced by anger. How dare he talk like this in front of her son, *their* son. How dare he dismiss him in such a way. She shouldn't have expected anything else.

She scurried after him, leaving Sam rocking backwards and forwards on the floor, his hands covering his ears. 'Jake!' she shouted, 'it's not his fault, he needs time to process information, to understand. He's only little.'

She desperately needed to defend her son. To show this brute of a man just how very special Sam was.

'Time to process,' he said, his tone mocking her, 'for fuck's sake!' He flung open the door.

Kate stood, hands on hips behind him. 'Jake, can you please stop swearing?'

Jake turned to glare at her, his face mere inches from her own. 'I'll say what I *fucking* well like, and *he*,' he gestured with his head towards Sam, 'needs help.'

'Jake, he's getting help, he goes ...'

Jake cut her off, 'I know he goes to a special school, blah blah blah.' He sighed and turned to walk down the path,

Kate nearly missed his next words.

'I just wish he was normal.'

That was when Kate saw red. Jake could call her names, insult her, but he couldn't do the same to her son. '*Normal*, what's normal?' she shrieked.

He turned back towards her, his face now puce. 'Well for starters, not some kind of ... I don't know,' he shrugged, 'just not like him. Not with signs all over the place. He can't even look at me.'

Kate felt the sting of tears and swallowed quickly. 'He is a normal little boy ...'

'There's no point talking to you,' Jake huffed.

Kate hoped that he meant it. She felt exhausted, she just wanted to be alone with her little boy. She strained her ears, heard him talking to the cars, happy, now that Jake had gone. Jake didn't understand; he had no intention of getting to know his son.

She watched as Jake stamped down the road then turned to go back indoors, but his final shouted words made her halt in her tracks.

'I'll be back Kate, this isn't over. I know my rights.' She stood open-mouthed as he strode onwards through the village streets.

'Are you okay?' a blonde-haired woman kindly asked. She gently placed a hand onto Kate's shoulder. Kate jumped, for she had neither felt, nor seen the gesture.

Kate blinked, tried to smile, failed. The woman looked friendly; she was no threat. 'Sorry, I was miles away.' Kate said, gritting her teeth. 'I'm fine, thank you,' she added when the woman made no attempt to move.

'You sure?' Lisa hesitated, 'it's just that he seemed really angry.'

Kate studied the older woman's face. A look of concern dominated her features; her eyes crinkled slightly, a frown forming, but it could not hide the fact that she was very pretty. 'I'm fine really, I am, he's gone now, so ...'

Lisa nodded, turned to go but then seemed to change her mind. 'I'm Lisa by the way, Matt's wife.' She held out her hand.

Kate bristled. So *this* was the infamous Lisa. She hesitated for a moment before returning the handshake. 'Kate.'

Lisa smiled, 'Well, ex-wife really, I keep forgetting.' She blushed, looked at her feet for a fraction of a second before once again looking up at Kate's face. She smiled, her mouth closed; Kate noticed it didn't quite reach the eyes.

'I'm sorry, I didn't mean to disturb you,' Lisa said as she followed Kate up the other path to the front door. Kate popped her head once more into the living room and found Sam, still sprawled on the floor surrounded by cars.

She turned around to face Lisa.

'You didn't disturb me at all, I'm just a little shook up, that's all.'

'Me too,' Lisa laughed, 'I nearly ran him over, he just darted out into the road. Didn't even bother looking.' She shook her head in disbelief.

Kate forced a smile. Her face was beginning to ache. Why was this woman still talking to her? She just wanted to be with Sam, to make a cup of tea. She wanted to cuddle her perfect little boy and forget the past half hour ever happened.

Lisa stepped back. 'Sorry, you must think I'm a crazy woman, it's just that Matt has talked so much about you, I was just concerned ...' She took another step backwards. 'I'm sorry.'

Although Kate hated the idea of Matt talking about her personal life to his ex, she couldn't be angry with him. She just didn't want to discuss it with the woman standing on her doorstep. 'Matt's been such a great help. I don't know what I would have done without him.'

Lisa's jaw clenched, and her features hardened slightly, but Kate noticed that the smile stayed in place.

'Well, that's Matt, a real-life knight in shining armour.'

Her words were forced, and Kate could read the warning signs a mile off.

'Yes, he is,' Kate smiled, this time her smile was genuine, 'you're lucky to have him.'

Lisa's smile widened, revealing perfect white teeth. 'Yes, I am. Anyway, I'll leave you to it. Maybe I'll see you later?'

Kate wondered what she meant. She was obviously a permanent fixture in Matt's life then?

Lisa's next words confirmed her thoughts.

'I'll be moving in soon, so we'll be neighbours,' she beamed. 'Catch you later.'

Kate watched as Lisa unlocked the door. So, she had a key, what did that tell her?

She quickly stepped into the hall and shut the door behind her.

Matt was back with Lisa.

It looked like they were serious about each other.

Kate felt a wave of disappointment, in the fact that she had lost something that had never been hers to begin with.

Chapter Twenty-Eight

Wednesday, 25th September 2013

The blackbird chirping outside the window woke Matt up from what was a troublesome dream. His head throbbed, which he made worse by rubbing vigorously at his forehead with the back of his knuckles. He scrunched his eyes up as he looked at the glare of the alarm clock. He ran his tongue over his dry, cracked lips and tried to swallow. It was only 6:00 am, but he had an early start at the aquarium; he needed to be there at 07:30 for a delivery. He closed his eyes for a few blissful seconds, pretending that it was just another normal day, that the woman sound asleep beside him should be there, in his bed.

But the fact was that she should not.

He had made a huge, terrible mistake.

His bladder was fit to burst, but he didn't want to wake her up just yet. He needed to clear his thoughts, think carefully about what he needed to say. It was the wine, alcohol was always to blame. *Just the one bottle*, she had said. But one had inevitably turned into three, followed by whisky shots, and all on a school night.

Matt slowly eased himself from under the duvet and slipped on his boxer shorts that were strewn on the floor by the bed. In the bathroom he urinated quickly, surprised that he wasn't more dehydrated. He decided not to flush, and then dry brushed his teeth, in the small hope that he would feel human again.

He poked his head back into the bedroom.

She was still asleep.

He needed coffee.

Matt was already on his second cup when he heard the gentle patter of footsteps on the stairs. He reached towards the coffee maker, poured coffee into a clean cup, and then sat back down heavily at the kitchen table.

'I've made you a cup,' he offered with a weak smile.

Lisa looked as bad as Matt felt.

She slowly lowered herself down and accepted the strong coffee with a flash of a smile. She took a long sip, her eyes focused on the table.

Matt sat and stared at his beautiful ex-wife. The woman he wanted more than anything to love.

But everything had changed.

Making love to her should have been so easy. He thought he would feel the same as he always had, but the experience had left him shaken, as if he had taken advantage of her in some way. It had been quick, almost rushed, and it had left him with a bitter taste in his mouth. He now knew that they could never go back to where they had been before. Neither could they move forwards. Once again, he found himself in limbo land. His worry was how to express these thoughts. How would he tell Lisa the truth?

Matt cleared his throat. 'About last night.'

'Matt, don't,' Lisa said, reaching across to touch his hand.

Matt felt the words that he so urgently needed to say evaporate on his tongue.

Lisa squeezed his hand. 'It's okay, I know.' She offered him a

watery smile, blinking back tears that were threatening to spill down her cheeks. 'It's not the same, I know' she continued, 'it'll never be the same.' She pulled her hand away to pick up her mug of coffee.

'I'm so sorry Lisa, so sorry that ... that we can never go back to how things were ... I want to go back and have what we had before, but ...'

'Everything has changed,' Lisa finished the sentence for him. 'We can never go back, I know that now.'

'I'm sorry, so sorry for everything Lisa, if I hadn't driven you away, with my constant working, my obsession to always provide for you,' he paused, looked up at her grief-stricken face, 'I ignored you. I pushed you away.'

'No Matt, I pushed you away too, with the whole bloody mess.'

Matt swallowed a golf ball sized lump in his throat – it wouldn't budge. He looked at Lisa and saw the daughter he never had.

'We are different people now Matt, I should have realised that. We can't just go back twenty odd years. I was just gripping on far too tightly to the past. I couldn't let go.'

Matt nodded. He knew exactly where she was coming from, as he felt exactly the same.

'Dave was a rebound, you do know that?' she asked, her eyes once again brimming with unshed tears.

Of course he had known that's what Dave was, but he didn't want to gloat. What was the point? They had both been hurt. 'I know Lisa, but we've both made mistakes.'

'You know we were practically kids when we married, and I loved being married to you,' her voice broke on the word 'love' but she carried on, 'but I never really got to know who I am. Does that make any sense?' She blushed slightly, redness appearing as a high spot on each cheek. Matt had never seen her so nervous, so unsure of herself.

He did understand.

'It's just that I've never lived alone, never! Isn't that strange? I lived with Mum, and then you, and then, well, Dave ...' She lowered her gaze. 'I feel awful about what I've done to him, he doesn't deserve any of this.'

'Have you heard from him?' Matt asked gently, genuinely interested. He could no longer hate the guy.

'I spoke to him yesterday, he's doing okay.' Lisa pushed the coffee away, looked down at her hands. 'He knows that the marriage was a mistake. He's better off without me.'

Matt reached across the table and took her hand, gently rubbing his thumb across her knuckles. 'Listen, about last night ...'

'Leave it Matt,' Lisa said quickly, 'it was lovely, and a final goodbye. I get it, let's remember it for what it was.'

'Okay,' Matt finally shrugged, knowing he had to let it go, but not quite able to do so. He still felt bad. 'It's just that, I don't want you to think ...'

'That you used me?' Lisa laughed. 'Really Matt? I practically threw myself at you.' She smiled, 'I have no regrets. It was nice, we're adults. We need to move on.'

'So, what now?' Matt tentatively asked.

'I move back home, rent somewhere, start over again.' She paused, and a huge smile lit up her face, 'But by myself. I need to work out who I am. I suppose I just need to be happy in my own skin.'

He smiled back at her, 'I get that, I really do. And, for what it's worth, I think it's a fantastic idea.'

'To be honest, I'm both afraid and excited, but I *need* to do this.'

'Of course you do,' Matt told her gently, 'and you know where I am if you need me.'

'No, Matt,' Lisa said firmly, 'this needs to be a clean break. For now, anyway.'

Matt's face fell. He had got so used to having her around. Things would never be the same.

He needed to find himself, just as much as Lisa did. 'You know that I'm here if you need me … for anything.'

'I know Matt, but I'm a big girl now.' She pulled her hand away. 'I'll be okay. You can't always be my safety net.'

Matt couldn't help smiling. She really would be okay. Being truly independent would be the making of her. She deserved this.

'You can move on too, you know.'

Matt raised an eyebrow. 'Move on? I'm doing great. I have my research work …'

'I know that,' Lisa said, cutting him off mid-sentence, reaching for the coffee. She poured herself another cup and placed the pot back down when Matt placed his hand over his own cup.

'You love work, you always have, but you need to live Matt, *really* live. Life's far too short.'

'I do live,' Matt snapped, feeling the indignation rising.

She gave him a warning look. 'No Matt, you don't,' she paused, staring down at her coffee cup, 'You stopped living when I, when *we*, couldn't get pregnant, and then the miscarriage …'

Matt opened his mouth to tell her she was wrong, that he had done all he could to support her, but the miscarriage, it had destroyed him too. He remained silent, just nodded in agreement. There were no words to describe that part of his life. He didn't like to think about how he was back then, that he hadn't been the supportive husband he so wanted to be, that ultimately, he had let her down.

'Matt, we were both grieving, *both* of us. But we moved on. I've now accepted that I need to live my life for me, and you do too.'

Shock clouded his features. 'I am happy.'

'Matt, I know you better than you know yourself.'

He thought she had a point.

'Matt, you need to move on, get on with your life,' she sighed, 'if I hadn't shown back up here, then you would have already done so.'

'Lisa, what are you on about? I have a new home, a new job.'

'Matt,' she shouted, 'does *she* know how you feel?'

Matt's stomach lurched; he needed food. This conversation was becoming far too serious for his liking. He pushed back from the table, the wood screeching against the floor. He stood and looked at the contents of the fridge. 'You fancy some eggs and bacon? Brian left some from the weekend.'

He heard her sigh before she answered.

'Scrambled eggs would be lovely, thank you.'

He rooted in the cupboard for the mixing bowl, cracked the eggs into it and then switched on the grill.

'You need to tell her.'

Matt's head whipped round to face her.

Lisa was sat staring straight at him.

She raised an eyebrow, 'You know who I'm talking about.'

'Just drop it, will you?'

'No, Matt, I won't. I can so tell that you have feelings for her, and she most definitely cares about you.'

Matt leaned against the kitchen counter, folded his arms. 'How the hell would you know? You've never met her.'

'Yes, I have,' she replied indignantly, 'I spoke to her only yesterday, and it was painfully obvious that she was jealous of me, and harbouring feelings for you.'

'What?' he spluttered. 'How long did you speak to her?'

'Not long,' Lisa shrugged, 'but long enough.' She grinned wickedly at him.

Matt sat back down, resting his head in his hands. 'When did you see her?'

'Just before I came here, she was on the doorstep, she was angry with that man, Jim? I just wanted to check that she was okay.'

'And you didn't think to tell me?' Matt said, his voice raised, knowing that he had no right to shout at her.

'She was fine, he walked off. There was no need to tell you.'

Matt supposed she was right. But he'd phone Kate later anyway.

'You need to tell her,' Lisa told him gently.

Matt suppressed a laugh. 'Really, that I *like* her? When she's seen you staying here? How *sincere* would that look?' He stood up and walked over to the stove, turning his back on her. 'We're just friends, that's all.'

'But you could be so much more.'

Matt bit back his response. Perhaps she was right. 'Perhaps in time? She has this whole Jake thing to contend with, as well as Sam. She has enough on her plate.'

'Really, you are full of excuses. She won't wait forever you know.' She pushed her chair back and walked over to the counter to where the eggs stood neglected in the mixing bowl. She retrieved the whisk from the holder and started to beat them vigorously.

After a few seconds, realising that there was nothing else to say, Matt placed the bacon under the grill.

'Just think about it Matt,' Lisa said quietly, 'please, just think about it, for me.'

'Lisa,' he began, 'I'm no good at this … it's not the right time.'

She smiled, 'Is there ever a right time?' She turned back to the eggs.

Matt had to agree with her. It was just that he had no idea of what to do next.

Kate knew that Jake wouldn't turn up. Sam was happily playing on his iPad. He hadn't asked any questions about his father. Kate wasn't

sure if this was because he was processing what had happened, or if he just didn't understand. According to his chat book, he'd had a good day at school, the best all week, so Jake hadn't upset him. She didn't know what to tell him. It was now half past four. She supposed he could be late, but she doubted it.

As if on cue her phone rang.

Jake.

'I can't make it today, sorry. I'll see you tomorrow.'

No apology. No preamble. No remorse.

'Okay, what time tomorrow?' Kate asked through gritted teeth.

'Just before four.'

'Okay.'

He paused, 'I'm sorry about what I said. I was just upset. I didn't mean to upset you.'

'It's fine,' Kate lied. It was far from fine, but the last thing Kate needed was another argument. She'd give him one more chance, and then that was it. She didn't trust him and after what he had said, she had to admit that she was frightened of him. She knew that he hadn't changed one little bit. Was she foolish to give him another chance? Yes, but what else could she do? He had only shouted; no exact threats were made. There was nothing she could do. He was Sam's father. She was back to that old nutshell. A never-ending circle.

'I'll see you tomorrow then.'

She swiped the screen to end the call and looked towards Sam. He had now moved on to one of his preschool apps, one where he had to match feelings to facial expressions. She ruffled his hair.

'Where's Daddy?' he asked.

The innocent words knocked the breath out of her.

He *had* understood.

There was so much to this little boy that she didn't yet understand.

'That was Daddy on the phone, he can't make it today, he'll see you tomorrow.'

'Tomorrow?' Sam asked, his eyes not leaving the screen.

'Yes, love, next day.' Her gut tightened at the thought.

'He shouts. Don't like him,' Sam said, still playing his game. He matched an angry face to the word *angry*. 'That's Daddy.'

Kate nodded, 'Yes love, he was angry, but he won't be on the next day.'

'Daddy here next day?'

'Yes Sam, Daddy here next day.'

His face fell.

Kate wondered what the hell she was doing.

Matt's phone call came at just the right time. They had eaten their tea; sausages and spaghetti for Kate, chicken nuggets for Sam. She once again swallowed down her guilt, as she had started to think about Jake. Should she just tell him to back off?

'I just don't know what to do,' Kate whispered, even though she had retreated to the solitude of the kitchen. 'He really scared me yesterday. He was like the old Jake.'

'You don't have to see him again you know,' Matt said gently down the phone, but Kate detected the annoyance in his tone. She was unsure if it was aimed at her, or Jake. She sighed. 'Well, he never called round today, and when he phoned he sounded apologetic.'

'Kate,' Matt snapped, 'this man will never change.' He took a breath, his tone softer, 'Look, I'm frightened for you Kate, you have no idea of what this man is capable of. Lisa saw him.'

'I know, I spoke to her, but she only really caught the tail end of it …'

'So, it was even worse than what she saw?' Matt spluttered. 'Christ Kate, Sam was there.'

'Don't you think I don't know that! This is all for Sam.'

The line went quiet.

'I know, I'm sorry. I'm just worried,' Matt said quietly.

Kate bit her lip. She really had no idea where she was with this man. Matt obviously cared about her, and Sam, but he was with Lisa. 'Look, I'll let you get back to Lisa.'

'What? I'm at work.'

'Oh, I thought you'd be at home.'

'I had some stuff to sort out in the office, and well, me and Lisa …'

'Listen, it's really none of my business Matt,' Kate interrupted, 'thanks for phoning, but we're fine, really.'

'Look Kate about me and ...'

'Matt,' Kate snapped. She had no intention of listening to him go on and on about his ex-wife, now girlfriend. 'I'm tired and Sam's calling me. I need to go.'

'Okay,' Matt said, 'I'll call by tomorrow late afternoon.'

'I don't need a chaperone Matt, I'll be fine.'

'I know, but I haven't seen you in days, I'm only working a half day tomorrow at the aquarium and then I just need to sort some stuff out at uni.'

Kate couldn't help the smile that spread across her face, nor the tingling feeling in the pit of her gut at the thought of seeing him. 'Okay, I'll see you tomorrow.'

She was still smiling when she ended the call. No matter how wrong it was, she needed to see him, and she needed him to be a part of her life, and if that was as a friend, then so be it. She would rather that than nothing at all.

CHAPTER TWENTY-NINE

THURSDAY, 26TH SEPTEMBER 2013

Kate surveyed the mess in the kitchen and forced herself to do a quick clean before starting the day's articles. Luckily, Sam had woken up happy, and had changed into his school uniform with minimum fuss.

He never mentioned Jake.

She quickly gathered the dirty plates, encrusted with the previous night's tomato sauce, and dumped them into the sink, adding a liberal squirt of washing up liquid. She squeezed out the dishcloth and rubbed at the stubborn jam, now dried on the kitchen table. Would she ever be domesticated? She busied herself with the mindless task of washing the dishes. Once the sink was empty, she knew she couldn't put it off any longer, so she headed to the living room and switched on her laptop.

She had emailed Bill earlier that morning, telling him that she would work from home today. She had all the information she needed to finish the articles, already having conducted the interviews, and would email him the final copy by the end of the day. He had replied telling her that there was no rush; she knew that he would, but she wanted them done. They still had no idea when Veronica would be returning to work, and she did not want to give her any ammunition to get rid of her. She needed the money.

Kate opened Word and clicked on the documents that she needed. It was while she was reading through her notes, reminding herself of what she had to write, that her mobile beeped. She picked it up and read the text, nearly dropping it in surprise. It was from Emily. She had assumed that it would be a while before she heard from her friend. But her text, albeit brief, told Kate that she was safe, well, and incredibly happy, and could she phone her in the next half hour?

All work was forgotten as Kate waited for Emily to answer the phone.

She picked up on the second ring.

'Emily,' Kate practically shouted, unable to contain her excitement, 'how are you?'

'I'm fine Kate, in fact we are both great. We're staying with Mum.'

'Oh, how lovely, I'm glad that you decided to go and visit her.'

'Yes, you were right Kate, it's the best thing I could have done. She was so pleased to see us.'

'How is Isaac?'

'Oh, he's so happy, not unsettled at all. He loves his nana and he's started to sleep through the night again.'

'Oh, Emily, that's wonderful.' Kate thought about her own gran and the bond that they had shared. Grandparents were so important, and she was so happy that Isaac could now spend time with his nana. 'Dare I ask about Gerald?'

The line went quiet, and Kate wondered if she had asked the wrong question. Getting as far away from Gerald was Emily's plan – she shouldn't have mentioned his name. 'I'm sorry, forget I asked that.'

'No, no Kate, you should ask, it's just that I try not to talk about him, but Isaac is out with Mum, so I have no excuse. Gerald has no idea where we are, and I want it to stay that way.'

'Oh, I completely get that Emily.'

'That's why I won't tell you where we are, apart from the fact that we are in Scotland, a tiny village. He'll never be able to find us.'

Kate really hoped that that was true. If Jake had managed to track her down after six years, what was stopping Gerald? But she hoped for the sake of her friend that she was right.

'So, that's it then? A new start for you both?'

'Yes, and I couldn't be happier. Isaac really seems to like it here. I think partly because of the freedom. There is so much green space, the house backs onto a field and he can just run and let off steam.'

'Oh, Sam would love that,' Kate laughed.

'It's such a shame that you can't visit, but …'

'I completely understand Emily, we don't want to put you at risk, I'm just so glad that you are finally happy.'

'Me too.'

'So,' Kate paused, unsure of how to ask the next question. 'What about *you*? What will you do with yourself?' Kate braced herself for the hostile response, telling her that this was none of her business.

Emily laughed, 'You know what Kate, I haven't thought about that yet, but I do want to work, after I have Isaac settled in a school. I've been to see one and it seems the perfect fit for him, but until then I am home schooling him, and it seems to be going well, so far.' Her voice lost its lightness. 'But, yes, I would love to do something creative, something like what you do. I've always been envious of you, you know that?'

'Me?' Kate gasped, her face turning a light pink. 'Really Emily, there is nothing to be envious about.'

'That's where you are so wrong. You're just so confident, know exactly what you want, and you're a fab mum.'

'So are you,' Kate said, meaning every word. Emily *was* a fantastic mum. 'I've told you this many a time, you've shown that by doing what you have done, to keep Isaac safe.'

'It's what you did too,' Emily added quickly.

Kate felt her eyes begin to sting and her throat tighten; she had done the opposite of what Emily had done. She had invited the monster into her home and she was now in too deep to know what to do. 'Oh Emily, if only you knew,' she said, and without warning, she began to sob.

'Kate, Kate,' Emily shouted, 'whatever is wrong?'

Kate forced the sobs down, ashamed; she was meant to be comforting her friend, the one who should be providing support. 'Nothing, nothing at all. I'm so sorry, it's just been a difficult few days.'

'Don't do that Kate. Don't shut me out. You've always done that, but I can help you, like you helped me. I can tell something is wrong. Is this about Sam's dad?'

Kate took a deep breath. 'He's back and I have been trying to help him ease gradually back into Sam's life, but it isn't going well,' Kate paused, 'he just doesn't get Sam, at all, he thinks that his autism is an excuse, and well, I can't put my finger on it, but it's almost as if he isn't bothered, that he doesn't really want to be there, which is off, as he's the one who tracked us down and begged for me to let him back into Sam's life.' All of this came out in one long rush of breath, the urge for the words to be spilled before she could swallow them back down. It felt fantastic to say exactly how she felt.

'Oh, Kate, things are really difficult for you. I just think that you need to tell him that enough is enough. Look at what you've

achieved without him, you don't need him and by the sound of things, neither does Sam.'

'But he's his dad, I was wrong to take him away from his dad.'

'Kate, what you need to remember is why you moved away in the first place. What he did to you, how he made you feel. Do you want the same for Sam?' She said all of this sternly, placing great emphasis upon Sam's name, knowing that this would make Kate listen to her. 'You are his mother, and you know what is best. Those are the words that you told *me*, and I now believe them. I don't need Gerald and his controlling, manipulative and aggressive ways, and by the looks of it, you don't need Jake. You've tried, and he obviously doesn't care, so tell him to leave you alone or you will get a restraining order out on him.'

'It's not that easy,' Kate began to argue.

'Of course it is, he hurt you in the past and if you're not careful, he'll do the same to Sam.'

'He's calling round tonight, after Sam finishes school. I can't phone him now and tell him to stay away.'

'Tell him when he gets to yours then.'

'Oh Emily, I just can't, I can't do that to him. I told myself he deserves another chance.'

'Kate, I remember you telling me about your gran and how she helped you. What would she tell you to do?'

Kate didn't need to think for very long; she knew exactly what her gran would say.

'You need to be careful with this man. How many second chances does he deserve?'

Kate thought about Emily's final words as she sat and finished typing up her articles. She really had given Jake far too many chances, but today, well, it really would be his last chance. She

would be brave. She would remember how strong she had been six years ago, but most importantly, she would think about her gran, and draw strength from what that inner voice would tell her.

The hours flew by as she immersed herself in work. She sat in the kitchen, to be near the radio, Radio 4 on in the background, giving her the stimulation she needed to form words, sentences, banishing all thoughts of Jake from her mind. What would be would be. She just hoped that this time his visit would go well. Now that he'd had a chance to think about what he had said. Now that perhaps he'd had the chance to do a little research on autism. Perhaps he would want to engage with his son?

As the time approached 3:00 pm, Kate closed her laptop and rubbed her eyes. She had met all her deadlines. Hopefully that would keep Veronica off her back. She would go to the office in the morning and see what other work was waiting for her. She needed to be out of this house. It was becoming oppressive. She needed to be with people, people other than Jake. She also knew that it was foolish to hide away like she was, scared to leave her own home. Isn't that why she had fled from him in the first place? Her thoughts turned to Matt. Matt who was always happy, smiling, there for her, unconditionally. She was so glad that she would be seeing him later. She had missed his company.

Jake would be here in less than an hour. She felt the anxiety creeping in, wondering how he would react today if Sam once again showed no interest in him. She would watch Sam, be near him, her phone clutched in her hand. She picked up her phone from the table, making sure that she had Matt's number – silly, as she had only spoken to him yesterday, of course she had his number, but her anxiety, her nervousness, was clouding her judgment. She couldn't think straight. She recognised the signs of the beginnings of a panic attack and sat down heavily on the

kitchen chair. This was how it had started all those years ago. Little jibes, shouted words, and she had let him, had simply become accustomed to it. She screwed her eyes shut and thought about her conversation with Emily.

The fact that she was Sam's mother, that she knew what was best for him.

That she was strong.

She would not be bullied again.

She was no longer Holly.

She focused on her breathing, *in and out, in and out*, and the kitchen once more came into focus.

She took a deep breath and wiped her damp hands on her jeans. She needed to keep busy until he arrived. The clothes still sat in the dryer. She'd sort the laundry.

Jake arrived ten minutes after Sam arrived home. Kate could tell instantly that he had been drinking. His gait was unsteady and his words slightly slurred, not to mention the reek of stale booze on his breath. She had attempted to gently push him away, had tried to tell him to come back when he was sober, but before she knew it, he had pushed past her into the living room.

'Still ignoring me then,' he shouted at Sam, as he sat down next to him on the couch. Sam's eyes were glued to the iPad. Jake peered over his shoulder, watching what was on the screen. Kate inwardly cursed – so much for staying close to Sam, and she had left her phone on the kitchen table. There was no way she was going to leave Jake alone with him to retrieve it. She stood helplessly as Sam angled himself way from his father, covering his nose. 'You smell funny,' he said, without looking at Jake.

Kate didn't correct him; he was right, he smelled awful. She hovered awkwardly in front of them both, before deciding to squat

down on the floor in front of Sam's feet.

'Charming,' Jake replied, 'that's a nice way to greet your dad.'

Sam carried on playing.

Kate held her breath; this was going just as she expected. She had to make him leave.

'No cup of tea today then?' he smirked.

Kate just shook her head.

Jake huffed; he obviously knew that she didn't want to leave them together, unsupervised.

'Jake, why don't we try again another day?' She forced a smile, tried to sound as nonchalant as possible, but her voice sounded strained even to her own ears.

Sam continued to play on his iPad.

'Turn that thing off so I can talk to you,' Jake demanded, reaching for the iPad.

Not this again, Kate thought. Had he not learned his lesson from last time? 'Jake, leave him, I'll get the timer.'

Jake continued to ignore her and gripping the iPad's outer frame, managed to pull it away from Sam with such force that it flew across the room, hitting the wall.

'Nooooooooo,' Sam wailed, jumping off the couch. But before he could make a dash for it, Jake snaked an arm around his waist, pulling him back to the couch.

'Jake, let him go,' Kate shouted as Sam began to punch Jake's arms, thrashing his legs about wildly, kicking where he could reach.

'You will talk to me, that *thing* needs to go in the bin!' Jake pointed to the iPad, now resting against the wall, thankfully intact due to the protective case.

'NOOOOOOOOO, NO BINNNNN!' Sam screamed, his movements becoming even more frantic, as he kicked and lashed out.

'Jake, let him go!' Kate shouted, reaching for Sam.

Jake swore and threw Sam at her, who clung to Kate's neck, his sobs wracking through his body, trying to gulp in air.

Kate closed her eyes, concentrated on stroking Sam, his hair, his face, his back, willing him to calm down. She had to diffuse this situation. She had to get rid of Jake.

'Jake, just go,' she said quietly over the top of Sam's shoulder. Surely, he could see the situation was hopeless. He was upsetting everyone.

He gave her a leer and leaned back into the couch, spreading his legs, King of the manor, letting her know exactly who was boss, and apparently, it wasn't her.

'I am here to talk to him, and that's what I will do.'

'Jake, what's the point of all of this?'

He started to laugh, but then abruptly stopped, his face losing all traces of humour. 'The point? What do you mean?'

'Sam, go and get your iPad, then, next, go to your room,' Kate said quickly. She wanted Sam away from this man. But Sam refused to budge, his arms still tight around her neck, face buried into her soft skin. 'You scare him, and you're drunk. I just want you to leave,' she hissed at him.

He stared at her for a few moments, his face expressionless, and suddenly the leer he had worn changed to that of disgust. 'You honestly think that I care about *him*? I don't even think he's mine.'

'What?' Kate couldn't believe what she was hearing. 'He's yours, of course he is.'

'Listen, I really don't give a shit about you or him.' He leaned forward in his seat, 'This was never about him. This was about getting *even*, taking back what's *mine*.'

Kate closed her eyes. She pushed herself up from the floor, taking Sam's weight, rocking him backwards and forwards. Matt

had been right all along – Jake didn't care about Sam.

It was never about Sam.

'I need money,' he shrugged, 'and the way I see it, you owe me.'

'Owe you? Owe you for what?' Kate spluttered as she now leaned against the kitchen door. She could see the phone on the kitchen table. So near, yet so far.

'You have got to be kidding me?' he snarled. 'Really, you don't know? When you left me I started to drink, I lost my job, lost the house and lived on the streets for a bit. It was only when I met an old school friend that I got back on my feet. He let me kip with him for a while, then I got a new building site job, got a bedsit, got back on track, but those lost years, that's down to *you*. I lost money. I want what's mine.'

'Jake, that was you, not me, I wasn't there. How you chose to live your life was up to you.'

'I was a laughing stock, I heard the comments from mates in the pub, saying that I couldn't keep my woman.'

Kate tried to control her breathing; if she wasn't careful she'd bring on another panic attack and she couldn't do that. She had to keep Sam safe. They had to get out.

She needed her phone.

Kate leaned back against the kitchen doorframe. Sam was growing heavier in her arms, but she refused to let go of him.

She needed to keep him safe.

'Jake, I have no money,' she said the words slowly, willing him to understand that his plan was completely futile.

'Don't lie to me, *bitch*,' Jake's voice was controlled, the emphasis placed upon the word *bitch*, knowing that it would only rile her.

'I'm not lying, why would I lie? I'm a single mum who works part-time. I have no spare cash. I have no savings.'

Sam started to wriggle even more, wanting to be free, away from

Jake. But Kate kept tight hold of him. He needed to stay with her until she could figure out a way of getting Jake out of her home. If only she could reach the phone. All she would have to do would be to press Matt's number; she wouldn't even have to speak to him, he'd hear what was going on. He would know she was in trouble.

She took a step backwards into the kitchen. Just a small step so as not to arouse suspicion. She made it look as if she was unbalanced with Sam's weight, just steadying herself.

Jake pushed himself up from the couch. Took a step towards then.

Did he know Kate's plan?

'I'm talking about Mary's cash, that's what I'm on about. I know that she left you her inheritance, and I want it. Give me the money and I'll leave you alone.'

'Blackmail,' the word came out of Kate's mouth as a whisper. How could she have been so gullible? 'There is no money Jake.' She tried to control her breathing; she needed to let him know that she was in control. That she was not afraid of him. She stopped herself from looking into the kitchen, forcing her eyes to stay put on Jake's face. She was now unsure of whether going into the kitchen to try and snatch the phone was such a good idea. From his position, he could see her every move, and surely he would stop her before she had a chance to grab the phone and call Matt, or the police.

There was also the fact that the kitchen was home to many knives and other sharp implements. So the kitchen was a bad idea. If Jake wasn't about to leave, then they would have to find a way out.

'Liar, you *fucking* liar,' Jake spat, 'tell me where the money is.'

'Jake, there is no money, my gran gave me money when I first moved here, to help get me started, but that was all. That was all she had. There was nothing left when she died.'

Kate began to sob. She couldn't help it; this whole situation was hopeless, and she had a horrible feeling how it was all going to end.

Kate managed to look past Jake. Would she have enough time to get past him and to the front door?

No, it was hopeless.

Sam started to squirm once more, oddly quiet. It was as if he knew that he needed to stay quiet to keep safe.

'Jake please go, I'm asking you nicely. I have no money, so please leave me alone.'

Jake took a step closer towards them.

Without any warning, Sam managed to wriggle free from his mother's tight hold and then to Kate's horror, ran straight towards Jake. After swiftly kicking him in the shin, Sam ducked under Jake's swinging arm and ran for the front door.

Jake was caught off balance, but he now separated Kate from Sam, who had somehow managed to open the front door and had made a bid for freedom. Had she forgotten to lock the front door? She must have.

Kate heard rather than saw the front door banging against the frame as Jake ran through it to reach out and grab hold of Sam.

It was as Kate stepped out onto the path, frantically searching for Sam and trying to reach him before Jake did, that she saw where he had headed.

She should have known.

Stood on Matt's doorstep, he was banging his small fists frantically on the door.

But Kate was too slow.

As if watching in slow motion, she saw Jake pull back his arm and then watched as he attempted to slap Sam across the face.

But Sam was too quick, and Jake too slow. Sam ducked once

more under Jake's swinging arm and hopped over the low wall towards Kate's outstretched arms.

But Kate wasn't as quick as her little boy. As she reached for Sam, who dived and buried his head in her chest, Jake lurched across the dividing wall and raised his outreached hand towards her, hitting her with such force that her head flew back and hit the wall.

Then the air was filled with a piercing scream.

Sam rocked forwards and backwards, his hands covering his ears, tears streaming down his face.

Despite the sheering pain in the back of her skull, for Kate, the world once again began to move at normal speed as she watched Jake raise his arm once more.

The sound of a man's voice shouting, '*You fucking bastard, you lay one more hand on her …*' made Jake halt in his tracks. He turned and then jumped over the garden fence before running down the street, away from Kate and a crying Sam.

Kate pulled Sam closer towards her and took him in her arms, flinching from the searing pain that felt like her skull was in two pieces. Tentatively she touched the back of her head, but she felt no trace of blood, just a slight bump. She'd be okay. She was just thankful that he had not struck Sam.

She heard a car door slam, followed by the sound of pounding footsteps.

'Everything will be okay, we'll be okay,' Kate told Sam over and over.

Matt was here.

Matt had seen and heard everything. His first thought was to run after the bastard, pin him to the ground until the police got to him. But Jake was a lot quicker than he gave him credit for and as he approached the house, the sight of a distressed Sam being

cradled by an equally distressed Kate made the decision for him. The police would catch up with Jake soon enough, plus, if he was to chase after him, he wouldn't be able to control his emotions and would probably be charged with GBH.

Swearing under his breath, he moved quickly up the path and knelt beside Kate.

Kate buried her face into Sam's blonde curls; she couldn't stop the tears. It was only when she felt a hand on her shoulder and Matt's comforting voice that she lifted her head. She was shocked by what she saw, which she knew must have reflected her own emotions. Those of disgust, shock and pain.

'I saw everything, as I pulled up on to the street. I can't believe that bastard hit you,' Matt's voice broke on the last word.

Kate saw the clenched jaw, the bobbing Adam's apple, as he tried to keep his anger in check. He reached out his hand, and with a nod of permission from Kate, gently touched her cheek. There was a red handprint, larger than his own, but no bruise.

'What about the back of your head?' Matt asked. 'I saw you hit the wall.' His hand moved towards the back of her head and again, he gently touched her skin, parting her hair with his fingers, examining for any breaks or bleeding.

He moved his hand away. It hovered mid-air for a fraction of a second before resting on top of Sam's head.

'Is he okay?' Matt asked as he gently ruffled Sam's hair. 'How are you Sam? How do you feel?'

Sam looked up, his cheeks bright pink, eyes red from crying. He said nothing, just burrowed himself back into Kate's embrace.

She had to stifle another sob. This was all her fault, all of it.

'We'd better get you both inside and then call the police,' Matt said. 'They'll need to find him.'

Kate nodded and attempted to stand, still holding onto Sam.

'Here, let me,' Matt reached down and scooped up a willing Sam into his arms. 'Okay buddy, you're safe now.'

Sam looked at Matt for a moment before nodding and wrapping arms around his neck, just as he had done with Kate.

Kate stepped into the house, followed by them both.

'Where should I pop you Sam? The couch? You want your iPad?'

Sam nodded.

Matt placed Sam gently down onto the couch. Kate bent down to retrieve the iPad from the floor and handed it to him. Luckily it had survived its trip across the room.

She gestured for Matt to follow her into the kitchen. She slowly sank down onto the kitchen chair and rubbed the back of her head.

'Do we need a doctor?' Matt whispered, crouching beside her. It was a nasty whack. His eyes bore into hers. 'Are you sure you're okay?'

Kate nodded before removing her hand and placing it on the table. 'I didn't lose consciousness, I'm not seeing stars or anything like that, and I'm not bleeding … I'm fine.'

Matt shook his head. He didn't like what he was hearing. If it was his choice, he would call for an ambulance. But it was Kate's decision. 'We do need to call the police. They can put a restraining order in place, make sure you are safe. They might suggest a trip to the hospital or for you to see your doctor. I honestly don't know. But we need to call them. Now.'

Kate started to shake, she couldn't help it. The shock was wearing off and she now began to realise just what had happened. How close Sam had been to becoming *really* hurt. If Matt hadn't turned up when he did …

'Kate,' Matt placed his hand gently on her shoulder. 'Phone the police and I'll sit with Sam while you chat to them.'

All Kate could do was nod.

'Hey, are you okay?' Matt asked, while he gently lifted her chin so that she could meet his eyes. 'If I'd have chased after him, I would have killed him, so I opted to stay with you. If he had *really* hurt you ...' He dropped his hand, turning his eyes towards the ceiling. 'I feel like killing him.'

Kate looked towards the floor; she couldn't bear this. The blame was all hers. She should have listened to Matt, to Bill. She had been so stupid.

'Hey, Kate, this isn't your fault.'

'Isn't it?' Kate said, 'I invited that monster into my home, after you told me what he would do, that he wasn't to be trusted, and you know what, you were right. He had no intention of bonding with Sam, of being a father, of making up for lost time. Oh no, it was all about the money.'

Matt took a deep breath before speaking, 'I gain no pleasure in finding out I was right about him, none at all. I'm just glad that he didn't do anything else.'

'He could have really hurt Sam, he could have …' Kate's words trailed off as she began to sob once more. She couldn't stop the tears, the guilt, the pain.

Matt pulled her towards him and wrapped her in his arms, stroking her hair. 'Shhh shhh, it'll be all right. He's gone, the police will get involved and they'll catch him. Just tell them the truth, from the very beginning, then this will all be over.'

Kate gently pushed him away and wiped her eyes with the back of her hand, 'I'm so sorry Matt, for all of this.'

'It's not your fault. All of this is Jake's fault.'

'I know that, I do, but I still feel responsible.'

'Kate, Sam seems to be fine,' Matt glanced to the sofa where Sam was still engrossed in his game. But Kate wondered about the

emotional scars. What he had *seen*? How would that impact upon her little boy? She felt sick to the stomach.

'I'm okay now, really it's just the shock,' she told Matt, as she wandered from the kitchen and sank down into the couch next to Sam.

'Sam, I just need to make a phone call in the kitchen and then I'll be right back. Matt is going to sit with you, is that okay?'

Sam, now fully engrossed in his app, the one where he had to match faces to emotions, nodded and carried on playing,

Kate stood up and Matt took her place, silently watching what Sam was doing. 'I'll be right here. Kate. I'm not going anywhere.'

Kate swallowed, offered a smile, and went in to the kitchen. She picked up the phone and turned to look at Sam, Matt sitting quietly beside him.

She had put her little boy in danger and she would never be able to forgive herself.

CHAPTER THIRTY

FRIDAY, 27TH SEPTEMBER 2013

Kate gratefully took the cup of coffee from Bill, the warmth seeping through her. She hadn't stopped shaking since last night. The police had been at her home until gone seven, asking her questions. Thankfully they didn't need to speak to Sam, the fact that Matt had seen what had happened, together with the bump that had slowly erupted on the back of her skull, was enough evidence of what had happened. After doing a quick name search, the police found that Jake was known to them on several counts: petty theft, driving under the influence, and threatening an ex-girlfriend. They wouldn't go into the specifics on the last matter, but the warning that they gave Kate was that this was one nasty piece of work and that things could have ended much worse.

What she had found the hardest of all was having to relive her past, having to tell them everything that had happened between her and Jake. The reason that she had legally changed her name, why she had fled and started a new life in rural Lancashire. She had started to cry at that point and was glad that Matt had taken Sam next door to play while she spoke to the police. She couldn't bear the thought of Sam seeing her upset.

'So, what happens next Kate?' Bill kindly asked, his words gentle. Kate saw no condemnation in his eyes, and he hadn't yet said, *I told you so*, and she knew that he would never say those words.

'Well, he now has a restraining order, so he can't go anywhere near the house or here. But, to be honest, I don't think he will try to make contact again.'

'So, he's not locked up then?' Bill's eyebrows had shot up in surprise.

'No, I didn't want to press charges against him, so they had to let him go. But, as I said, there is a restraining order.'

'Kate, is that really enough?'

'I just have to hope that it is.' She took a sip of her coffee. 'Matt seems to think that he won't be back, he has nothing to gain from us, now that he knows we have no money.'

'Mmmm,' Bill didn't sound convinced.

'Bill, he didn't even try to hide from the police. They found him here in the village, drinking at the pub. I really do think that he knows the game is up.'

'Not the sharpest tool in the box then, eh?' Bill said.

Kate laughed, 'No, he really isn't that clever, but manipulative, yes, he's good at that.' Kate shook her head, wincing slightly at the dull ache. She was sick of talking about Jake, about what he had done. She wanted things to go back to normal. 'Right, what do you have for me today then?'

'What? I was going to give you the day off.'

'Bill, I need to work ...'

'Kate, you've had a terrible shock, and I know your head is hurting.' He gave her a knowing look. 'Take the day off. Read a book, go and watch a movie ...'

'Bill, I need to keep busy, otherwise ... I'll just think about him, about what he could have done to Sam.'

Bill reached across the desk and handed Kate a tissue. She hadn't even realised she was crying. She quickly dabbed at her eyes, embarrassed. She didn't want to cry in front of Bill.

'I must look a right mess,' she blubbered.

'No need to apologise, you've been through a terrible ordeal, it's just the shock. You need to rest.'

Kate knew he was right. She wouldn't get any work done today, but neither did she want to go home. She'd sit and stew all day about Jake; she needed to occupy her mind, to be surrounded by people. Perhaps she could go to the library and take a drive out somewhere? Maybe she could sit on the pier, eat chips and people watch. That was a good distraction.

'Okay, I'll go, leave you to it. But, I'll be back on Monday and normal service will be resumed.'

Bill grinned, 'Sounds good to me, but if you need a few more days, just let me know.'

'I will.' Kate stood and picked up her coffee. She'd sit in the staff kitchen for a few minutes, get her head straight. Then she'd go for a walk along the pier. The fresh air would do her good.

'It was good that your young man turned up when he did.'

Kate sat back down.

'What? *No*, he's not my young man, we're just friends,' Kate said far too quickly, her voice a touch higher than usual.

'Are you sure about that?' Bill asked, one eyebrow raised. A smile flickered across his face.

'Bill, he's my next-door neighbour and I am eternally grateful for what he did yesterday, and for all the help he has given me, but that's really all there is to it.'

She felt her face warming up and quickly picked up her cup, suddenly absorbed in drinking her coffee. She knew that she had given the game away.

Bill just sat and stared at her.

No words were needed. He knew exactly how she felt about Matt.

'Oh, for God's sake Bill. What am I supposed to say or do?' Kate said, finally giving in to the silent treatment. 'I do like him, yes, I do. There, I've said it. Happy now?' But she didn't wait for an answer. 'The fact is that my life is far too complicated for any kind of relationship now. Who in their right mind would want to get involved with me? And if that isn't bad enough, he's just got back with his ex-wife, so even if I wanted to tell him how I feel, there really is no point.'

Kate sat back in her seat, hardly believing that she had just said everything that had been bottled up inside her for days. But what she had said out loud was true; her feelings for Matt would stay buried. They would have to, otherwise she would ruin their friendship and she couldn't afford to do that.

She looked up and met Bill's eyes, which were so full of sorrow and understanding that it made her want to cry.

'The good ones are always taken,' Bill said.

Kate burst into tears once more.

'Are you sure next weekend is okay, it's just that Beth is taking the kids to her mum's over the weekend, *again*, so I might as well come and see you.'

'Of course, it is, it'll be lovely to see you. Is everything okay between you and Beth?' Matt asked.

Brian laughed. 'You don't need to worry about us. Her dad's not been too well, so she thought that the kids would cheer them up. I only ever get in the way.'

'Okay, well, you always know that there is a room here, especially if you want to bring the kids for a long weekend, Beth too, of course.'

'That'd be great, but are you sure about all of us invading your space?'

'Brian, you're all more than welcome, really, think about it. Perhaps in the half term?'

'I'll talk it through with Beth,' he hesitated, 'listen, is everything really okay with you, you know with Lisa and everything?'

'Everything's fine, really it is. I suppose what happened between us, had to happen, for us to be able to move on. Does that make any sense?'

Matt wondered if his friend with his loving and seemingly perfect marriage of over twenty years could really understand what he was going through. But he knew Matt better than anyone else and he also knew Lisa. And the fact that he had a happy and successful marriage, just as Matt once did, well, at least he would know where Matt was coming from. It would be good to talk to him.

'Of course it makes sense, listen, I just want to ask, have you had a chance to chat to Kate yet?'

Matt sighed, 'Things are a bit complicated now, things between her and her ex, well, he won't be on the scene anymore, something happened yesterday. He tried to attack Sam, but Kate got in the way.'

'What? Is she all right? How's her little boy? Bastard, what happened?'

'He tried to hit Sam, but Kate got in the way and was shoved into a wall, right outside the house in broad daylight. If I hadn't showed up when I did, it would have been much worse.'

'Shit, you didn't hit him did you?'

'Sadly not, he ran off before I could get him. To be honest I was shaken up, I just wanted to check that Sam and Kate were okay.'

'Of course, mate, how are they now?'

'Well, I haven't seen them today, but they both seemed okay last night. Shook up obviously. Kate had a slight bump on the back of her head, but other than that she was unhurt. It's just lucky he didn't break any bones, with the force that Jake pushed her. The police caught Jake by the way, he's on a restraining order, so …'

'What a bastard, men like that need locking up. They should get the crap beat out of them.'

Matt nodded. He agreed, but if he started to talk about Jake he'd never stop.

'So, you've not seen her today then?'

'No, I've been at work all day, but I'm going to call round once I get home this evening.'

'And?'

'And what?'

Matt could hear his friend's chuckle down the line.

'You known what, you really need to tell her how you feel.'

'It's not a good time.' Matt took a deep breath; he had to share his feelings with someone, and Brian would get him, he'd understand. 'I was going to tell her, I have this speech in my head, I know exactly what I need to say to her, but the words, they just don't seem appropriate, not after what she's been through.'

Brian started to laugh, 'Always so serious mate. You don't need to declare your undying love for her. All you have to tell her is that you care about her, that you have feelings for her.'

'But she's been through so much. She has Sam, and now Jake turned up in her life and ruined things.'

'But he's now gone from her life.'

'I know, I know, but everything is still so mixed up.'

'No, it's not. You're just making excuses. Lisa has *gone* and Jake has *gone*. You care about her and she has feelings for you, so what's so complicated about that? Plus, I really think that you

underestimate this woman, she's a lot stronger than you give her credit for. After all, she left her abusive partner and travelled with a new-born baby to a new part of the country to start a new life for herself. Now, that takes guts.'

Matt mulled the words over in his mind. What Brian said made absolute sense, it was almost too simple. But him barging into Kate's life, telling her how he felt could ruin everything; he could lose her friendship, and he didn't want that to happen. Plus, how did Brian know that Kate felt the same way? Lisa had said pretty much the same thing. Could they both be right? Did she really have feelings for him?

Matt couldn't believe the next words that came out of his mouth.

'Yes, maybe I will.'

Kate was busy preparing Sam's tea when the doorbell rang. She knew it would be Matt. He had phoned earlier to say that he would be calling around, but she still peeked through the glass to make sure that it was him. Her stomach was in knots at the thought of seeing him again. How could she remain friends with him when she wanted so much more? But for now, it was his friendship that mattered to her, and although she hated to admit her strong feelings, she needed him in her life.

His wide, open smile greeted her as she flung open the door, and even though she hadn't meant to, she flung her arms around his neck, pressing his strong, firm, and reassuring body to her own.

They stood like that for a moment, just hugging, until Kate took a step backwards, her face slightly flushed.

'Well, it's not every day that I get a welcome like that,' Matt said, his grin now even wider.

Kate beamed back at him and ushered him into the living room. It was only then that she noticed the bunch of flowers that

he was carrying. He thrust them towards her, and then once she had taken them, took a step backwards.

'Thank you,' Kate whispered. She inhaled the floral fragrance, a smile spreading across her face. It was such a different feeling to the one when Jake had brought her flowers.

Sam came scampering down the stairs and ran at Matt, wrapping his arms around his waist.

Matt, momentarily taken aback, put an arm around the little boy and patted his head.

'I think someone else is glad to see you,' Kate said with a chuckle. 'Sam, look at these beautiful flowers. Aren't they lovely?'

Sam nodded and then bounced over to the couch where he picked up the iPad. 'I had a wee Mum,' he told Kate proudly.

'Okay love, tea won't be too long.'

Kate turned towards Matt, who was still stood in the same position, watching her every move. 'Do you want to stay for tea? There's plenty to go around. I'm making spag bol.'

Matt grinned. 'If that's all right with you, then yes, I'd love to.'

Kate walked into the kitchen and fetched the jug that she had used for Jake's flowers, the ones that were now rotting in the bin. She filled it with water and placed the flowers into it. 'So, is Lisa not around tonight then?' she asked quickly, while fiddling with the flowers. She didn't want to bring her name up, but she knew she couldn't avoid talking about her.

'What? No,' Matt cleared his throat, 'listen, I wanted to talk to you about that, about Lisa.'

Kate spun around, her face red. 'There's no need.' she forced a smile, 'I'm so happy for you Matt.' She knew that he was probably embarrassed as he had talked about how wrong Lisa was for him, that they were over, and here he was telling her that they were back together. Kate told herself that it really was none of her business.

Matt reached towards her, grabbed her hand and pulled her towards him. 'No, you don't understand.'

Kate snatched her hand back. This was all wrong. 'Matt, you don't have to explain to me, really …'

'No, Kate, I do, you've got it all wrong. Shit …' He rubbed his temple with the tips of his fingers. 'I'm crap at this.'

Kate stood there, silent, wondering what the hell he was talking about.

'Me and Lisa, well, there is no *me and Lisa*, she's gone.'

Kate stood there dumbfounded. *Lisa had gone*. She hadn't expected him to say that. 'Oh, Matt, I am sorry.'

'No, don't be sorry, it's the best thing to have happened to us. It really is.' A huge grin broke out on his face.

A thousand thoughts whizzed around in Kate's mind. Lisa was gone, and he was happy about that. So too was she, but she couldn't tell him that.

'Kate,' Matt said as he took a step towards her, grabbing her hand once more, 'I really like you, and if it's okay with you, I'd like to get to know you more, and Sam,' he swallowed, 'if you'll have me around.'

Kate just stood and held his hand, his fingers interlaced with her own. It was so natural, she felt as if she had known him for years, not weeks.

She was completely lost for words.

'I'd like that, I'd like that a lot,' was all that she could say. She couldn't get her words out.

They stood looking at each other, grasping fingers, unsaid words, the flowers in the jug.

Sam on his iPad. The sound of cows mooing in an interactive world.

Kate just knew that everything would work out.

She felt it in her bones.

EPILOGUE
THE ENDING

JUNE 2007

I find myself sitting opposite Mary on the train that is quickly heading towards the north of the country. Sam is strapped to me in a baby carrier, fast asleep, a shared picnic lunch of cheese and pickle sandwiches, crisps and grapes spread out on the carriage table. Gran told me that I needed to keep up my strength, and that grapes were good for me. Just as she had done when I was a little girl. We had both refused to pay the extortionate amount declared by the onboard food and drinks trolley, but we were going to treat ourselves to a cup of tea later. For now, we sipped flavoured water from plastic cups.

I'd had to quickly decide what to bring with me. I had quietly squirrelled away my belongings during the previous week, under the bed in the spare room, where Jake would never see them. The rest of my belongings were to be boxed up by the removal company that Gran had sorted out for me. Although I should have felt guilt in this deception of my partner, I felt none. This was self-preservation.

So, above me in the overhead rack is a stashed suitcase and one carry bag crammed full of Sam's clothes and my most treasured possessions, a few books and photographs of my parents. I have brought nothing that will remind me of Jake. Holly is now dead, gone forever, and I have been reborn as Kate Sullivan. I have always liked the name Kate, and it is simple, easy to remember. I chose Sullivan because of the connections to my parents. My mother's friend had been a Sullivan and she had looked after me as a little girl. I wanted a link back to my past, although it is only a tentative one. I never want to hear my old name again.

By my feet lies Sam's changing bag, and apart from that and the two other bags, everything else will be in the removal van. Apart from my clothes. I can buy more clothes when I get there. None of them fit me anymore anyway, and I hate them. I need new clothes for a new me. I can buy a pram when needed. Gran has secured a travel cot, that is now ready and waiting in the house, as well as a fully functioning kitchen and practical furniture. Gran has warned that the old furniture has seen better days, but that it's clean and functional. I had heartily agreed that that was all that mattered.

'Kate, are you okay love?'

It takes me a few seconds to realise that Gran is talking to me. I tell myself that I need to get used to my new name, and quickly. '*Kate Sullivan, Kate Sullivan*' I repeat over and over in my mind. I want to say the name as often as I can, so that I will believe it, that it will become engrained within me. It is who I must be.

'I'm fine, just thinking,' I smile. I really am. I'm as nervous as hell, I admit that, but I am also excited for this new chapter of my life to begin. In my mind, I see the rooms in my new house. I can decorate them as I wish. I can buy what I like. But most importantly, I will no longer have to live in fear.

I glance at my watch; it's just coming up to noon. Jake has been at work since 7:00 am, and he has a further six hours to go. I will be in Muddletown by the time he gets home. The silence will greet

him, the absence of baby clothes, my books. What will he think? More importantly, what will he do?

I banish these thoughts to the back of my mind. What he will think and do are no longer my concern.

I am now Kate Sullivan, and I am going to live my life.

The End

Jo Worgan is a freelance copywriter, columnist and book blogger. She has published 4 non-fiction works aimed at parenting children on the Autistic spectrum, based upon her experiences as a mother of an autistic son.

Writing is what she truly loves and *Picking up the Pieces* is her second novel following her first, *An Unextraordinary Life.*

Today Jo lives in Lancashire with her husband and their two young sons. When she is not busy writing, she likes to take her boys to the local museums, cafes, cinema, the Lake District and lots of playgrounds.